MYSTERY DAUGHTER

CHUCK GLEASON

BLACK ROSE writing™

The final approval for this literary material is granted by the author.

First printing

ISBN: 978-1-61296-852-0
PUBLISHED BY BLACK ROSE WRITING
www.blackrosewriting.com

Printed in the United States of America
Suggested retail price $18.95

Mystery Daughter is printed in Adobe Garamond Pro

To Janet, the love of my life,
and to our Great Grandchildren, Aaron and Gabe.
Thank you for the joy you have brought into our lives!
I also want to mention Ann Whitley Singleton,
who has constantly been my strongest supporter.

Special Thanks

I wrote this novel several years ago. No one would publish it, so I gave it a rewrite. My editor for the original novel was my loving wife, Janet. She also had help from Penny Goodell. Thanks to you both and thanks to Ann Whitley Singleton who has constantly been there for me.

I am deeply grateful to Black Rose Writing, to Reagan Rothe and to David King who have supported me every step of the way.

Mystery Daughter

PROLOGUE

He pushed the door of the jewelry store open. The pusher was obviously a confident young man. If he owned the store, he couldn't have been more self-assured. He marched right up to the diamond ring counter. No one could doubt that this was a customer who demanded attention.

It wasn't this youngster's looks that made the two male sales clerks watching shake their heads. He appeared to be almost six feet tall, a tad on the heavy side, long dark hair with a sallow complexion. It was the undesirable attitude of contempt emanating from him that was so objectionable. One clerk muttered quietly to his associate. "The expression *pompous ass* comes to mind, big time. Do you want him?"

"It's my turn, I guess I don't have a choice. Watch my fake smile in action, Pal."

The clerk approached the diamond ring counter. "May I help you?"

"My name is William Knowlton. I am here to purchase a diamond ring."

"For yourself? Or perhaps, for a young lady?"

"I want an engagement ring. She is a beautiful woman. I want a spectacular, very large diamond."

Pompous ass or not, thought the clerk, *this could be a nice commission.* The clerk was correct. In a few minutes, William selected an exceptionally expensive ring.

As the clerk wrapped the ring he announced, "Beginning this year, 1985, we have a new policy. When we sell an engagement ring, our store policy is…if the lady happens to say no, you have thirty days to return the ring."

Knowlton looked down at the clerk as if he was daft. "Are you implying that a woman would turn down a proposal of marriage from me?"

"Oh, no sir, not on your life. It's just my job to inform you of the store return policy."

"Humph!"

Nose in the air, purchase securely in his hand, young William Knowlton marched out.

Once outside, Knowlton stuck the ring box in his pocket, climbed into his Mercedes and started driving from Indianapolis to Ann Arbor. Spring vacation was over. He was off to begin his last quarter before graduation at the University of Michigan. In the fall, he would attend Harvard Business School to begin work on his MBA.

Before he left the Ann Arbor campus, there was an important piece of business to complete. He wanted to *lock up* the vivacious Margaret Weatherby. She was only a freshman; however, she was a very attractive girl. William had taken her on several dates. He'd reached a decision. *Margaret socialized well. She would make a good hostess. Business leaders need wives who compliment their husband's responsible positions.*

As he drove along he began to compose the words he would use in his proposal. *I know, I'll simply announce I have selected you to be my wife. Simple and right to the point. She will be exceedingly happy. Furthermore, I will announce my decision to marry her on our date tonight! Why wait? She will have the entire spring quarter to show off her ring around the campus.*

• • •

At about the same time as William's Mercedes flashed across the Indiana - Michigan state line, things were happening at the freshman dorm in Ann Arbor. Margaret Weatherby tossed her suitcase on the bed and hugged her roommate, Joanne Dartforth. It was great to be back on campus.

The two roommates were good friends. They exchanged their spring break adventures. Joanne had simply gone home. Margaret went to Florida with her parents. She spent lots of time on the beach and she had a gorgeous tan to prove it. Blue eyes twinkled with joy and excitement under her sun bleached short blond hair. She was a 'happy camper.'

Then a sad thought crept into her mind. It soon reflected on her face. Joanne picked up on the change immediately.

"What's wrong, Margaret?"

"I have a date with William tonight. I've made up my mind; it's time to dump him."

"Break it off? I thought you liked him."

"I guess I've never explained William, have I? His Mom and my Mom are old friends. They arranged our first date. I knew immediately I didn't like him. He's way too full of himself. Because of Mom, I felt obligated to be nice to him. We've had several dates and I continue to feel absolutely nothing for him. Zip. Nada. The only reason I kept going out with him was I didn't want Mother upset with me.

"But, enough is enough. I talked to Mom on vacation and she understands. So, I need to get this over with tonight. I hate to shoot anyone down but I know this is going nowhere. To be fair to William, I need to tell him."

"I understand he is awfully rich."

"Well the rich part's true. He's been very careful to let me know that his parents own a chain of some kind of appliance stores. My plan, however, is to marry for love and not for money. Besides, William is a pompous ass. My only problem is how to let the guy down gently."

As soon as William picked her up, Margaret knew letting him down gently was going to be tough. She could tell something exciting had changed his usual boring manner. She decided to wait until they finished eating before giving him the news.

Unfortunately for William, he decided to spring his good news as soon as they'd ordered their dinner. The minute the waiter left he announced, "I have a surprise for you. I've decided we should be married. Here's your engagement ring!" He removed the box from his pocket, opened it and pushed it across the table toward an astonished Margaret.

She was thunderstruck! The only thing she felt for William was disgust at his incredible conceit. How could he possibly imagine she would be willing to marry him? Then she realized, *William never thinks of anyone's feelings except his own.*

While she pondered this, William became aware of what one could call an awkward silence. He asked, "Don't you think it's a beautiful diamond?"

"It's a lovely diamond, William, however I can't accept it."

Completely ignoring her reply, William continued. "I thought you'd enjoy showing it off this last quarter of school before I head for Harvard."

Margaret shook her head as she continued to be appalled at his self-centeredness. Then she realized … *he never even asked me to marry him! The pompous son of a bitch simply announced that he decided we should marry!*

"William, I told you I cannot accept your diamond or your *'declaration of intentions.*'" As she said this her anger began to boil over. "Do you realize you never even asked me to marry you? You self-centered goat, you simply announced that you decided we should marry. Did it ever occur to you that I might want to have some input in a decision of that importance?"

Temporarily stunned, William exclaimed, "You don't understand, Margaret. I, William Knowlton have consented to take you as my wife. When someone as eligible as me asks you to marry, you accept. With eagerness, I might add. The lady's consent is a given."

"Well, this lady's consent is no given," Margaret shot back. Then she softened. "William, I don't love you. I don't even enjoy being with you. There's no magic between us."

"Margaret, a wise person doesn't marry for love. A wise person chooses a mate with his head, not his heart. Now, if you will use that pretty little head, you will see that I am a terrific catch for you."

Margaret stood up, snapping the ring box closed as she pushed it back across the table toward him. "You can pick your spouse any way you want, William, but when I pick mine, it will be with a heart full of love. Good bye. I'm taking a cab home. Please don't call me again. I promise you, I won't change my mind!" Squaring her shoulders, she left the astonished young man staring at the empty seat across the table.

When Margaret got back to the dorm she was still steaming. Luckily, her roommate hadn't left for her date yet.

"What happened? You're back so soon," Joanne asked.

Margaret unloaded. "That pompous ass asked me to marry him. No, he didn't...He announced that HE decided we should marry! Then he shoved this big diamond ring across the table at me as if he were buying my consent!

"It never occurred to him that I might want some input in selecting the man I want for my husband! I was so angry! I called him a self-centered goat, shoved the ring back at him and walked out. I took a cab back. How can any human be so totally immersed in himself?"

Joanne's face quickly twisted from concern to a broad smile. She tried to keep from laughing, but it was useless. "I can just picture the look on his face when you called him a self-centered goat!" Her snicker became a giggle which quickly turned into outright uproarious laughter! Seconds later Margaret joined her. The two roommates laughed for a long time.

• • •

Margaret's refusal became intensely personal for William. His wounded ego took a long time to recover. He pretended it didn't matter. There were other women out there who would realize he was a fabulous catch. But it did eat at him. Within a few weeks his supposed affection for Margaret turned into genuine hate.

Several months later, William met a woman named Shirley Lansing. After a six-month courtship, she accepted his very similar marriage declaration. In William's mind, Shirley would be more of a hostess than a wife. Of course, Shirley didn't realize this.

William and Shirley had two daughters, Betty Ann Knowlton and Laurie Lansing Knowlton.

Margaret fell in love with a wonderful man, John Randall. They had one child whom they named Brad.

Twenty-five years after the rejected proposal, in the year 2010, Laurie and Brad wound up as college freshmen at the same institution…

CHAPTER 1

As Laurie walked out of the University library that cold November night, a strange sound reached her ears. Someone was crying. Really sobbing.

Apparently, the sound was coming from a bench located part way down the hill to her right.

Should she intervene? It was patently none of her business. But maybe someone needed help. Laurie's tender sensitivity came into her consciousness. If someone needed help, she needed to at least inquire. Cautiously, she headed down the hill toward the bench.

Laurie was one of the few in the freshman class who spent lots of time studying. Long brown hair reached half way down her back. Most of the time, she confined it in a ponytail which was the way she had it this night. When she was younger, she'd had complexion problems. However, by the time her college freshman year came around, her skin was clear and softly attractive. Brown eyes twinkled with merriment and mirth. A narrow nose and generous mouth completed an attractive face. Laurie was no beauty queen, but she was certainly a woman any man would examine more than once.

Laurie was quite tall, just over five feet eleven. Her 155 pounds distributed themselves beautifully over her strong body which meant her curves were in all the right places. In high school, her complexion problems, her height and her terrifying father, frightened away most of the boys. Because of this, Laurie was quite used to being alone.

The lack of social attraction in high school, reflected itself in Laurie's personality. She learned to be sensitive. It amazed her how often she could feel what people were thinking. Helping others became a part of her character. That gentle sensitivity was easily felt by the other girls in the dorm. It was easy to be friends with Laurie. One other reason she was so popular with the women on campus was that her shy, introverted personality would never compete for the good-looking guys.

It was a Friday evening. Laurie had been studying in the carrels of the library. The carrels were tiny cubbyholes furnished with a desk and a good light. They were located amongst the stacks of books in the back of the building. It was a quiet place to study. Because the carrels were surrounded by that wonderful library smell, serious students loved to go there. It was much easier studying in the carrels than in the noisy college dorm. Much to her surprise, she came to the end of her homework early. It was only 8:00 o'clock. She decided to walk back to the dorm and clean her room.

It was then that she heard that sad sound.

She wasn't afraid. The campus at Denison University, whose enrollment is only about 2,000, is high on a hill above the little town of Granville, Ohio. There was virtually no possibility of a non-student being down on that bench crying.

As she eased her way down the darkened path to the bench, she could vaguely make out the figure of a tall man. He was sitting on the bench with his hands over his eyes trying to suppress his grief. If she heard him way back on the library steps, he was obviously not very successful.

Laurie hesitated. In her entire life, she could not remember seeing a grown man cry. His anguish seemed so real, she finally approached. "Are you okay? Is there something I can do to help you?"

He looked up at her through tear stained eyes. There was silence for a minute. Then he blurted out, "I came out here to be alone with my pain, but right now I could really use a shoulder to cry on."

Without hesitation, Laurie sat down and put her arm around him. His head came to her shoulder. When she did this, he started to cry again. He cried so hard she could only wonder what had happened. Then he started sobbing, deep gulping sobs. She could feel his tears dampening her jacket. Laurie didn't attempt to talk. She just held him, waiting for the tears to stop.

It took a long time. Finally, she heard him take a deep breath. Then he quietly whimpered, "I just got word my Grandpa died. We were very close. I loved him dearly."

Laurie politely murmured, "I'm so sorry."

"You can't truly understand until I tell you more. My mom and dad were killed in a car wreck when I was just one-year-old. Gram and Grandpa raised me. Gram died last year. Now Grandpa is gone too.

"I'm all alone. I've no mother, no father, no siblings, and now, no grandparents. My loneliness is total." The crying almost started again, but he managed to check it.

"I have no recollection of the pain from when my parents died. I was only one. But right now, I'm feeling serious pain. You're awfully nice to let me borrow your shoulder. You've no idea how nice it felt to be hugged just now."

Another short bout of tears came. She hugged him again, stroking his face with her soft hand. She tried to absorb his pain as best she could. Gradually, he stopped crying. He lifted his head to face her.

"I think I'm okay now. I just can't thank you enough," he whispered. "You've truly been a life saver."

Laurie replied, "I can understand from what you described how lonely you must feel. I'm aching for you and I don't even know your name."

Slowly he sat up, pulled a handkerchief from his pocket and attempted to compose himself. "My name's Brad Randall. I'm a freshman. My home is in Chelsea, Michigan, a suburb of Ann Arbor."

"My name is Laurie. Also a freshman. Or maybe I should say fresh woman … No, wait, fresh woman doesn't sound right."

In spite of his sorrow Brad smiled as he extended his hand, "Nice to meet you Laurie. Thanks for saving my life."

Laurie laughed, "I'm sure it wasn't that serious. Do you think a cup of coffee over at the Student Union's in order?"

"You know, a cup of coffee sounds like a great idea." He took her hand. Together, they started for the Union.

The second they stood up Laurie immediately noticed Brad's height. It seemed all her life the boys she dated were shorter. Even though this was not a date, it was nice to walk with someone taller than her five feet eleven inches.

Laurie wondered as he clung to her hand, if she should disengage. She decided he was so alone he really needed to connect with someone for a little while. She left her hand in his as they walked the short distance to the Union.

In a few minutes, they found themselves on opposite sides of a booth sipping hot coffee. Laurie forced a smile as she examined him in the light of the room.

Brad's eyes were red. Tears streaked his face. When he looked at Laurie, he was astonished. An extremely beautiful face was looking back at him.

After a minute, Brad fumbled out, "You're not only a lifesaving, sensitive person Laurie, you're an incredibly beautiful woman. I bet you have a million boyfriends. I hope you don't, because if there's an opening, I'd sure like to apply for the job."

Laurie smiled. "Why don't you go into the wash room and get some warm water on your face. I'll wait."

When he left, Laurie considered her response to his query. He seemed like a really nice person. He would never have gotten into the freshman class at a tough university like Denison if he wasn't pretty special.

Face washed, short hair slicked back, Brad sat back down offering a cautious smile. Laurie smiled at him, "Brad, I like to be straight with people. It will be difficult for you to apply for the job as my boyfriend because I'm not looking for romance. I'm happy just being me. I don't need a boyfriend to define who I am."

Brad thought for a minute. "In light of that, may I rephrase my question? Let me ask it this way. Would you allow me to be your friend even though I am a boy? I mean, maybe we could just hang out sometime."

Laurie laughed. Her smile was bright enough to light up a room. "After what we've been through tonight, I suppose we're already friends. But now, it's time for me to go back to the dorm."

"May I walk with you?"

"I don't see why not. At least part way."

As they walked out together, Brad took her hand again. For the second time that evening, Laurie decided not to say anything. *Actually, holding hands with him feels kinda nice.* There was silence between them; however, it wasn't a strained silence. Apparently, they were simply lost in their own thoughts and peaceful in each other's company.

In spite of his fog of grief, one thing was becoming clear to Brad. Laurie was the most sensitive person he'd ever encountered. She was also very attractive. *I feel some serious chemistry working here. I wonder if she feels it too?*

As Laurie walked, she confronted what was going through her mind. Perhaps it was because she felt warmth and caring from the tall freshman. Perhaps she just felt sorry for him. Whatever the reason, she decided maybe he could turn into someone important in her life. If that was going to be true, she needed to tell him something that she felt sure would seem weird to Brad. *Oh well, if he can't handle my weirdness, he's probably not worth it anyway. It'll be a way to find out.*

She turned to face him. "Brad, if you're going to be my *friend who is a boy,* you have to know that I come with a lot of rules. Some of these rules will seem strange to you I feel sure. But I have some very specific reasons for my rules."

"This sounds intriguing," Brad replied. "Can you share a rule or two with me?"

Laurie thought a minute. Then she made this statement. "Do you realize that I kept the conversation tonight entirely directed on you? I know your name, where you're from and a whole bunch about your life. All you know about me is my first name is Laurie and that I'm a freshman."

A stunned Brad responded, "You're right. I've been so upset; I haven't focused on getting to know you. That's very selfish, isn't it?"

"Not really, under the circumstances. Besides, I deliberately kept the conversation away from me. Which brings me to my number one rule."

"And rule number one is?"

Laurie took a deep breath, "Rule number one is.... I will not answer any questions about myself or my background for a significant period of time. I don't want you to even know my last name. Someday, if we remain friends, I promise to answer those questions. However, for right now, what you see is what you get, a Mystery Daughter. My background and my history are off limits. Furthermore, if you make a serious attempt to investigate those areas, I will terminate our friendship ASAP."

"Wow," Brad exclaimed. "Hey, you're serious, aren't you?"

"Yes I am. Dead serious. This is the one area where a person may not trespass if they want to become my *friend who is a boy*."

There was a silence for some time. Then Laurie added, "Please understand I have some very strong, logical reasons for this rule. For now, you're just going to have to go along with my wishes, no questions asked. Now, to prove my point, we're going to part company right up ahead where the path forks. You see, I don't want you to even know the name of my dorm. If you knew the dorm, it'd be simple to learn my last name and something about me."

"But how can I reach you?" asked a confused Brad.

"Humm.... I'll give you my cell number. It is 574 231 0655. You can always reach me on my cell."

Brad entered her number on his cell. When he offered his number to Laurie, he was pleased to see that she entered it into her phone. As they neared the fork in the path, Brad began to think aloud.

"Laurie, I hate to leave you because now I'll be forced to be all alone with my thoughts. Besides, I have to rent a car in the morning so I can drive home for the funeral. I really hate the thought of walking into that house all alone."

After a minute of further reflection, Brad decided to take a risk. "Laurie, by any miracle, would you consider going home with me? It's just a four-hour drive. The funeral's Monday morning so we could probably drive back to campus Tuesday. You'd have to miss your Monday and Tuesday classes … I guess that's way too much to ask……but I sure would appreciate some company."

The invitation stunned Laurie. Her initial response was…. silence. As they reached the place where the paths forked, she turned, still holding his hand and looked up into his sad eyes. "Brad, I had a talk with my mother right before I left home. She told me something that seems to apply to your request. She told me, "*Laurie, you are a child of God. When facing a difficult decision, believe your heart. You will know what to do.*

"Right now, looking at you, I feel trust. I also feel you really do need me. I haven't cut a class since I came to school. My grades are good. It might be all right if I missed a few classes. What time are you planning to leave?"

With soaring hopes, Brad replied, "I figure by the time I rent the car, it'll be around 9:30."

"OK, I'll be right at this spot where the path forks tomorrow at 9:30. I'll have my bag packed."

"Thank you so much," exclaimed Brad. "You can't imagine how much comfort you've just given me."

Without warning, he tipped up her chin and bent to kiss her. She exclaimed in a shocked voice, "I have a rule against kissing on a first date!"

Brad stopped. "Laurie, this isn't a date, and the kiss I'm planning to give you is not in the least romantic. It's simply a way to express my deep gratitude for all you've done for me tonight."

Without waiting for her to reply, he kissed her gently and tenderly right on the lips.

Laurie never understood why, but she didn't fight the kiss. Quite the contrary, she met it half way. When they broke apart she exclaimed, "You've violated my no kissing rule. You are in big trouble."

"What's the penalty for violating your no kissing rule?"

Hesitantly, Laurie replied, "I don't really know; no one's ever broken my first date no kissing rule before."

Brad countered, "Well, when you think of the penalty, think of a good one because I'm going to have to pay double."

With that, he took her face in his hands, kissing her again. This time the kiss slipped past the tender phase. His firm mouth transfixed Laurie, as did the way he put his arms around her pulling her close. It definitely was not a *platonic kiss.*

Laurie's breath caught. She felt herself flush. As they broke apart, she wanted her eyes to show anger. Instead, much to her dismay, they twinkled at him. "Now you really are in big trouble. Tomorrow at 9:30 you're going to find out how bad your punishment will be."

As Laurie walked the rest of the way to the dormitory, she pondered the events during those past two hours. *The poor guy is truly upset. I did a good thing helping him get through his grief. My agreeing to go home with him for the funeral was a kind, thoughtful thing for me to do. If he was an 'ugly duckling,' would I have agreed to go home with him? Probably not. He sure is good looking. Moreover, truth be told, I really liked it when he kissed me. I wonder what tomorrow will bring?*

Brad walked slowly home. The grief of losing his grandfather started to overwhelm him again. He forced himself to think about Laurie. *She's such a thoughtful, gentle person! She probably has a million boyfriends. I never should have kissed her once she agreed to go with me. She probably just feels sorry for me. I sure hope she doesn't change her mind.*

CHAPTER 2

Brad ran into trouble when he tried to rent a car the next morning. He was under the twenty-five-year age requirement. However, when he explained the circumstances, the kind rental agent bent the rules. Brad was able to get a decent Chevrolet for the one-way trip. He planned to return the rental car in Chelsea and drive back in his grandfather's car.

With fingers crossed, he started up the hill to the meeting place with Laurie. He was almost praying she would be there. First and foremost, he felt he truly needed company on that lonesome trip home. Taking those first steps into the empty house would surely be excruciating. But there was a second reason. He wondered if that was even more important than having company on the trip. *I'm feeling serious attraction towards Laurie. The wonder of kissing her was special. Even more importantly, I feel a true connection with her warm sensitivity.*

Suddenly he realized he was ten minutes late! He hadn't anticipated the delay at the car rental agency! *I should have called her on her cell! I bet she's left ... if she even showed up in the first place.*

Wonder of wonders, Laurie was still waiting! A small suitcase stood on the ground at her feet. A white scarf wrapped beautifully over her tan coat. The effect made a striking contrast with her long brown hair. She looked so good. Brad discovered his throat was dry.

Pulling up next to her he rolled down the window exclaiming, "I thought you were gorgeous last night. In the daylight, you're even more spectacular!"

She laughed as she came back with, "You're not fooling me with that line, Mr. Smooth!"

Jumping from the car to help with her bag, he explained the problem he'd encountered at the car rental agency. *God, I want to hug her!*

As he started the car he told her with absolute sincerity, "I'm so grateful to you for coming with me. Thank you a million times."

Laurie smiled, "Did you get any sleep?"

"You know, I really did. I think all that hard crying really sapped my energy. It was very cathartic. I hope you realize Laurie; your shoulder is a fabulous place for catching tears."

As they left tiny Granville he asked, "Have you eaten breakfast yet?"

"No I only grabbed a cup of coffee. I'm not hungry now, so maybe we should drive an hour or so and then stop. It'll help break up the trip."

"Have you thought of the penalty I have to pay for kissing you last night? I still say it wasn't a date. Consequently, I cannot be guilty of breaking your no kissing on the first date rule."

"As a matter of fact, I've spent a good deal of time thinking about this. My rules are very important to me and you blatantly ignored them. You're *it wasn't a date* argument has been considered and rejected by the court. So be prepared, because big trouble is about to descend upon you."

"You're making this sound really bad."

"Your penalty is… I'm putting you in *kissing purgatory*".

"What may I ask, is *kissing purgatory*?"

Laurie answered with a serious look. "When a person is in *kissing purgatory* he may not initiate a kiss with his friend who is a lady. He must refrain from kissing her totally."

"I see," acknowledged Brad……. "Ah, how does one get himself out of *kissing purgatory*?"

Laurie continued in her serious tone. "The only way a person can get out of *kissing purgatory* is to be so contritely good that the lady involved decides she cannot go any longer without a kiss from her friend. Consequently, she initiates a kiss. Now we need to discuss the second kiss. While I might agree that the first kiss was a kiss of gratitude for my allowing you to cry on my shoulder, the second kiss was of a much different nature. As a consequence, that second kiss has caused me to *double your fine.* Which means you will remain in *kissing purgatory* until I have kissed you twice."

"Wow. You're really tough, Laurie. Will you please define for me the meaning of *contritely good*?"

"No I will not. When you have affected me in some way that makes me want to kiss you, you will be informed."

"On that note." Brad countered, "I wish to appeal to a higher court."

"Sorry, Brad, there is no higher court."

"This is most unfair. However, I shall be noble and accept my punishment. Now, to start off my *contritely good* program, I'd like to invite you out for breakfast at that Cracker Barrel yonder."

The verbal sparring got both of them laughing. As they returned to the car after breakfast, Brad cornered Laurie against the car door asking, "I took you out for a nice breakfast. Does that constitute enough *contrite goodness* to warrant a kiss?" Their faces were only inches apart.

Laurie took a quick intake of breath. She realized her juices were flowing. She wanted that kiss. However, her common sense prevailed. "Not even close. I can see, Mr. Randall, you have no idea how much trouble you caused yourself by breaking one of my rules."

They climbed into the car and began driving. A long silence ensued. Laurie decided to add, "Just to reiterate, I want to remind you the most important rule in my book is the one regarding finding out my last name, where I live, or anything else about me prior to my entrance at Denison last September. I'm sorry Brad, but I need to remain The Mystery Daughter for now. Please assure me you understand that rule is extremely serious."

"I noticed you said Mystery Daughter, not Mystery Woman."

"Every female is a daughter. I mean, even though your parents have passed, you are still their son. But you are correct, I guess I could have said Mystery Woman."

"But you didn't. I think that's psychology significant."

A moment of silence occurred in the car. Then she said, "Adds to the intrigue, doesn't it?"

"Are you trying to intrigue me, Laurie?"

"Brad Randall, are you fishing to discover if I have some feelings for you?"

More silence.

At last Brad admitted, "I guess maybe I was. But can you blame me? Let's face it, you are a pretty spectacular female, Laurie. You're kind, sensitive, as well as damn good looking. You're the kind of a girl a guy is proud to bring home to meet his parents. You are definitely the marrying type."

"Brad Randall, we haven't had a date yet and you have brought up the 'M' word."

"The 'M' word?"

"The 'M' word is marriage."

"Oh … I don't think I ever heard the 'M' word expression. I guess I did bring it up, didn't I? ... Adds to the intrigue, don't you think?"

Laurie laughed as she said, "I think it's time to change the subject."

"We might as well do exactly that. One thing's for sure, I can't begin to come up with a reason why I can't ask you about your past life."

"You'll just have to trust me, won't you?"

"I guess. But your rule creates a problem. We're going to meet several people in Chelsea. What shall I tell them is your last name? If I just introduce you as Laurie, won't people wonder about your last name?"

"I suppose you're right....... Why don't you just tell them my name is Laurie Lansing? That kind of rhymes and it sounds innocent enough, don't you think?"

"Is Laurie Lansing your real name?"

"I refuse to answer on the grounds that it would violate my rule number one."

After a silent period, Laurie added, "You know Brad, I'm enjoying my time with you. Please trust me. I have a very good reason to keep you in the dark regarding my past. Let me assure you that I'm not a criminal or an axe murderer."

"I always thought an axe murderer who was female would be an axe murderess."

"I suppose that's true."

"Well, I'm a lot more comfortable now. Having an axe murderess accompany me is not high on my list of things to do."

When more silence fell, she added, "Okay, here's the deal. It's early November. If we are still friends on Valentine's Day, I'll take you out for dinner. At that dinner, I'll answer any questions you want. Is that fair?"

"Valentine's Day? That's three months away! Unfair!"

"Take it or leave it."

More silence ensued. Brad decided to fire another shot. "Laurie, suppose for a minute, I agree to go along with this mystery of yours. Would that constitute enough *contrite goodness* that I can get a kiss?"

"Oh, you are so naïve. Absolutely not."

There was another pause in the conversation. Strangely, Laurie was not upset by the silence. Usually, on those rare times when she was with a man, a lack of conversation felt awkward to her. Today, it just felt … *right.*

After several minutes of silence, Brad said, "I guess I have no option except to go along with your wishes. So, okay, I agree to your mystery status."

"You have made a very wise decision."

A few minutes later Laurie remarked, "Sometimes it helps ease a person's grief to talk about the loved one who died. Would you feel comfortable sharing with me something you recall about your grandfather?"

"Are you asking for the story of my life?"

"I guess I am. Please try and tell it in chronological order."

"Well, I was only one when my parents were killed. Consequently, I don't remember anyone except Gram whose name was Cathy, and my Grandpa, who everyone called Jay… They used to tell me stories about when I was a little boy. Do you want me to share those?"

"You know Brad, I really do."

"Well, let's see…There was one Christmas story Grandpa said he would never forget:

I guess I was about two. Apparently, I had a bad cold. It seems I woke up every night, coughing. This kept my grandparents awake all night. Grandpa knew Gram was exhausted.

On Christmas Eve, Gram and Grandpa put me to bed and then put the presents under the Christmas tree. After sharing some precious minutes together beside the tree, they went to bed. About 1:30 in the morning, Grandpa heard me cry out. He jumped up quickly because he wanted to get to me before Gram woke up.

When he entered my room, he found me standing in my crib. Tears were running down my face. Stuff dripped out of my nose. Apparently, I looked up at Grandpa and pleaded, "Rock-a-bye."

Grandpa told me he changed me, wiped my nose and cuddled me into my special blanket. That blanket went everywhere with me. Grandpa realized the only rocking chair they owned was in the living room. It was placed right next to the Christmas tree, which was surrounded by presents. Grandpa thought, it's dark. I think it'll be OK.

He took me down by the darkened Christmas tree at 1:30 in the morning and began to rock me. He started by singing the song Grandpa's mother used to sing to him when he was a baby:

Sweetest little fellow,
Everybody knows,
Don't know what to call him
But, he's mighty like a rose.
Lookin' at his mammy,
Eyes so shinny blue,

Makes you think that heaven
Is comin' close to you.

He told me that was exactly how he felt… that heaven was close to him, as he hugged and rocked me.

In a few minutes, I fell into a deep sleep. It was time to take me back to bed. But somehow, Grandpa didn't want to stop hugging and rocking. He said to himself, this is my Christmas! Rocking my grandson by the darkened Christmas tree, is the best Christmas present I could ever have.

Soon Grandpa ran out of songs to sing. He didn't know any more lullabies. Then he remembered how many of the Christmas carols actually are lullabies. So he sang Away in a Manger, The Friendly Beasts, Silent Night, and all of the Christmas songs, while we bonded together, there in the dark.

Every Christmas, Grandpa would share that story with me. For him, it had been an unforgettable moment.

Laurie found a tear in her eye. Then she looked and saw that Brad's eyes were also moist.

"What a beautiful story! But I didn't mean to make you sad. Maybe telling me Grandpa stories isn't a good idea."

"No, I think it's good for me to pull out the past. It's sort of cathartic."

"Are you sure? I love hearing the stories, but I don't want to upset you."

"Laurie, having you here with me is so comforting. I'll continue if you want to hear more."

"Please go on."

One cold winter night when I was about seven, the three of us went for a walk. A couple of streets away from our house we heard children playing in a back yard. When we looked, we realized the children were ice-skating on a back yard rink!

I asked if we could make an ice rink in our yard. Grandpa said, "I wonder how they make it?" Then he walked into the yard to ask the oldest boy how they made the rink.

The boy explained to Grandpa that the trick was not to flood the yard but to spray very thin coats of water on the grass. The boy told him, if you flood the yard, the water is warm enough to melt the ground. When that happens, the water simply drains into the ground.

You have to get a night when it's colder than 16 degrees. Then you go out and spread thin coats of water on the grass about every 30 minutes. Toward morning, you'll have a number of coats of thin ice on the ground. When you get to that phase, the thin ice coats will hold water. Then you can begin to flood the yard.

Grandpa thanked the boy. When he rejoined our walk, he reported what he had learned. "If you want, Brad, when we get the next cold snap, maybe we can try it."

I jumped with excitement.

"Laurie, you realize by age 7, I'm talking from my own memory, not a story handed down."

"Of course."

The following week a cold front moved into Michigan. As Grandpa drove home from work, he noticed the temperature was already down to 12 degrees. When he came into the driveway he could see I had already started spraying thin coats of water on the back yard.

We worked together until my bedtime. Then Grandpa kept making thin coats until after midnight. By 2:00 a.m. Grandpa felt he could start the flooding process. Sure enough, by 4:00 a.m. it was really beginning to look like an ice rink.

Grandpa finally hit the sack to get a few hours' sleep. He recalled later, the cold dry air was so stimulating he never got sleepy until he went to bed.

The next night the ice was in decent shape, however there were a few holes. Fortunately, some light snow had fallen. We discovered that we could plug the holes with snow. Then, with a touch of water, the hole would freeze over. Once we filled all the holes, the rink took shape quickly.

It wasn't long before all the kids in the neighborhood were skating on our backyard rink! Mothers and fathers joined in, too.

The next day, Grandpa bought a string of lights, which he hung in the trees over the ice rink. He also bought an outside loudspeaker, which he connected to the CD player. Now we skaters had music!

It stayed cold for many days that year. The ice rink made a very exciting, happy winter.

"Sounds like great fun. Did you ever build another rink?"

"Oh my, yes, we had ice rinks every year. We knew last year's rink was the final one because I wouldn't be home this January. We were lucky. It was cold for a long time last winter so we had lots of days to skate."

CHAPTER 3

"Am I boring you?"

"You most definitely are not. Please tell me another story."

On my ninth birthday, Grandpa gave me a chess set. Fascinated by the various chess pieces, it didn't take long for the two of us to lock in mortal combat. Grandpa let me win a few games at the beginning. As I progressed in my knowledge of the game, Grandpa played tougher.

After a year or so of strenuous competition, I complained, "I used to win most of the games. Now you beat me every time."

As I complained, I looked into Grandpa's eyes. The twinkle that was there gave it away.

"You let me win!"

"Yes," Grandpa admitted. "I thought if you won, it would be the best way to teach you. After a few months, I realized I was wrong. In life, we learn much more when we lose than when we win. This is especially true in Chess. People learn from their mistakes."

Grandpa continued, "From now on, we are going to write down every chess move. Then we can replay the game and see where the mistakes occurred. When we do that, we'll both learn to improve our games.

"I want to make a promise to you, Brad. I promise that from this point forward, I'll never let you win. If you beat me, it'll be because you earn the victory, not because I allowed you to win."

"Our games improved sharply after that. However, I found I couldn't beat Grandpa, no matter how hard I tried.

"I may have gotten out of chronological order but one night when I was just a kid, the three of us were sitting around the fire after dinner and I asked them to tell me about my parents.

"There was a pause, then Gram began. "Our son, your father, was named John. He was a good looking young man. He did well in college and got a good job in downtown Detroit when he graduated. He met your mother Margaret, his senior year in college at the University of Michigan. They were married right after graduation. They had a small apartment in Detroit, which is where they brought you when you came home from the hospital.

"When you were about one-year-old, your mom and dad went to a play at the Fisher Theatre in downtown Detroit. Coming home, there was a huge smash up on the expressway. Your parents were in the middle of it. They died instantly. John and your mother would have loved you terribly, Brad. They would be extremely proud of you because you are a very good boy. I still miss them every day."

"I remember looking up at my grandfather and asking, "Where do you go when you die?"

After some reflection, Grandpa began, "No one really knows, Brad. Your body remains here on earth. Some people are buried. Others choose to cremate, that means to burn the human remains into ashes. Often, people scatter the ashes into the air or on the water in some beautiful place. That's what we did with John and Margaret. Their ashes were scattered to the winds up there in the field behind the house.

He continued, "What happens to the spirit or the souls of people who die? No one really knows the answer. I like to think those spirits are up there somewhere looking down on us; watching and helping us do the right thing. In a sense, that's where you have an advantage, Brad. The other kid's parents might be miles away when their child needs help. But your mom and dad are always watching over you, no matter where you go."

"If you ever have a problem and don't know what the right thing is, you can always ask yourself, what would mom and dad want me to do? If you do that, I bet you'll find the answer to your problem."

"Grandpa then taught me a good lesson. He said, "There's an old saying I would like to share with you, Brad."

'To live in hearts we leave behind is not to die.'

"Your job is to remember that your mom and dad were good people who loved you very much. Your further job is to continue to grow into a strong, honest person, so your parents will always be proud of you."

I recall looking at Gram and Grandpa and saying "Thanks for loving me, you guys. I love you a whole bunch."

Then we all three hugged each other and cried. When we went to bed that night, the kisses were extra special. That serious discussion created some real closeness in our little family. The closeness remained always.

Laurie quietly, almost reverently, interjected. "Brad, I wonder if you realize how fortunate you are to have had all that love and tenderness in your home. Lots of kids never have that privilege, you know."

"I'm sure you're right, Laurie. I think that's why Grandpa's passing hurts so much. We had such a special relationship."

"More stories, please."

"Are you sure?"

"Oh Brad, I really am. You have no idea how your stories help me to get to know you."

"Laurie, is it becoming important that you get to know me?"

"There's no way I'm answering that question. Get back to the stories, please."

In high school, I tried out and made the football team. I was tall and fast, so the coach put me at end. By my junior year, I was starting tight end. I love football. Gram and Grandpa were always in the stands, cheering for me. I also became interested in the school newspaper. I liked writing articles. I did well in academics, so a college education appeared to be within reach.

The social pressures of high school were many and concerning. One group of students was into dope and drinking. Fortunately, I was a little shy. The fast crowd intimidated me, so I stayed away. This decision delighted Gram and Grandpa.

Girls were another matter. When you're tall and on the football team, girls get friendly.

One sexy looking brunette named Nancy became important to me.

Apparently, Gram expressed her concern to Grandpa one night after I left for a date with Nancy.

Grandpa agreed, "She's nothing but a hussy. She scares me to death."

Gram exclaimed, "What if they get pregnant?"

Grandpa remained silent a while. Then he responded, "We have to trust that sooner or later Brad will see through Nancy. When he does, they'll split up. If we get involved, it could backfire and drive them together rather than apart."

Grandpa had a collection of poetry and important sayings he kept in a box on a shelf in the living room. After he thought a minute, he got up, picked up the collection and started leafing through it. In a few minutes, he began to read some excerpts from The Prophet by Kahlil Gibran:

Your children are not your children.
They are the sons and daughters of life's longing for itself.

Though they come through you,
They come not from you.
And though they are with you
They belong not to you.
You may give them your love, but not your thoughts.
They have their own thoughts.
You are the bows from which your children as living arrows are sent forth.
The Archer sees his mark upon the path of the infinite.
He bends you with his might that his arrows may go swift and far.
Let your bending in the Archer's hand be for gladness
For even as he loves the arrow that flies,
So loves He also the bow that is stable.

When Grandpa finished reading he told Gram, "I think this is one of those times when we give Brad our love but not our thoughts. He has his own thoughts."

Just then, the doorbell rang. It was Mary Sue Johnson, their next-door neighbor. Mary Sue's son, Tim, had spent many days on our back-yard ice rink.

Mary Sue was upset because Tim was involved with the fast crowd. There was a girl in Tim's life too. Mary Sue was not happy with this 'piece of trash' as she put it.

"We are thinking of confining Tim to the house on weekends. Do you think that's a good idea?"

Gram said nothing. She just looked at Grandpa. Grandpa pondered what to say for a moment. Then he said, "A high school senior will be in college next year. He'll be doing stuff then which you cannot control. To lock him up now might create more problems than leaving him to work out of the situation by himself.

After a minute's reflection Grandpa asked, "What would happen if that 'piece of trash' became your daughter in law?" He let that sink in a minute and then he reflected, "It's a good idea in dealing with a teenager to make no lasting scars."

Then Grandpa asked Mary Sue, "Did you ever hear the Aesop Fable, 'The Wheat and the Oak?'

"No I don't think I have," replied Mary Sue.

Grandpa related the story:

There was once a great strong oak tree growing on the side of a wheat field. One day a great windstorm came and blew down the oak. As the oak was lying on its side watching the wheat swaying in the wind, the oak said. "Why does a great strong oak like me fall in this wind and you are still standing?"

The wheat said to the oak, "It is better to bend than to break."

Grandpa concluded, "When dealing with teenagers, it's better to bend than to break."

Mary Sue considered this for a few minutes. "Thank you, Jay. You're a wise man. I appreciate your advice."

"Laurie, do you want me to quit?"

"No way. Your stories are fascinating."

CHAPTER 4

Brad announced, "We're in Bowling Green, Ohio which is about half way. Do you need to stop for a minute?"

"No, I'm OK. I want more stories."

"When do I get to ask about you?"

"I told you, Valentine's day."

"But what about from the time you arrived on campus till now?"

"We can talk about that on the way back. It won't take long because we're only going to talk about eight weeks of time."

"Maybe I should share some happy times. When I was little, Grandpa would make up stories. Would you like to hear one?"

When Laurie agreed, Brad said, "Okay, now pretend you are six years old. You are visiting your grandfather."

The NO BOY Story

Once upon a time, there was a nasty little boy who always told everyone "Nooo" in a very crabby voice. Because he was so negative, everyone called him the NO BOY.

It just happened that the NO BOY went to visit a mean old man who owned a house in Florida. In front of the old man's house was a fresh water bayou populated by alligators.

The mean old man believed everyone should help with the household chores. The man told the NO BOY, "By helping with the work, everyone will appreciate how nice it is to have a house to visit in Florida."

The old man asked the NO BOY "Will you please help wash the dishes?"

The NO BOY snarled "NAOO" in a very irritating voice.

The old man then asked the NO BOY, "Please take out the trash."

The NO BOY again snarled "NAOO" in a nasty irritating voice.

The old man told the No Boy, "If you say NO to me again in that nasty irritating voice, I will throw you into the Bayou where all the alligators are! Now, will you please help sweep the floor?"

Once again the NO BOY snarled "NAOO" in his nasty irritating voice.

The old man grabbed the NO BOY. He threw him into the bayou. There was a great SPLASH and then a huge SWIRL in the water.

And there was NOO BOY!

"I love it!" Laurie giggled. "I can just see that six-year-old's face when he heard that there was no boy!"

She continued, "I think I'm becoming very fond of your grandfather."

"Maybe I should share this story."

"Toward the end of my junior year, Gram got pneumonia. She tried to fight it at home for a while. Finally, as the disease worsened, she went to the hospital.

"I'll never forget the last night with Gram in the hospital.

"Grandpa and I drove to the hospital right after dinner. The staff nurse told us Gram was going downhill rapidly. When we got to her room, it was evident the nurse was correct. Gram was really weak. Even with the oxygen tubes in her nose, it was easy to see her breathing was very shallow.

"Grandpa asked, "How are you feeling, Cathy."

"She replied in a weak voice. "Jay dearest, I suspect I'm going to see John and Margaret soon. I'm excited, because I'll have such a wonderful report to share with them about Brad."

She turned to me. "Thank you, Brad, for all you did to make my life significant and wonderful. You're a terrific young man. You will always have a warm spot in my heart. Never forget, I love you deeply."

"Then she turned to Grandpa, "Thanks my darling, for all my wonderful memories. I'll be waiting for you!"

"A few minutes later Gram fell asleep. It was as if she just waited until 'her boys' got there to say goodbye. We kept a vigil by the bedside. After a couple of hours, we realized Gram had stopped breathing.

"We hugged each other, as we sobbed.

"Later, we scattered Gram's ashes on the same hilltop where my folk's ashes were scattered. I remember Grandpa saying, "I'm sure Gram will be waiting by the door for us when our time comes. Oh, my darling wife, how much I miss you."

"I began my senior year in high school without Gram. Grandpa faced a life without his loving wife. As we each struggled with our loss, we became closer to each other. However, we both knew college would begin the next fall. Our days together were ending."

There was an interval of silence in the car. Laurie broke it. "I'm beginning to comprehend why you were so upset last night. First your Gram, who was for all purposes your mother, and now Jay, who was in reality your father. You know, Brad, sharing these stories with you has helped me understand you a whole lot. It makes me really glad I decided to come with you."

"You have no idea how much I appreciate your coming with me, Laurie. Can you imagine what it would be like if I was all alone in this car right now?"

"Not fun, that's for sure. Tell me about your senior year in high school."

It began with my last football season. For the second year, I was a starting receiver on the varsity. We had a good team that year. We won our first four games. We were looking forward to the game against Dexter, another undefeated team, in game six. Ahead of the Dexter game there was an 'easy game' against Saline, a team that had already lost 3 times.

Grandpa told me he had a feeling our team was looking past the 'easy game' to the 'big game' the following week. It was a premonition. An upset was in the cards. It was an away game for one thing. It was pouring rain for another.

We had two powerful running backs. In the rain and mud, however, their speed slowed to a walk. There was no score at the half. Late in the fourth quarter we fumbled deep in their territory. Saline recovered the fumble. They were able to push across a touchdown. The game ended with a 6 – 0 defeat for us.

Grandpa always had permission to travel on the team bus. He was sort of a voluntary coach. On the way back home, he asked the head coach if he could speak to a very disheartened team. The coach agreed. Jay stood up and got everyone's attention.

"Did you ever ask yourself why sports are included in high school education? Trust me, it's not just so you can have fun. Students learn 'lessons for life' through sports.

"Today you have an opportunity to learn two of those important 'lessons for life.' The first lesson, which I'm sure you all realize by now, is to play each game, one at a time. Don't look ahead to the next week. However, guys, that's not the important lesson.

"This is the important lesson you can learn from the game tonight. ***The true measure of a man is not what he does when he wins; it's what he does when he loses.***

"Does he start moping around feeling sorry for himself? Or does he pick himself off the floor, congratulate his opponent, put a grin back on his face, and go forward?

"You have a great opportunity to show the world you have the 'inner fire' that allows you to come back from defeat with a positive, upbeat attitude.

"If you can do that, I feel sorry for that Dexter team you play next week. They will expect you to be down and feeling sorry for yourselves. They will be the overconfident team. However, you can fill yourselves with that inner fire that makes true champions. You have learned one of the great lessons of life. That lesson is what to do after you lose.

"What is it going to be, guys, depression or inner fire?"

There was silence on the bus for a few seconds. Then the entire team rose to their feet and yelled "inner fire!"

"The coach was thrilled with Grandpa's little talk. The boys became upbeat. The conversation shifted to ways to win the game next week.

"In the Dexter game, on the very first play, I caught a short pass over the middle, dodged two tacklers and ran the ball in for a touchdown. The play covered 80 yards. It set to tone for the entire game. We pasted Dexter 33 to 14.

The following week was my last game. At breakfast on game day, Grandpa asked if I planned to try out for football in college.

"I've been thinking about that a lot Grandpa. "I truly don't think I'm heavy enough to compete at the college level."

"So, this will be your last game?"

"I guess it will."

Grandpa reflected, "You know, every player in every sport reaches a spot where he has to 'hang up his spikes.' The odds of making it into the professional ranks are almost impossible. There are only about 3,000 professional athletes in the entire United States in all professional sports. Even the pros reach a spot when they have to 'hang em up.'

"He continued, 'Competing teaches great lessons for life. It teaches the value of hard work. It teaches the importance of practice. It teaches what to do when you lose. In addition, it teaches us to be gracious when we win. You've learned those lessons, well, Brad. I'm proud of you. I know Cathy, your mom, and your dad would be very proud of you too."

"That night I caught five passes and scored a touchdown. The team won for the sixth time against only one loss. By any measurement, it was a successful season. On the next to the last play of the game, coach took me out. I got a huge ovation. It was a very heady moment.

"When Grandpa caught up to me after the game, there were tears in his eyes. I had tears too. Grandpa quietly spoke to me, "You're growing up, young man. And growing up always hurts a little."

"As Grandpa walked away from me, he realized there was a girl there waiting. Since I made no move to introduce the girl, Grandpa immediately made an assumption. She's not the kind of girl a boy wants to *bring home to mother.*

"The next morning at breakfast, Grandpa brought up the subject. "A girl was after you last night, does she have a name?'

"I was stunned for a minute. Then I blushed and replied, "Yes, her name is Helen Maloney."

"Grandpa remarked, "Was there a reason you didn't want to introduce her to me?"

"I fumbled around to find the correct words. Finally, Grandpa let me off the hook by saying, "Would you say she's just a practice girl?"

"Yes, that's it, she's just a practice girl.

"Grandpa nodded and then warned, "You want to ruin your life, just get a girl like that pregnant."

"I opened my mouth to say something, then I thought better of it.

"Grandpa continued, 'Girls like that know if they get a super kid to get them pregnant, they can force you to marry. Marriage at age eighteen is a very tough way to start life. I imagine being married to a girl who's only interested in sex can be satisfying for a while. However, if a couple have no common interests and no similarity of intellect, the marriage will be fraught with danger.

"Sexual attraction is very easy. It's normal for young people. However, sex without love is a very selfish act. Each person is in it for his or her own enjoyment.

"True love is not something you take; it is something you give away."

I asked, "Grandpa, how do you know when it is true love?"

"You are asking a tough question to answer, but I'll take a shot at it. If the girl is the kind of person you don't want to introduce to your Grandpa, it's almost certainly not true love. That's a person who you are ashamed of in some way. If sexual gratification is the only thing in the relationship, you can be pretty sure that's not true love.

"When it's true love, you generally become friends with the person first. You find you truly enjoy being together. You think about ways to please your friend and make them happy. After that stage, when the sexual desires come to the fore, your sex act becomes a way to please your partner. Your own selfish desires take second place. When that happens, sex gets truly wonderful."

"I expect your Gram could have explained all this much better...but she isn't here and I felt this subject needed to be covered."

I remember saying, "Thanks, Grandpa. I'll try to remember true love isn't something you take; it's something you give away."

CHAPTER 5

Laurie broke in. "Brad that story makes me jealous."

"Jealous?"

"No one in my family ever had a conversation on that subject with me. You were very lucky to have such loving, caring people around you."

"I never thought of it quite like that, Laurie, but of course you're right."

"So how did you select Denison?"

"After football season ended we decided it was time to start thinking seriously about where I would go to college the next fall. Grandpa proposed a trip into Ohio. He said, "Many small colleges in Ohio have splendid reputations. I think you might enjoy going to a small school."

"I remember saying, 'Well, living where we do, I have already seen Michigan State and the University of Michigan. I agree those big schools with 40,000 plus students don't feel right for me. I have also seen Albion. I kind of thought Albion might work. However, nothing is certain at this point. I'll talk to the counselor at school and get the names of some Ohio schools to think about."

"A few weeks later we headed south for a weekend trip to look over the Ohio small colleges. We looked at The College of Wooster and then Kenyon College. I had some interest in those two schools, but not a lot. Late in the day, we drove into Granville. I was immediately attracted to the small town. As you know, Laurie, the beginnings of the Appalachian Mountains are sensational, especially in fall colors. I was stunned by the beauty of the Chapel, which towers over the main drive up the hill to the campus. We parked the car and began walking across the main quadrangle. Both of us were impressed with the beauty of the campus buildings and the layout across the quadrangle.

"As we walked, we noticed almost all of the students who passed by said

"Hello." Later we found out it was a campus tradition to say "Hello" whenever you pass someone. That tradition gave a warm friendly feeling to the campus. Then we found out the enrollment was limited to about 2,000 students. I became intensely interested.

"We went into the admission office and interviewed the admissions director. It appeared with my good grades it would be possible for me to gain admission to the freshman class starting in the fall.

"Then I asked how much it would cost to go to Denison. The answer stunned me. I looked at grandfather. He was grinning. When we got back outside I asked grandpa why he was smiling.

Grandpa then explained my financial situation. "When your Mom and Dad were killed," he began, "they had a modest amount of life insurance. It wasn't a whole lot. I invested it with the hope it might grow large enough to pay for your college education. If you save money and invest it for 18 years, the interest and capital gains can really be substantial. Of course, this meant all your growing up costs came out of our income, but your Gram and I were happy to provide those things for you.

"So, Brad" smiled Grandpa, "I'm happy to report to you there is enough money in your college account to pay for your tuition and costs at Denison. Please remember, all of the money came from your mother and your father. Your college education will be their lasting gift to you."

"I was speechless. I hugged Grandpa really hard. When we returned home, my mind made up, I applied for early admission at Denison."

Laurie said, "More stories please."

"You are insatiable."

"Well, maybe it's because I met this nice guy and for some strange reason, I want to know more about him."

Brad smiled. Then he continued.

"As graduation approached, I was selected by my classmates to be the graduation speaker. I decided not to tell grandfather of the honor, I wanted to surprise him. I worked hard on my speech. I wanted it short and straight to the point. My speech teacher had taught me the secret to speaking without notes. I recall him telling the class, "To memorize a speech is extremely difficult. The secret is to outline the speech, then memorize the outline."

I wrote out the speech. Then I made an outline of the speech, stressing the important points. Next, I memorized the outline. By the time graduation day arrived, I was ready to deliver the speech without notes. As the time approached,

I found I wasn't exactly nervous. I was excited to get up and do a good job and at the same time to surprise Grandpa.

When the time came, I stood at the microphone and paused until the room became deadly silent. I think I can still remember what I said:

"Today's a very important day in the lives of everyone in this room. It's an important day for the graduates. It's also an important day for our teachers and for all the parents and grandparents who are out there in the audience or who are with us today, in spirit.

As graduates, we look forward to the future. However, we also look back to the four happy years we've spent here. We've learned to work hard, to use our time well, to strive constantly to learn and to become better citizens. As we go forward, these characteristics will enable us to face whatever is in our future with optimism and confidence. For that, we owe a great deal of thanks to the faculty and administrators of our school.

As the saying goes, 'Make good habits and the good habits will make you!'

We also owe a great deal to our parents and, especially in my case, to our grandparents. As a special tribute, I want to share with you a poem by Erma Bombeck. It's called "Kites."

KITES

"I see children as kites.
You spend a lifetime trying to get them off the ground.
You run with them until you are both breathless...they crash...they hit the rooftop...you patch and comfort, adjust, and teach, you watch them lifted by the wind and assure them that someday they'll truly fly.
Finally, they are airborne, but they need more string... so you keep letting it out. But, with each twist of twine, there is sadness that goes with your joy.
The kite becomes more distant, and you know it won't be long before that beautiful creature will snap the lifeline that binds you together and will soar, as it is meant to soar, free and alone.
Only then do you know... you did your job."

"And now Parents and Grandparents, Teachers and Administrators, the time has come to watch these graduates fly!"

As the crowd stood to applaud, I looked right into grandpa's eyes. As I did so, I could see joy, pride and sadness. The look resulted in some gentle tears for both of us.

• • •

About an hour after crossing the Michigan state line, they approached Chelsea. Brad decided to drive by the high school so he could point it out to Laurie. Then they headed toward his grandfather's house. "Our neighbors, Mary Sue Johnson, her husband Tom, and their son Tim will probably be the first people you'll meet."

When they pulled into the driveway, Brad turned off the car. He just sat there looking at the little house. He was certain walking into the empty house was going to be one of the hardest things he'd ever done.

Laurie examined the house. A ranch model, with white aluminum siding, filled much of the 150-foot lot. Behind the house, she could see a hill. Some cows were munching on the grass. It was certainly not pretentious, just an average house located on the edge of a small Michigan town.

There were gardens with evergreen trees in front to soften the harsh lines of the ranch style house. A large scattering of colorful autumn leaves covered the front lawn. Most were under an enormous oak tree with a swing attached. The yard obviously needed a good raking.

Brad took a deep breath. "Okay Laurie, this is why I needed you to come with me. Let's go in and face the memories."

Slowly they walked up to the front door. Brad got out his key, turned the bolt and pushed the door open. She took his hand. Holding tightly, they went in together.

Apparently, the Johnson's had turned the heat on, so the house was warm, not cold or clammy. Brad was grateful. The Johnson's also must have picked up everything in the house and vacuumed.

Laurie found herself impressed with the big picture window in the living room. The afternoon sun was shining through. It gave a nice warm glow to the room.

Brad turned, guiding her into a kitchen-family room combination. He walked over placing his hand gently on a big easy chair. Judging by the way he stroked it, it was easy for Laurie to realize… it was his grandfather's favorite chair. He touched a smaller chair, beside the fireplace. Laurie guessed it was his grandmother's chair. When they reached his grandparent's bedroom, Brad just stood at the door, searching the room. He took a deep breath. Then he turned to Laurie. "You know; I've truly been dreading this moment. It may sound funny to you, but it's not as bad as I expected. I feel as if the house has sort of wrapped its arms around me. I'm feeling close to my Grandparents here rather than lonely. Having you with me, has helped a lot too."

Laurie silently managed a warm smile. Then Brad added, "Let's check the fridge and see if there's anything to eat." When they did, they found out the pickings were very slim.

"Maybe we should take the rental car back so we can get lunch in town and pick up some groceries. You can follow me in Grandpa's car. I suspect the keys are on his dresser."

They went out to the rental car and retrieved their bags. He took Laurie's bag and showed her to the guest room. His bag went into his own room.

Just as they were leaving to head for town, Mary Sue Johnson came over. She threw her arms around Brad. They hugged for a long time. When they broke apart, they were both crying.

Brad said, "Mary Sue, I want you to meet a friend of mine, Laurie Lansing. She was kind enough to make the trip with me so I wouldn't have to be alone facing all of this."

Mary Sue went up to Laurie giving her a warm hug. "You must be a kind, sensitive person to come into this situation."

Laurie responded, "I truly don't understand why I agreed to come. However, I'm glad I did. No one should have to go through this alone."

"Will you two come over for dinner tonight?" asked Mary Sue.

"We'd be glad to," Laurie responded. "I'm not a cook, so you'll be doing a real service."

Mary Sue took a deep breath. "Brad, a few nights ago, your Grandfather came over and gave us a letter. He told us, *If I forget to wake up some morning, please read this. It's got all the information you'll need, including how to reach Brad.*

"At the time, we didn't think it was anything but his being cautious, but he died so soon after he gave us the letter……. It makes me wonder if he had a premonition."

Mary Sue then added, "Brad, you probably better plan a stop to see Mr. Denks at the funeral parlor. We asked him to cremate your grandfather as he instructed us to do. You may be able to pick up his ashes."

"OK thanks, Mary Sue. We'll see you at dinnertime. Thank you so much."

CHAPTER 6

Brad went back into the house so he could sit down and carefully read his Grandfather's instructions. When he finished, he handed the letter to Laurie so she could read it.

The letter was businesslike and terse. He wanted to be cremated and his ashes strewn with his wife and children's up at the top of the hill behind the house. No viewing at the funeral parlor, just a small funeral at the church. He suggested Brad confer with his attorney in town, Mr. Olsen. The letter was dated two days before he died.

"Did you and your Grandpa ever discuss this situation, Brad?"

"Yeah, a few times. Do I think he had a premonition?... Yes, I do. The last time we talked on the phone he seemed extra anxious to tell me how much he loved me and how proud he was of the person I was becoming." Softly, in an anguished voice, he exclaimed, "God, how I loved him!"

It was then that the tears came. Laurie hugged Brad as he let them flow. After a while, he smiled through tear stained eyes at Laurie. A few minutes later, they were able to head back out to the cars.

Brad drove the rental car back to the car return location. Laurie followed in Grandpa's car. After they returned the car, Brad stopped by to pick up his Grandfather's ashes at the funeral parlor. According to his grandfather's wishes, Mr. Denks had placed the ashes in a small cardboard box. There would be no expensive frills to this funeral service. After that, they bought a few groceries.

The dinner with the Johnson's was pleasant. Laurie liked Mary Sue and her husband Tom. Laurie could easily discern their son, Tim, was in the fast crowd. He and Brad had little in common.

When the main course ended, Laurie noticed Brad jumping up to help Mary Sue clear the table and load the dishes into the dishwasher. In her house, servants did the dishes. She admonished herself. *If I want acceptance from these hard-working people, I'd better start helping.*

When dessert was over, Laurie began to clear the dishes. Soon she found herself alone with Mary Sue in the kitchen. Mary Sue was burning with curiosity. "Have you and Brad been dating long?" she asked.

"Actually," Laurie answered, "we've never even had a date. I was walking home from the library last night. I heard this boy sobbing." She related the story to Mary Sue.

She continued, "One of my goals in life is to be kind to people in need. When Brad explained his total loneliness, I realized how tough this was going to be for him. I just couldn't refuse to join him when he asked me to come. Now you know my being here is not because we're romantically involved. I'm just being a friend."

Mary Sue remained silent for a long while. Then she said, "I sensed from the start, Laurie, you were a special person. I really was hoping you two were 'involved.' Brad is one of the finest people you'll ever meet. He needs someone thoughtful and loving, exactly like you. I hope you'll not close your eyes to a possible romance…… If I'm not being presumptions, judging by the way Brad looks at you, I think he's already smitten."

"Mary Sue, I think you're just a romantic at heart!"

Shortly after dinner, Brad and Laurie excused themselves. It had been a long day. They were both tired.

When they got to Brad's house, he simply locked the front door. Then he turned to look at Laurie. "Is it all right if I just go bed?" he asked, "I'm really bushed."

Laurie replied, "Of course. I brought some studying to do, so I'll be up for a little while."

"If you need anything let me know." Brad headed for his room.

About a half an hour later, Laurie found she could not keep her eyes open. *Time to hit the hay*, she thought. She turned off the living room lights and headed towards her bedroom.

As she approached her door, she heard sobbing coming from Brad's room. *The poor kid*, she thought, *I wondered when he was going to let go.*

Quietly, she opened Brad's door. He was lying on his side staring away from the door and crying hard. Laurie's heart melted. "Would you like a shoulder to cry on for a minute?" she asked.

He turned, "Yeah, I really would."

Laurie lay down on the top of the blankets. She correctly figured, with the blankets between them, nothing would get out of hand. Gently pulling Brad's head onto her shoulder, she just let him cry. Brad's grief overpowered any other thoughts.

They lay there together a long time. Finally, Brad's crying stopped. "I just can't thank you enough for all the comfort you're giving to me Laurie. I'd never have been able to get through this alone. I'm eternally grateful to you."

Laurie simply stroked Brad's face. She hugged him firmly. Slowly he drifted off to sleep. When she was certain he was asleep, Laurie extracted her arm from under his head and went off to bed.

As tired as she was, sleep refused to come. Laurie got up, threw on her robe, went into the living room and found the rocking chair. She rocked herself in the dark. As she rocked, she began to think.

Coming here was crazy. However, I'm glad I came. Brad really needed a friend. I feel good because I'm helping someone. The interesting question is... am I falling for Brad, or do I just feel sorry for him?

She rocked and thought. He seems to be a really nice sincere guy... She continued rocking... Finally, she gave up. The answer, she guessed, *was...maybe a little bit of both.* After she returned to bed, sleep finally came.

Instead of being a restful day when a person could get some studying done, Saturday turned into a zoo. Because of Grandpa's request was that there "was to be no 'viewing' at the funeral parlor," many of Grandpa and Brad's friends dropped in to visit and to extend condolences.

Laurie found herself serving the guests with whatever she could find or borrow from Mary Sue next door. When the parade of guests finally stopped, Brad offered to take Laurie out for dinner. She gratefully accepted.

• • •

They drove to East Lansing. In the car, Brad explained why he decided to take Laurie to his favorite restaurant which was the State Room on the campus of Michigan State University.

"The students in the Hotel Management curriculum staff the restaurant. The food's always good. I enjoy the warm friendly service the students provide."

After they ordered, Brad looked at Laurie, "Can we call this our first date?"

Laurie smiled at him. He wore a blue shirt with dark blue slacks. His glowing eyes smiled adoringly into hers. She realized the decision to get away from Brad's home had been a good one.

Laurie thought aloud, "Well, you asked me out for dinner and I accepted. But it was very 'spur of the moment.' I didn't have time to get all dressed up, so it's not a date."

Brad examined her clothes carefully. She had on a white blouse, which one could see through. It revealed a lacy slip. The effect bordered on provocative. Beneath her dark brown pleated skirt, which stopped just above her knees, were her shapely calves. Her feet were tucked into matching brown heels. Laurie's light brown hair fell softly against her face. It made a wonderful frame to a smiling mouth topped by shining brown eyes.

"You look awfully pretty to me, Laurie."

After dinner, they decided to go for a walk. The MSU campus looked beautiful in the streetlights. He took her hand and she let him hold it. After a while, they reached a dark spot in the path. Brad turned to her. "I guess I'm still in *kissing purgatory,* aren't I?"

Laurie's reply came out a little more sharply than she intended. "You certainly are. "Please remember, I came with you to be your friend, not your girlfriend."

As soon as she said it, she realized she'd made a mistake. Brad's shoulders sagged. The enthusiasm she felt from him earlier, drained right out of him.

He mumbled, "I guess we better be heading back." Laurie realized she had ruined the evening with her thoughtless remark.

As they approached the house Brad asked, "Do you want to go to church tomorrow or sleep in?"

Laurie replied, "I really need to get some studying done."

Brad responded, "I need to study too, however, I think I'll go to church. It's probably a good plan if you don't come. In this small town, tongues will wag if we go to church together. And I know you don't want anyone to think you're my girlfriend."

Laurie winced. His remark reflected how badly she'd hurt him.

When they got inside, Brad turned to her. "I can't thank you enough for hugging me last night, Laurie. It was more comforting than you'll ever know. Thanks for tonight. I had a really good time on our… not date."

He went to his room. Laurie went to the rocking chair and rocked away her misery. *Why did I say such a thoughtless thing? The way Brad feels right now about his Grandfather, he sure didn't need me squashing his romantic ego. Laurie, you have undone a lot of the good you were doing.*

• • •

Brad left early for church.

When Laurie woke up, she realized Brad was gone. After coffee and toast she tried to study. It was useless. She found herself looking at the page, however nothing was recording in her head. She announced to the empty room, "*I'm still upset because of my thoughtless remark last night.*"

She quit trying to study and headed for the rocking chair. *Am I falling for the guy, or do I just feel sorry for him? That is the problem. I squashed him because I'm very unsure of what's going on in my heart.*

Laurie rocked and thought. She remembered something her grandmother once taught. "*When you are in a 'situation' the best plan is to be absolutely truthful.*"

That became the temporary answer. *Just sit down with Brad and tell him the truth.*

A few minutes later Brad returned. She looked at him asking, "Did you eat before you left for church?"

"No. Well, just coffee. While I'm changing out of my suit, why don't you fry up some eggs and bacon? We can have a Sunday brunch."

A shamed Laurie admitted, "Brad, I don't know how to fry eggs and bacon."

"You can't be serious!"

"Unfortunately, I am serious,"

"Would you like to learn? I'd love to teach you."

'I'd like that very much."

"As soon as I change, I'll show you the kitchen ropes."

This will be good Laurie thought. We'll be sort of *starting over*. He can teach me something I always wanted to know. After we eat, I'll talk with him.

Teaching Laurie to cook bacon and eggs turned out to be fun for both of them. Brad proved to be a patient teacher. Instead of demonstrating how to do it, he just offered instructions and let her do the actual work. As she did it, her confidence grew. Cooking was fun. She was able to fry four eggs, over easy. To her credit, she only broke one yolk, which Brad assured her, was really good for a first timer. Breakfast over, Laurie told Brad as they refilled their coffee cups, "We need to talk."

"We do?"

"Yes, we do. I need to apologize for the stupid remark I made last night. In addition, I need to explain things to you."

Brad could sense she was serious, so he wisely remained silent. He just let his eyes caress her face.

Taking a deep breath, Laurie began. "Remember the other night when you were crying and I came in and lay on the bed beside you?" When Brad nodded, she continued. "Well, after I left you, I found out I couldn't sleep.

I went into the living room and sat in the rocking chair. I thought and thought. I've spent a lot of time in that rocker this morning too, because I wanted to get all this thought out before we talked."

She continued, "Now please don't interrupt me until I finish. What I have been wrestling with is the question 'Am I falling for this guy or do I simply feel sorry for him?'

If I'm falling for you because of who you are that's one thing. However, if I'm falling for you because I feel sorry for you, that's completely different. If we 'became an item' because I felt sorry for you, it would be for the wrong reason. Do you understand what I'm saying, Brad?"

"Yes, I think I do."

"I don't see how any relationship between a man and a woman could be on a solid foundation if it occurred because one person simply felt sorry for another," Laurie added.

"The other night my conclusion was ...... probably a little bit of both. I'm attracted to you because you're a terrific person. I'm also feeling sorry for you. Last night, when you started to get romantic, my defensive mechanism ignited. I said a thoughtless, cruel thing. I'm very torn, Brad, so please forgive me for my quick tongue.

"Now I'm almost finished so here goes the rest of it. Right now, this is what I'm thinking. My attraction has nothing to do with feeling sorry for you. I'm certain of that. Which means, I'm drawn to you for the right reasons. ...Maybe I'm not attracted a whole bunch, but if falling for a guy constitutes sliding down a 100-yard slope, I'm probably 25 yards down the hill." She looked up at Brad with those soft brown eyes.

Brad was elated with Laurie's admonitions. He reached across the table taking her hand in his.

"Laurie, I really appreciate your honesty. It's extremely important to be open and honest with each other. From my viewpoint, what you said last night did crush me. However, I can certainly forgive you. As nice as you have been to me, how could I not?

He continued, "More importantly, I want you to know I'm falling for you, big time. On your 100-yard hill, I am at least 60 yards down the slope. In my whole life, Laurie, there has never been a serious girlfriend. More and more I feel… you're the girl I've always dreamed about."

"Oh Brad, please do both of us a big favor. Please climb back up the hill. I'm terribly afraid when I tell you all my history on Valentine's Day, you'll wind up being badly hurt. Brad, I never want to hurt you. However, I'm truly afraid I will."

"Laurie, that is such a puzzling statement. Whatever you tell me Valentine's Day can't be that bad, can it?"

"God, I hope not, Brad. But it involves…'outside forces' over which I have no control. So just climb back up the hill a little, okay?"

They went for a long walk. Brad held her hand. Laurie decided holding hands with Brad created wonderful warm feelings. He was always gentle.

When they returned home, Brad went into the garage to grab a rake. "I need to get those leaves off the lawn or come spring it'll be a real problem."

"Why?" asked Laurie.

"The leaves now are dry and easy to rake into a pile. By spring, they'll be wet and awfully heavy. Raking wet leaves is extremely hard work. If I do it now, it's actually kind of fun."

"I've never raked leaves. Do you have an extra rake?"

"You never cooked and you never raked leaves? What kind of a sheltered life did you live?"

"The Mystery Daughter refuses to answer."

"Oh, I'm sorry. I bet you never rolled in a pile of leaves, either.

When Laurie nodded, Brad announced, "You've a real treat in front of you."

With two rakes going, it didn't take long to create a huge pile of dry leaves.

"Now, you just run and jump in," Brad instructed.

Laurie looked suspicious. "Watch me," called Brad, as he threw himself into the leaf pile.

Laurie thought, that does look like fun. Seconds later, she too dove into the pile. They lay there hugging for a while. Then one thing led to another and a major leaf fight broke out. Brad threw leaves in Laurie's face. She shoved leaves down Brad's back. Laughing as if they were tiny tots, they rolled together all over the leaf pile.

When they got up and started to rake the pile back together, Laurie teased,

"Someone who throws leaves in my face is a long way from 'contritely good'.

"That's no fair, you fight like a girl! You shoved leaves down my back."

"Brad dear, I am a girl." Delighted with his shocked expression, Laurie tossed some more leaves in Brad's face, then ran to the shower, locking the bathroom door behind her.

Later, Brad explained that the minister thought he should say something at the Funeral tomorrow morning. "I need to go through Grandpa's 'Treasure Book' so I can find something appropriate to share."

Sometime later, Brad told Laurie that Grandpa's attorney, Mr. Olsen had approached him at church. They'd made an appointment for Monday afternoon.

Laurie decided to 'hit the books.' Because she felt she had been able to 'clear the air' with Brad, she was able to get some serious studying done.

CHAPTER 7

Early Monday morning, the sound of the back-door closing, wakened Laurie. She looked at her watch. It was still dark out, apparently just before dawn.

Thinking perhaps Brad was upset on the day of his Grandfather's funeral; she threw on her robe and walked toward the door. As she passed through the living room, she happened to glance at the mantle where Brad had placed the box containing grandfather's ashes last night.

The box was missing.

Stepping outside, she spotted Brad walking up the hill behind the house. He'd mentioned earlier the hilltop was where the ashes of his parents and his grandmother were scattered. Laurie started up the hill after him.

The view was surprisingly good in the pre-dawn light. Brad's silhouette stood out in sharp contrast as he walked into the breaking dawn. She decided to stop and watch, wisely choosing not to interfere.

When Brad reached the hilltop, he took a deep breath. He knew he was doing what his Grandfather wanted. He remembered from last year when they scattered Gram's ashes that dawn was the proper time.

Laurie watched Brad's silhouette as he bowed his head. After a few minutes, his head came up. She could see him as he watched for the sunrise. It seemed to Laurie he was waiting for something.

Then she felt a strong early morning breeze sweep past her and up to the top of the hill. When Brad felt the breeze, he threw the ashes up into the air as high as he could. He stood there for a long time.

The breeze whisked some of the ashes away. Some settled back onto the dew drenched grass. The sun hit the dewdrops, causing the grass to sparkle in the early dawn light. Brad took another deep breath. He realized he had done a good thing. His soul filled with peace…It was time to move on.

Laurie waited as he came down the hill. When he approached, she remained silent, just put her arms around him. They hugged for a long time. Finally, she said, "Someone taught me to fry eggs yesterday. Can I try and see if I remember?"

Brad smiled, "Go for it."

• • •

After breakfast, Brad reviewed what he would say during the funeral service. In a little while, it was time to leave. When they got to the church, the minister showed them to a small room just a few steps away from the podium.

"If you sit here, you can see what's going on in the service, however, no one in the audience can see you. It's nice to have some privacy at a time like this. I recommend you use this little room."

Brad accepted. Then he asked Laurie if she wanted to stay with him or sit in the audience. She replied, "I'm here to be with you."

The service began with everyone singing the up-tempo hymn *Bringing in the Sheaves*. It was the one Grandpa had requested when he wrote out the instructions he had given to the Johnsons. After a few remarks by the minister, a couple of people gave short eulogies. Then it was Brad's turn.

Laurie watched him as he confidently strode to the podium. He was dressed in a dark blue suit with a white shirt and matching blue tie. He looked both handsome as well as vulnerable as he stood before the crowd. She thought - *he is so young to have to go through this.*

Surprising her, Brad's voice filled the room with warmth and strength.

"*I want to thank all of you for coming to this service. Your presence here is a real tribute to my Grandfather. I'm deeply grateful to each of you.*

As many of you know, Grandpa kept a 'Treasure Book.' The book is filled with poems, special stories and sayings that were especially meaningful to him. I went over that Treasure Book yesterday. I've selected two poems, which I feel are appropriate for today. The first selection is not the entire poem, just four powerful lines from the poet Edwin Markum:

Brad took a deep breath. Then he recited from memory in a strong voice:

And when he fell in whirlwind,
He went down.
As when a lordly Cedar,

Green with boughs.
Goes down with a great shout upon the hills.
And leaves a lonesome place against the sky.

After a pause, Brad continued. "It's my hope each of you will feel that this is a celebration, not a funeral. My Grandfather had a great life. He did a very good job. He and Gram raised a son who was a good, fine person. When their son and his wife died, they started over with one-year-old me.

Grandpa was 52 years old when they brought me home. He was 65 when I became a teen ager. Can you imagine being the parent of a teen at 65?

Despite his age, he stood out in the freezing weather and made ice rinks for all of us to enjoy. He did this year after year.

He and Gram did their job exceedingly well. They did it with kindness, courage and hard work. They did it with wisdom and great love.

As Ms. Sullivan wrote in her book about Helen Keller:

"He who loves his own child walks with nature.
He who loves another's, walks with God."

This morning I woke up before dawn. I walked up the hill behind our house. I went to the same place where we had scattered the ashes of my Grandmother last year and where Gram and Grandpa scattered my parent's ashes almost 19 years ago.

I waited up there until the sun began to peek over the trees. I waited until a cool breeze sprang up and brushed against my cheek. When I felt the breeze, I threw Grandpa's ashes as high in the air as I could.

Somehow, when I did that, a strong feeling of peace came over me. They are all together now. It was the way Grandpa wanted it…It was time for me to go forward. Jay Randall...He was my Grandfather…. He was my Father…Most important of all, he was my Best Friend.

It's not possible for me to put into words, how much I'll miss him.

I leave you now with this beautiful poem from Grandpa's Treasure Book. It was one of his favorites. The author is Henry Van Dyke.

A PARABLE OF IMMORTALITY

I am standing upon the seashore. A ship at my side spreads her white sails to the morning breeze and starts for the blue ocean. She is an object of beauty and strength. And I stand and watch until at last she hangs like a speck of white

cloud just where the sea and sky come down to mingle with each other. Then someone at my side says, 'There she goes!'

Gone where? Gone from my sight…that is all.

She is just as large in mast and hull and spar as she was when she left my side and just as able to bear her load of living freight to the place of destination. Her diminished size is in me, not in her.

And just at that moment when someone at my side says, 'There she goes!'… there are other eyes watching her coming…and other voices ready to take up the glad shout… 'Here she comes!'

Brad turned then and walked back into the little room where Laurie waited. With tear-filled eyes, she put her arms around him, kissing him right on the lips.

"You did a great job, Brad. Your Grandpa would be very proud of you!"

Before he could react, the funeral service ended. It was time to greet the friends who had come. The women of the church served coffee and cookies in the church parlor.

In a little less than an hour everyone left. Brad took Laurie home so she could study. As they were driving along he remarked, "I really liked the kiss you gave me, Laurie. It was wonderful. Does that mean I'm out of *kissing purgatory?"*

"Half way out. Only half way."

"Did you kiss me because I was *contritely good* or did you do it because you felt sorry for me?"

"Considering what has happened between us, I feel you're asking a fair question." She paused……. I'll give you an honest answer."

There was silence in the car for a moment. Then she began, "I kissed you for neither of reasons you mentioned. Let me put it this way. I saw you up there in your blue suit. You were very poised and speaking so strongly. You looked, well, handsome. The reason I kissed you was… because I must have fallen another five yards down the hill."

They looked into each other's eyes for a minute. Then their hands met. They remained and in hand, saying nothing, until they reached home.

• • •

Laurie went in the house to study and pack for the trip back to school in the morning. Brad returned to town to keep his appointment with the attorney.

Mr. Olsen was a grey haired, slightly stooped old gentleman, with kind sensitive eyes. After some preliminaries, he got right down to business.

"Your Grandfather did not have a lot, but he wanted you to have all of it, Brad. There are some securities, a small IRA retirement account, and the house. The house has no mortgage, so that's your largest asset."

Brad replied, "Grandpa and I reviewed his financial matters last fall before I left for school. He showed me everything and told me what to do if anything ever happened to him. Sometimes I wonder if he had a premonition about his death."

"He may have. I've known others who've had similar feelings."

"Is it okay for me to drive the car back to school?" asked Brad.

"Of course. However, I'd call the insurance company and let them know you are now the owner of the car and that the policy must be changed," replied Mr. Olsen.

"Brad," he continued, "If I were you, I don't think I'd do anything right now with any of these assets. You'll be back at Thanksgiving and Christmas. That'll give us plenty of time to get into the legal estate necessities. When you return we'll need some time together. I'll try to have everything, including the car registration, ready for your signature by then."

After Brad left Mr. Olsen, he made the call to the car insurance agent. The agent assured him he could take the car back to school.

When he returned home, he took Laurie in his arms. He hugged her for a long time. "I don't know how I could have gone through all of this, without your being here. I've no idea how I'll ever be able to make it up to you."

"There is nothing to make up, Brad. I'm glowing inside because I know in my heart coming with you was the right thing to do."

Laurie had already packed. After Brad packed, they went for a walk. Brad seemed to be calming out nicely. Obviously, he was happy the funeral was over. He also felt good because he knew his grandfather would've been pleased with the memorial service.

They went out to dinner. The conversation was a mixture of what was ahead at school and reminiscing over all that had happened since they connected on the campus bench Friday night.

When they returned home, Brad turned Laurie into his arms and tipped her chin up. "You know, if you would kiss me once more I'd be out of *kissing purgatory.* Then we could spend the rest of the evening on the couch necking."

She replied, "Brad, whether you want to admit it or not, we just met each other last Friday. This is Monday. I admit our time together has been rather extensive. However, having you in *kissing purgatory* is one method I have of controlling the situation.

"Furthermore, if we get up at 6:00 A.M. we can get back to school in time for me to make my important 2:00 o'clock lab. Therefore, I'm going to do what I ought to do, not what I might like to do. I'm going to bed. Which is what I ought to do. As to what I 'd really like to do, and here she paused for several seconds, I'll leave to your imagination."

CHAPTER 8

The next morning Laurie helped Brad lock up the house and turn down the heat. No one spoke a word. They went through each room. She could sense Brad was reflecting on all of the memories that followed him around the house.

Brad started the car. He looked at Laurie. "Gram and Grandpa always stood on the lawn to wave goodbye when I drove away. This is going to be tough."

As he took a deep breath, he noticed moisture in Laurie's eyes. She smiled at him, "Tough on me too."

Another deep breath, another look at the empty yard. Slowly...... they pulled away.

Laurie spoke in a muted tone, "If your grandfather stood out in weather colder than 15 degrees and held a hose to make an ice rink until 4:00 in the morning, he had to be one super guy. Hearing all your Grandpa stories and seeing all the people who came to the funeral, has made it easy to understand how difficult this has been for you. On the positive side, you've got to realize Brad, how lucky you are to have had the love of Grandparents that are so special."

"You know, Laurie, you're absolutely right. Thanks for pointing that out."

After several minutes of silence, Laurie expressed another thought. "I know it's none of my business, and I know nothing of your financial situation, however, I feel the need to make a suggestion."

"Oh?"

Laurie took a minute to verbalize her thoughts. "That house is your rock. It's your home base. You have millions of happy memories there. If I were you, I wouldn't be in a hurry to sell it. I think you'll find the house to be a major comfort when you return. People need familiar things to help deal with grief and loneliness. And loneliness Brad, is sure to be a part of you for a while."

She felt certain Brad was reflecting deeply on her suggestion, because he remained silent for a long time. Finally, he answered, "Thank you for that suggestion Laurie. I think you're absolutely right. I suppose there'll be a time to sell the house, but it's definitely not right now."

As they drove south, away from Chelsea, Brad turned the conversation to Laurie. He started this way, "As I understand your rule, you won't share with me any information about yourself before you came to Denison in September. So, can you tell me about you from September to now?"

"That's fair enough. Let's see…I settled into my dorm room. My roommate is okay… not great.

"What seems to be the issue?"

"If I could sum it up in one word, she's a slob. She leaves her stuff all over the room. Her lingerie is all over the bathroom. I'm a neat orderly person. She also plays music all the time, which makes it impossible for me to study. That's why I go to the carrels in the library so often. It gets me away from her.

"Have you ever studied in the carrels, Brad?"

"Yeah, I go there often. I love that library smell, and it's really quiet. Funny we never saw each other there before. I always go to the top floor."

"I always go to the third floor. That's probably why we never ran into each other."

"I'm switching to the third floor."

Laurie laughed. Then she continued, "Early in the fall, I had some dates with guys in the fast group. There was a lot of drinking. Since I don't drink, it was somewhat boring. Once the boys found out I wasn't 'easy' they have left me alone."

"You don't drink at all?" asked Brad. "Is there a reason?"

Laurie thought a minute. Then she replied, "Someone in my family had a serious problem with drugs and alcohol. I decided never to start. I feel I don't need to get drunk in order to have a good time."

"That's really interesting," Brad responded. "My grandmother promised me $100 if I never drank or smoked until I reached 21 years of age. I promised I would try to live up to that. By the time I resisted all the pressure in high school, it has become kind of a challenge to live my life without getting involved in the drinking scene. In college, it's interesting how some in the fast crowd really resent that I don't drink. They do their best to humiliate me and to make me feel uncomfortable."

"I've experienced those feelings too," replied Laurie. "I keep telling myself they have the problem not me."

"You know, Laurie, we seem to have a lot of important stuff in common. Have you decided on your major yet?"

"Would you believe I'm majoring in economics and finance?"

"A strange major for a beautiful woman."

"The Mystery Daughter chooses not to respond to your sexist remark," was her puzzling reply.

"Sexist remark?"

"You sound like you think all women want to do is become housewives and mothers."

"I'm so sorry. I don't think that, but I can see why you thought I did. I apologize."

"Well, okay, now we're even. The other night in East Lansing I said a dumb thing and today you said a dumb thing."

To fill the silence after her abrupt statement, Laurie asked Brad about his classes. "I'm taking a writing course which I really enjoy. My other courses are Accounting, English Lit and Speech. I enjoy my classes and I think my grades will be okay."

Having driven an hour, they decided to stop for breakfast.

Back in the car, Brad began speculating on why Laurie would not tell him her history until Valentine's Day. "I've several guesses, can we play guessing games?" he asked.

"Maybe, however, I reserve the right to invoke the 5th amendment whenever I wish."

Brad began, "On Valentine's Day you will reveal to me you are an Arab Terrorist."

Laurie laughed, "That does not dignify a response."

"On Valentine's Day, you will reveal to me you earned your money for college by working as dancer in a strip club."

Laurie giggled. "Well, that's certainly a possibility. However, my figure probably means I wouldn't be very attractive to the patrons."

"Your figure, Laurie, is absolutely gorgeous. How can you make a statement so totally inaccurate?"

"I guess my friendly personality has blinded your eyesight."

"On Valentine's Day, you will reveal to me you are the mother of three children all born out of wedlock."

"Really, you're terrible. I don't want to play this game."

"I've thrown out three suggestions. You haven't denied any of them," countered Brad.

"Increases the mystery, doesn't it?"

"On our way over Brad, you hadn't quite finished your life story when we got to Chelsea. What happened that last summer after high school graduation?

"Well, let's see. I got a job that summer working at a local coffee shop waiting on tables. "Grandpa and I spent many hours doing things together that summer. I loved being with him. Even if we were working, Grandpa usually found a way to make it fun. It was always a game or maybe a competition. Both of us realized our time together was growing short. I never imagined it would be this short, but we did try to make every minute count last summer.

"In late July, Grandpa announced, "Why don't you give them notice at the coffee shop? You've made enough money for this summer. Let's go on a trip."

"Sounds good to me. Where are we going?"

"I think west. We've about a month before you go off to college. I'd like to take you to see Mount Rushmore, The Grand Tetons, Yellowstone and, if we have time, The Grand Canyon. These places are part of our American heritage. I don't feel you've completed your education 'til you've seen them. Besides, I've never been there, either. If we motel it and share the driving, we can cover a lot of ground."

"I was excited. Actually, we both were.

"The days on the road began early. Usually, we were able to get in 60 miles or so before breakfast. In deference to Grandpa's hatred of big cities, we drove around Chicago. Soon we were looking at the splendor of Mount Rushmore. The huge faces of Washington, Lincoln, Jefferson and Teddy Roosevelt were not only impressive; they spread a sense of awe. Have you been there, Laurie?"

"Yes, I have."

"As we stood there, I told Grandpa 'I think sometimes Jefferson doesn't get enough credit. He wrote the Declaration of Independence. He had the vision to make the Louisiana Purchase. In my opinion, he was the brains behind America. Then I asked Grandpa what I'm going to ask you now. Do you know what it says around the top of the Jefferson memorial in Washington?"

"I've been there...but I don't remember what it says."

"I can quote it from memory...

I have sworn eternal hostility against every form of tyranny over the mind of man.

"You may be right, Brad, Jefferson was definitely a great thinker."

"The Tetons were inspiring. We loved the bears and the Geysers in Yellowstone. The Grand Canyon of the Yellowstone River is incredible. Finally, we worked our way down to the south rim of the Grand Canyon.

As he stood transfixed by the incredible splendor Grandpa murmured, "If I ever saw anything as humbling as this, I don't know what it was"

"I remembered a poem by Bliss Carman, which I shared with him there in the stillness.

I took a day to search for God
And found him not: but as I trod
By rocky ledge, through woods untamed,
Just where one scarlet lily flamed,
I saw his footprint in the sod."

"The trip was over. We knew we had long days ahead of us on the road so I could get home in time to pack for college. We stood there by the Grand Canyon and looked at each other. Finally, I took Grandpa in my arms. "Thanks a bunch, Grandpa, I'll never forget this trip with you."

With moist eyes Grandpa responded, "That makes two of us. It's a trip to last a lifetime."

"Laurie, you have no idea how glad I am we took that trip together. I've been wondering after what Sue Ann said, if Grandpa did have a premonition. Maybe that's why he proposed the trip?"

"Maybe it was, Brad. Now we'll never know. But surely it's a wonderful last memory for you."

"You got that right."

"When we got home, I had only a few days to pack for college. I hated the thought of leaving him alone.

"For our last night together, I planned a special dinner. I made a cream sauce by melting butter in a pan and adding flour. Once the flour browed, I added milk. Next came sliced up hard-boiled eggs. I created one of Jay's favorite dinners, creamed eggs on toast.

After dinner, Grandpa asked, "One more chess game before you leave?"

"You betcha. This time I'm going to win," I vowed.

"Early in the game, Grandpa made a mistake. He moved a pawn, which exposed his unguarded rook to my bishop. At first I thought it was a trick. I studied the board for a long time. Then I took the rook.

"Grandpa muttered, "Dog gone it, as soon as I moved that pawn, I realized

I'd made a mistake. I kept hoping you wouldn't see it. Now I'm really in a hole. However, 'When the going gets tough, the tough get going.' I'm not out of this yet."

"Grandpa battled valiantly. I put my full concentration into the game. I was able to keep trading pieces, which allowed me to keep my material advantage. Finally, I nailed his king. "Checkmate."

"Grandpa tipped over his king. As he shook my hand he said, "Great game. First time you've won since I promised not to let you win years ago. Congratulations."

"After we'd put away the chessboard, Grandpa sank back into his chair by the fire. 'You always enjoy my little poems or sayings. Since this is our last night together for a while, I want to share another one with you.' He thumbed through his Treasure Book for minute, then he began to read.

CREATIVITY

The one who follows the crowd, will usually get no further than the crowd. The one who walks alone is likely to discover places no one has ever been before.

Creativity in living is not without its attendant difficulties, for peculiarity breeds contempt. And the unfortunate thing about being ahead of your time is that when people finally realize you were right, they'll say it was obvious all along.

You have two choices in life:

You can dissolve into the mainstream, or you can be distinct. To be distinct, you must be different. To be different, you must strive to be what no one else but you can be....

(Author unknown)

I responded, "I have a poem for you too, Grandpa."

"This poem reflects exactly what you've done for me. I want you to keep it always as a reminder of that." I began to read:

THE BRIDGE BUILDER
BY WILL ALLEN DROMGOOLE

An old man, going a lone highway,
Came at the evening, cold and gray,
To a chasm, vast and deep and wide,

Through which was flowing a sullen tide.
The old man crossed in the twilight dim –
That sullen stream had no fears for him;
But he turned, when he reached the other side,
And built a bridge to span the tide.

'Old man,' said a fellow pilgrim near,
'You are wasting strength in building here.
Your journey will end with the ending day;
You never again must pass this way.
You have crossed the chasm, deep and wide,
Why build you the bridge at the eventide?'

The builder lifted his old grey head.
'Good friend, in the path I have come,' he said,
'There followeth after me today
A youth, whose feet must pass this way.
This chasm, that has been naught to me
To that fair-haired youth may a pitfall be.
He, too, must cross in the twilight dim;
Good friend, I am building the bridge for him.'

"When I finished, I handed the poem to Grandpa who had a tear or two in his eyes. 'I love you, Brad. You've fulfilled all my dreams for you.'

"Oh Brad, you're going to make me cry," Laurie confessed.

"That night, after I was asleep, Grandpa must have crept in to my room and opened one of my closed suitcases. He slipped in a 3 x 5 card, closed the suitcase and left.

"No one spoke very much on the trip to Denison the next day. It's hard to make conversation when you feel like crying. After we piled my stuff in the dorm, Grandpa said, "Well, I think I'll run along and let you unpack. I want to get home before dark. If I leave now, I'll just make it."

I walked him down to the car. We hugged. We were both crying. Grandpa got in the car, waved goodbye and left. I'd never felt so alone in my whole life.

CHAPTER 9

Brad continued his story. "I walked upstairs to my third- floor dorm room. Luckily, my roommate hadn't arrived so I could be sad all by myself. To get myself busy I opened a suitcase. There was the 3 x 5 card Grandpa had snuck into it the night before.

The Road Not Taken
Robert Frost
Two roads diverged in a wood, and I --
I took the one less traveled by,
And that has made all the difference.

"I tucked the card under the glass on my desk so I could look at it often...

"You want me to continue, Laurie?"

"I sure do, only please don't make it so sad from now on."

"Well, it isn't sad. It's just the story of my first few weeks at school.

"Okay, I can handle that."

"It didn't take me long to realize that even though Denison consisted of only 2,000 students, I was definitely a small fish in a big pond. Like you did Laurie, I quickly sorted out the same two groups of students.

"I knew I belonged in the 'not party group'. I had no interest in being a 'party boy'. My motivation is to make Grandpa proud of me. My roommate, a boy named Dave Minor, is from Dayton. He and I have little in common. Dave is a Chemistry major who wants to be a doctor. He virtually studies all the time.

"The course I enjoy most is a writing course. Creating something via writing feels good to me. I inquired about a job on the school paper. They told me to submit an article whenever I wanted. If they liked it, they would print it.

If I got several articles printed, they might make a student staff position available to me next fall.

"One Friday evening in late October, I was sitting alone in my room writing an article called 'Grandpa's Scrapbook.' I remembered all the wonderful poems and articles that Grandpa had saved over the years. I thought I could write an article, which would include some of those treasures. I was even planning a series of articles about them.

"Then my cell phone rang. It was Mary Sue Johnson…My world turned upside down… I guess you know the rest, Laurie."

• • •

As they approached the campus, Brad opened a new topic. "As I recall, you promised to reveal your mystery on Valentine's Day, if we're still together. Since I have every intention of being with you February 14th, I'm going to ask you for a date. What about Friday night?"

Laurie replied, "Sorry, on Friday night I have a date at the library until it closes at 10:00 P.M. I always study Friday nights so I can have the rest of the week end off."

"Well then, how about Saturday night? We can walk down into Granville and catch a movie. Will that work?"

"Brad, I'm just not sure. I truly don't want you to find out my real name for a while. If we are seen around campus someone who knows my name, might ask you about me and you'd find out."

"Laurie, I promise, on my word of honor, that I will avoid all such conversations. I promise I'll do everything in my power to keep your secret. And if it does somehow come out, I promise to tell you right away."

"Well…In that case, I guess we can go to a movie…Brad, I truly appreciate the way you are respecting my wishes in this matter. Trust me, it may prove to be very important."

"I haven't a clue as to why you want to be so secretive. Can't you give me a little hint?"

"Ok here's a hint. Laurie grinned as she said, "Suppose you were an Arab Terrorist, or a strip club dancer, or an unwed mother of three. You'd keep it a secret, wouldn't you?"

"Oh Boy… you got me good!"

He parked at the fork in the path where they had to separate. "I'm looking forward to Saturday night, Brad."

• • •

The college rules forbade freshman students from having a car on campus. Brad knew this when he drove his grandfather's car back to school. He also knew how to solve the problem. Some upper classmen rented a house off campus. For a monthly fee, they would allow freshmen to park a car in their back yard.

This arrangement meant Brad had to walk downtown to the rented house every time he needed his car. It was inconvenient, but far better than having the car up in Michigan.

The next Friday night, Laurie found herself bent over a book in the library carrel on the third floor. Deep in concentration, she paid no attention to the other students who were also using the carrels. Around 9:00 o'clock, someone walked by dropping a note on her desk. When she picked up the note, she read:

I know someone who thinks you're great
He was hoping this night to have with you a date
But you turned him down to study your lit
Can he walk you home? This guy for you has bit!
B

Laurie giggled. She looked around to see which desk Brad was using. She spotted him easily. A few minutes later she dropped this poem on Brad's desk:

The guy who wrote a poem to me
Can't write his whole name, only a B.
But if, at ten, he's on the library deck
I might let him kiss me on the neck.
L

Needless to say, a smiling Brad was waiting when she came out of the library. He blurted out his first question. "If I kiss you on the neck, will I be released from *kissing purgatory*?"

"Of course not. The rules are it takes two kisses on the mouth. You have only been awarded one." Then she put her hand in his. They headed for the student union.

When they sat down over coffee, Laurie looked him straight in the eye asking, "Okay, tell me, how're you doing?"

Brad knew she was referring to the loss of his Grandfather. He thought a minute. "You know, on the whole I've done pretty well. The other night when my roommate was gone, I had a really good cry. After that one time, I've pretty much been all right." A few seconds later he added, "It's helped a lot to look forward to our date tomorrow night and to my plan to kidnap you for coffee and a walk tonight."

Laurie smiled across the table at him. "I've been thinking about all the poems and inspirational stuff your Grandfather shared with you. He must have been a really wonderful person. He always seemed to be trying to inspire you to do better and to become a better human being."

"Yes, he truly was an inspiring man. However, I'm determined to look forward not back. So, let's talk about tomorrow night. What restaurant do you enjoy and what movie do you want to see?"

"I'd rather you surprise me. However, the movie better not be X rated."

"Is there any possibility I will get off *kissing purgatory*?" asked Brad.

She smiled at him. "Young man, in spite of all our time together, tomorrow is our first official date. As you recall, I don't kiss men on first dates. That's what got you into *kissing purgatory* in the first place."

He countered, "After I kiss your neck tonight I'm hoping you'll be just dying to kiss me by tomorrow night. Therefore, I'm extremely expectant you will change your rules just this once."

In your dreams, big guy, in your dreams," was the playful answer. "Now, what's this about kissing my neck? Surely you realize I was only making something to rhyme with deck."

"I'm sorry, I have it in writing, tonight I can kiss your neck," responded Brad as he waved the little poem in Laurie's face.

Laurie countered, "You know what? You're fun. Let's start our walk."

The campus was a wonderful place to walk on a cool November evening. The color came into Laurie's cheeks and a twinkle into her eyes. Even though his heart felt heavy, Brad could feel his spirits lifting. Laurie was really helping him to get through his grief.

They sat on an empty bench, which overlooked the little town. Beyond the hills, the clear sky reflected a breath-taking myriad of stars.

"Do you ever wish on a star?" she asked.

"All the time."

"What do you wish for, Brad?" The sincerity in her voice told him she really wanted to know.

Brad thought a minute. "When I was in high school, I used to wish for success in football. Now things are so different. I've been thinking about becoming a writer. It would be cool to be able to write a novel and get it published."

Laurie responded, "I think being a writer would be a great life style. You could live wherever you want and, within limits, work when you felt like it. However, I fear it's terribly difficult to get a book published."

Brad added, "In my journalism class the professor told us only one book gets published out of 1,150 submissions. These are practically impossible odds. However, I wouldn't have to write a book. At least not at first. Maybe I could just get a job as a reporter."

There was silence for a while. Then Brad admitted, "If I were to wish upon a star right now, I would wish to get out of *kissing purgatory.*

Laurie laughed. She rose to continue the walk. "You're dealing with my principals, mister. You haven't got a chance."

Eventually, they reached the fork in the path where Laurie insisted they part company. Laurie turned her back pushing into Brad. Then, as his arms came around her, she pulled her long hair away, exposing her neck right below his lips. Instead of kissing her hard, Brad just laid his lips gently on the back of her neck.

Did he hear a moan? The sound was so faint he couldn't be certain. However, Laurie didn't move, so he again gently kissed the back of her neck. Then he felt her wiggle up against him. Her body language begged for another neck kiss. Brad obliged with enthusiasm.

Suddenly, she spun out of his arms and walked away. As she did, she called over her shoulder, "See you tomorrow, Brad."

Brad stood there in the path shaking his head for a long time. As he walked slowly back to his dorm room, he realized he was utterly captivated by Laurie. *She's attractive, intelligent, extremely sensitive and fun. What's not to like about that?*

Laurie also did some serious thinking as she walked to her dorm room. *Brad is loads of fun, she reflected. He is also handsome, intelligent, and sensitive. When he gave me the gentle kiss on my neck, wow! He actually made my whole-body shiver. I'm going to have to keep him in kissing purgatory a long time because I won't be able to control what happens when I let him out.*

I'm really glad I didn't tell him my last name. If we stay together, it's going to be extremely important. I can just picture father saying, 'Brad only wants you for my money.' Now I can respond, 'Brad didn't even know my last name for almost 4 months.'

CHAPTER 10

Since this was their first official date, Brad wanted it to be special. As he drove through tiny Granville, he stopped off at the florist shop to buy Laurie a gardenia for her hair. The word excited, could not begin to reveal his emotions.

He arrived early at the rendezvous watching for her from his car window. Soon Laurie came walking down the path. She was dressed in a white cashmere sweater which he could see because her tan coat was unbuttoned. She'd untied her ponytail. Watching her lovely brown hair bounce against the tan coat and the white sweater, Brad felt heat in his chest. Her brown eyes shone atop her brilliant smile. He opened the door so she could slide into the passenger seat.

Brad handed her the flower box declaring, "I bought you a present to match your sweater." She opened the gardenia, and smelled its wonderful aroma. She smiled at Brad thanking him. Joyfully, she pinned the flower into her hair. Then she got this puzzled look on her face.

"How did you know I'd wear a white sweater?"

"I have mystic powers. I can tell what you're thinking."

"You know I don't really believe you, because I just decided on the white sweater about 5 minutes ago. You must have bought the flower before that."

Brad responded, "Well, my powers are very strong. I actually directed your mind to pick the white sweater, so it would match the gardenia."

"All right mister smarty pants, let's test your power.

What am I thinking right now?"

Brad paused a minute pretending to listen for mystic vibes. "You're thinking; he was so nice to buy me a gardenia I want to kiss him. However, if I did, it would remove him from *kissing purgatory*. Kissing him would be a serious mistake."

"Humm," responded Laurie. "Ah, where are we going for dinner?"

"Miss Lansing, are you trying to change the subject?"

"Who me? Whatever gave you that idea?"

The happy repartee began a fun evening for both of them. Dinner was in a quiet restaurant in Newark, Ohio, about 7 miles from the campus. Then they took in an exciting movie. As they returned to the campus, Brad explained the car parking arrangement. He suggested they park the car so they could walk together back to the rendezvous spot. He told her, "I love walking and talking with you."

As they walked, he began to talk about the future. "Thanksgiving vacation starts next Wednesday. We need to have our second date before you go home. Can you go out with me tomorrow?" asked Brad.

"No, but Tuesday night would work. There won't be any tests on Wednesday before the vacation," replied Laurie.

"OK Tuesday night it is. Can I call you on over Thanksgiving vacation?" Brad asked.

"Somehow, I don't think that's a good idea. I don't want my parents to know about you until...until after the Valentine's Day revelations."

Brad looked perplexed. "I sure am puzzled about those revelations."

She replied, "Well if you don't like dealing with the Mystery Daughter you can always break it off before Valentine's Day."

"Even if I wanted to break it off, my curiosity would never allow it. The Christmas formal is December 12th. May I have the honor of escorting you?"

"Is the Christmas Formal where I get to wear a fancy dress and get to see you in a tux?"

"I think it is technically a semi-formal. This means the girls get all dressed up but the guys can get by with just a suit and tie."

"What if I told you I wouldn't be seen dead at a formal, unless my date was in a tux?"

"I'd report you for cruel and unusual punishment. However, I know you too well by now. My mystic powers tell me there's no way you would force me to wear a tux because..... I don't own one."

"No, I'd never force you to do anything. However, I might hint that if you wore a tux you'd get out of *kissing purgatory*."

"Laurie, the Christmas Formal isn't for three weeks! Surely I'll be out of *kissing purgatory* before then?"

"Humm," was her only reply.

They reached the rendezvous spot. Her shining brown eyes looked into

Brad's blue ones. "I had a really nice time, Brad. Thank you for the gardenia. Yes, I'll be glad to go the Christmas Formal with you and no, you don't have to wear a tux."

Then she turned around and backed up into his arms. She bent her neck so he could kiss it again. He kissed very gently and once more, he wondered if he heard a moan. She didn't leave, so he kissed her neck a second time.

Then she spun out of his arms. "See, I told you I don't kiss guys on a first date." With a little wave, she walked away.

He watched until she was out of sight. Reluctantly, he turned for the dorm. He found himself shaking his head from side to side. There was a huge smile all over his face.

Laurie found herself smiling too. *What a neat guy!*

• • •

Tuesday afternoon an idea occurred to Brad. He wandered through the dorm floor asking if anyone had a tux. Across the hall, one of his friends replied, "Yes." Brad asked to borrow it for about an hour. "Can you fit in it?" asked the tux owner.

"Don't worry I'll make it work," replied Brad.

He took the tux back to his room. It didn't take long for him to realize the tux was way too small. He could get the pants on but he couldn't button them or even zip up the fly. He put on his belt. By pulling the belt really tight he discovered he could keep the pants up. With the pants problem solved, he tried on the coat. By some miracle, the shoulders were only tight. However, the arms stopped about 5 inches from his wrists. Fortunately, the coat was long enough to cover his open fly, so he figured it was worth a shot. He put on a white shirt and tied the black bow tie. He looked in the mirror.

From the neck up, it looked okay. From the neck down, it looked absolutely ridiculous. Fortunately, he possessed a long raincoat, which, when he put it on, covered the entire outfit. He buttoned up the top button on his raincoat so even the bow tie wouldn't show. Then, walking very gingerly so not to split the back out of the borrowed tux, he walked down to town, got his car, and went to meet Laurie at the rendezvous.

It happened to be a cool November evening. Laurie appeared again in her tan fuzzy coat. She'd left her hair loose again, because she knew Brad liked it that way.

"You know, Laurie, with your pretty brown hair, that tan coat really looks great."

She smiled. Then she noticed him all buttoned up in his raincoat. "Are you cold or something, you're all bundled up?"

"I've a surprise for you. We have to go to the library to get it. When we get there, you have to just follow me blind. The surprise will explain everything."

"Sounds like fun."

Brad parked the car. Luckily, they found a space open near the library. Then very stiffly, he walked with Laurie into the library. She noticed how funny he was walking. He was not using the long lanky stride his six foot three frame usually revealed.

He steered her back into the stacks. Just as he suspected, on the night before the Thanksgiving break, the stacks and the carrels were empty. He stood Laurie in an aisle in a remote part of the stacks. He asked her to close her eyes. She heard a rustling sound, which told her he was removing the raincoat.

Then she heard Brad say, "Ta Da!" She opened her eyes. There stood Brad... in a tuxedo! Well, it was sort of a tuxedo she surmised, and sort of a comedy routine costume. She burst out laughing!

"You promised me," Brad began, "If you saw me in a tux you would kiss me and remove me from *kissing purgatory*."

"I remember what I promised," laughed Laurie. Then she asked him, "What is your full legal name?"

"What? Here I am holding my breath in this crazy too small tux and you are asking about my name?"

"Just answer the question please."

"My full name is Bradley Weatherby Randall."

She smiled up at him, "You have to promise if I kiss you, your arms will remain at your side. You cannot put them around me."

"Why not?" countered Brad.

"I'm afraid if you hug me you will tear the back out of that borrowed tux coat."

"Oh...I guess you're right. Okay, I promise to keep my arms at my side."

Then she whispered, "Bradley Weatherby Randall, I adore you!" She threw her arms around him and kissed him...right on the lips.

When she broke off the kiss, she said, "Now let me help you out of that coat before it splits down the back."

"Okay. However, you have to keep your eyes up. The pants were too small to zip up. They are only held up by my belt."

Laughing together, they struggled. Finally, they managed to remove the coat.

"Oh, how I wish for a camera," laughed Laurie. Then she looked up at his face. *Oh Oh……. I'm about to really be kissed.* They stood there, for a long time, among all those stacks of books, with their arms around each other, laughing, kissing and hugging.

Laurie whispered, "We better get out of here. I'm sure the University has a no kissing in the library rule. We don't want to get caught."

Brad put on his raincoat and they went back to the car. He drove to his dorm running in to change out of the rest of the tux. Laurie stayed in the car, laughing. *He sure knows how to make me happy.*

Brad returned to the car now clad in comfortable clothes that fit his tall frame. Laurie said, "Brad, from this point forward, you have to remain contritely good at all times."

"At all times, why?"

"I don't want to have to put you back in *kissing purgatory*."

"I don't understand."

"Well then you better think about it for a while."

Brad pondered her statement. *If she doesn't want me in kissing purgatory, it must mean she likes kissing me!!!*

A few minutes later they were having sandwiches in the town coffee shop. After the food arrived, Brad pleaded, "I can't believe you won't let me call you over the Thanksgiving holiday. I'm going to be all alone in the house. I'm sure I'll be lonesome. I'll need to talk to you."

"I've been thinking about that too. I've decided to give you my email address. My parents would know if I received a phone call, however, they don't check my email. Hand me your phone."

When he did, she typed in Llansing@gmail.com

"You'll hear from me frequently," promised Brad.

"What will you do while you're home?" Laurie asked.

"The lawyer tells me I've some legal stuff to do for the estate. Which means, I'll have to meet with him. Mary Sue Johnson asked me to come over to their house for Thanksgiving dinner. That'll help a little. Then, I think I'll try to write something. If I'm going to be a writer, I'm going to have to start sometime. What are your plans, Laurie?"

"I can't tell you a lot until after Valentine's Day. However, I'm sure there'll be many parties. Which means I'll be fending the off hundreds of men who'll be seeking my attention."

"You really know how to upset a guy, don't you?"

"Being the Mystery Daughter is fun."

"Fun for whom?"

Laurie chose to remain silent.

Brad chose to break the silence with a serious thought. "Laurie, are you ashamed of me?"

"Why on earth would you think that?"

"Well, it's becoming pretty obvious you don't want your parents to know anything about me. I have no clue why that is or why you have invoked all this Mystery Daughter stuff, but I'm beginning to wonder if somehow I'm not good enough for you."

Laurie immediately sensed this was important. She reached across the table grasping his hand. "Brad, it has absolutely nothing to do with you. The last thing I would ever want you to think is that somehow, I am ashamed of you. This situation, for want of a better term, is entirely on my side of the equation. It has nothing to do with you, except for the fact that you are a super guy and I am falling for you. If you weren't so wonderful, I wouldn't need to be the Mystery Daughter. Can you just leave it there till Valentine's Day?"

"Do I have a choice?"

"No, I guess you don't. But Brad, it's becoming increasingly clear to me that we will still be together Valentine's Day. So please, just hang in there a few more weeks.

"Okay, if you're sure it isn't something about me."

"On February $14^{th,}$ you will understand. I'm positive.

Brad thought, *time to change the subject.* "Now that dinner's over, we have to decide what we want to do next. We can go to the movie, or we can drive up to Sugar Loaf Hill, find a quiet spot to park and make out."

"Those are my two choices?"

"Can you think of anything else you might want to do?"

She thought a minute. Then she declared, "Mr. Randall...... Laurie Lansing is a proper young woman. She'll always make the proper choice, which is, of course, a movie....However, Laurie the Mystery Daughter, might just have a bit more spunk. Especially when she has recently had the distinct pleasure of seeing her handsome boyfriend in a tuxedo. I vote for Sugar Loaf Hill!"

He grabbed her hand as they ran for the car.

CHAPTER 11

Brad's last class before the Thanksgiving Holiday ended at noon. He had plenty of time to drive home before darkness arrived. As he approached the house, he found himself driving slower and slower. He was not anxious to walk into his empty house.

He pulled into the driveway. Hesitantly, he walked to the door unlocking it. Taking a deep breath, he opened the door and stepped into the living room. No Grandmother, no Grandfather.

It felt just as empty as he'd expected. After he turned up the heat, he took a slow walk into each room. Memories flooded his depressed mind.

He encountered the first problem when he opened the closet in his grandfather's room. There were all of Grandpa's clothes. He'd have to spend some time sorting through them and giving them away.

He went over to Johnson's to say hello. They were really glad to see him. Mary Sue told him to plan for a 4:00 P.M. dinner tomorrow. She offered him supper. Brad replied, "I'm going to have to learn to eat alone sometime, I think I should start now.

When he talked about Grandpa's clothes, Mary Sue suggested the church rummage sale would accept anything he wanted to give away.

Then Tom Johnson, Mary Sue's husband, asked Brad to accompany him to the basement. "I have something I want to show you."

When they got to Mr. Johnson's workshop, Brad noticed a whole bunch of memorabilia hanging on all the walls. Mr. Johnson explained, "This is my Family Hall of Fame. Everything on those walls has a special memory for me."

Mr. Johnson continued, "I've been thinking……When you go through all the things over there, you'll probably find a lot of stuff you're not emotionally ready to give away. When you do, toss whatever it is into a box marked 'Hall of

Fame.' Then someday, when you have your own home and family, you can open the box and hang that stuff around. If you try this idea, I'm sure your sorting out process will be less painful, because you won't be parting with your really meaningful memories."

"You know, that's a great idea. Thank you so much."

When he returned home he thought, *a fire in the fireplace will help.* In a few minutes the warm glow helped him feel better. A dinner of scrambled eggs, bacon and toast also contributed to his feeling of well-being. Then he set up his computer right there by the fire so he could send an email to Laurie.

Hi Laurie:

I arrived safely. On the drive, I remembered the last trip here when you were at my side. You were so thoughtful to make that awful trip with me. I'm forever in your debt.

My idea of doing some creative writing this weekend may be put on hold. My first priority is to clean out Grandpa's clothes and stuff. I plan to start in the morning, first thing. Mr. Johnson next door suggested I make a Hall of Fame box. If I find something too precious to throw away, I can just toss it in that box for later. You were right when you told me the house would put its arms around me. Thanks for suggesting I hold off selling it for a while. You gave me great advice.

Don't eat too much turkey tomorrow! I miss you a whole bunch!

As ever,

B

His 'in box' was empty. He was disappointed, but not surprised. She would be busy with lots of people, no doubt.

He woke early. Laurie had replied to his email.

Thanks for your note. I miss you too. The 'Hall of Fame' box sounds like a great idea.

Do you have to go through your Grandfather's things yourself? Maybe someone else could do it? It'll be very sad for you.

I wish I could be there to give you a big hug!

Xxx

L

He smiled as he typed off this fast reply.

No, it's something I have to do myself. There's no way I could ask a neighbor to do it.

Are you having many relatives for Thanksgiving Dinner?

I wish you were here too!
Xxx
B

• • •

Thanksgiving morning, Laurie woke up around 10:00. She stretched, then put her head back on the pillow, closing her eyes again. Sleep did not return however, so she just lay there thinking. It felt nice to be back in her gorgeous bedroom. The walls had soft pink wallpaper on them. The windows faced east and south, so the sunlight streamed in onto the reddish hue of the oriental carpet. In spite of its formality, the room gave off a warm atmosphere. There were some attractive art pieces on the wall. It'd never been anything resembling a teen ager's room. No one ever asked her what décor she would enjoy in her room. It was a requirement that everything in the mansion be formal because of all the business entertaining her father did.

As Laurie dozed, thoughts of Brad filtered into her mind. *I really like him. He's gentle and sensitive. The fact that he's taller than I am and handsome, is a big plus. He's also a lot of fun. That too small tuxedo trick was such a laugh. I'm so glad I became the Mystery Daughter for him. Now when father grills me I'm going to stand my ground. If I don't have the courage within me to stand up to father, I'm going to do it for Brad. I don't want to lose him.*

After a few minutes, Laurie got up to exercise. As she looked for her sweats, she glanced at her formal gowns. She would need to wear one for the Christmas dance with Brad. A quick glance told her those formals were too 'high school.' She would need to go shopping tomorrow for a new one. For Brad, she wanted to look extra special.

The Thanksgiving guest list was, as she suspected, filled with a few relatives and a lot of business associates. When you own a chain of stores, as her father did, you do a lot of business entertaining.

Laurie never had to help with the entertaining. There was a cook and a butler as permanent staff. Her job was show up at the proper time and be gracious and charming. All her life, she had been trained to be exactly that, so it was no big deal.

The formality of the entire affair seemed rather banal. After all the fun in the college dorm, and the warmth she felt when she and Brad were together, Thanksgiving dinner turned out to be major boring.

After what seemed like an eternity to Laurie, the guests departed. Laurie found herself in the huge living room with only her mother and father. Mother sat by the fire, enjoying a glass of wine. Father was reading the paper.

Laurie's father, William, conveyed a commanding presence. He was tall, about six feet and heavy. He wore suits and kept his ties up tight even when home from the office. His face appeared fleshy. His checks were red, probably because of the amount of alcohol he consumed.

His manner bordered on rude. He demanded attention whenever he spoke. There were no displays of tolerance for anyone who disagreed with him. As for expressions of affection for Laurie from father?,...... Forget about it.

Laurie's mother, Shirley, was an attractive brunette. A tad overweight, perhaps, however her enthusiasm made her fun to be around, when William was absent. Whenever William was around, he trampled her self-esteem, badly. As a consequence, Shirley came through as a shy retiring person.

Laurie's Mother's brown eyes were lovely. They topped a small mouth and a demure nose. She kept her hair back in a bun. Laurie didn't care for the bun because it didn't show off her mother's long soft strands of hair. Shirley did well in her role as host for the family. Although William treated her with distain, Shirley was plenty smart. Years of mental abuse from William had taught her to keep her intelligence well hidden.

Laurie took a breath before she opened the conversation. Then she plunged in. "Mother, I've been asked to the Christmas Formal. The dresses I have upstairs are sort of 'high school.' I need to go shopping tomorrow for a new formal. Would you like to go with me?"

"Oh, how lovely to be asked. Is he a nice boy?"

Laurie noticed her father lowering the paper. He was listening intently.

"Yes, he's very nice," answered Laurie. Playing it low key she added, "The dance is an important event on campus. I was pleased to be invited."

As Laurie expected, William Knowlton started what Laurie called the third degree. Every boy who had ever looked at her, caused father to open up the question barrel.

"Does this boy have a name?" he began.

"His name is Brad. Brad Randall."

"What does his father do?" William shot back.

"His father and his mother were both killed in an auto accident when Brad was just a few months old."

That was sort of a stunner. William, even with all of his pomposity, didn't exactly know how to respond.

Taking advantage of her father's silence, Laurie looked at her mother asking, "I plan to leave for shopping around 10:30. Does that work for you?"

"Of course, dear."

Laurie got up to leave. Before she could escape, her father recovered. He bellowed, "No doubt that boy is just out for your money. I have warned you repeatedly, Laurie, money grabbers will be the only ones who show interest in you. Remember, we Knowlton's pick our mates by using our heads not our hearts."

This conversation had occurred all through her last two years in high school. This time, however, strengthened by her affection for Brad, Laurie found herself ready to pounce.

"Father, I'm now going to inform you of a few things which apparently, you have no wish to know. Number one, I'm not the tall ugly girl with the pimples on her face any more. My complexion is clear and very attractive. In addition, now that the boys I'm around have grown up, my five feet eleven inches of height no longer requires me to stoop to keep my date from feeling foolish. I now wear high heels. I can square my shoulders. This causes my breasts to stick out and I look damn good. I have a very attractive figure. The boys at college ogle me all the time.

"Furthermore, Brad is six feet three inches tall. He is slim, broad shouldered and handsome. Together, we make a striking couple. More importantly, he's honest, fun, and hard working.

"Number two. All my life you've been telling me how no one will want me for who I am. They will only want me for your money. Well, this time I have put your argument to rest.

"When I first met Brad, I felt the distinct possibility that he would be a special person. Consequently, I've never told him my last name. He knows absolutely nothing about my family or me.

"Furthermore, I have refused to tell him anything regarding my background until we've dated for three months. I don't even let him know where my dorm is, so he cannot look up the information without my knowledge. We meet for our dates at a rendezvous on the campus.

"If he is still interested in me after three months without knowing my last name, maybe you'll realize he's my boyfriend because he likes me, not your precious money. Good night, father. Happy Thanksgiving!"

She stormed from the room.

After a few minutes of silence, William turned to Shirley, "This Brad person sounds like bad news. I think I'll put someone on it to find out his background."

"If you do," Shirley replied, "you'll mess up Laurie's efforts to find out if he likes her without knowing she's rich."

"But I need to know something about him." replied William.

"There'll be plenty of time to find out, if they last three months. Why don't you let me see what I can find out tomorrow before you set your private investigators in motion?"

"Oh, all right. But I don't like the feeling of this," he grumbled.

"William, when are you going to stop your constant downgrading of Laurie? Remember, you were the major cause of Betty Ann's revolt. Please be cautious this time. I don't want to lose our only other daughter."

William blanched at this. "How can you possibly say I was a factor in Betty Ann's downfall? It was that wretched boy who caused all the trouble." With a scowl, William casually strolled out of the room.

Shirley remained alone with her glass of wine.

Upstairs, Laurie seethed. She lay on her bed crying silent tears. A gentle soul, it hurt to cause her father grief. In addition, she feared her mother would be blamed for the stress she'd just caused her father.

Into her thoughts came a sentence from her Shakespeare class. "Hamlet is the story of a young man who couldn't make up his mind." She thought a minute. Then she said to herself, *I hope and pray Father doesn't force me to decide between someone I love, and someone he wants me to marry! But I have a gut feeling that's exactly what's going to happen!*

Later she opened her computer, read Brad's message, and then sent this reply:

I wish it was Valentine's Day. I would like to tell you all my troubles
I can hardly wait till we're were back at school
XXX OOO. L

CHAPTER 12

When Brad returned from the Johnson's Thanksgiving feast, he found Laurie's email message.

He sent this reply:

Sounds to me as if you need to talk. I know you said not to call you, but maybe you could call me?

B

A few minutes later, the phone rang. He picked it up. Laurie's soft voice whispered, "Hi."

"Are you all right?" asked Brad.

"I'm surviving," was her depressed reply. "I can't talk to you about anything because of the Valentine's Day restrictions. I called because……. Because… I just want to hear your voice."

"Laurie, you made the Valentine's Day rule. You can also break it."

"Sorry, that is not an option."

"Laurie, there's no way we are not going to be together on Valentine's Day. I'm so nuts about you I can hardly think about anything else all day long."

After a pause, Laurie changed the subject, "Tell me about your day."

He described the Thanksgiving turkey, dressing, cranberry and mince pie. Then he related the story of his morning when he cleaned out his Grandfather's room.

"The clothing phase was not too difficult. I just made a big pile to take to the church rummage. I made a list of it all for the income tax deduction of a charitable gift.

"Then I opened his top drawer. I found a bunch of pictures and some stuff of my parents he had been loath to throw away. I put a lot of stuff into the 'Hall of Fame' box."

"Were you crying?" asked a concerned Laurie.

"Yeah, once in a while. Some of the old photos hurt. Some were quite interesting. I found one of my Mom at college with another guy in the picture. I'm sure it wasn't my dad. I wonder who he was?

Then I found a picture of a pretty girl. On the back was written, *Joanne Dartforth, my college roommate.* I suspect it's in my mother's handwriting. Someday, I might look up this Joanne Dartforth via the University of Michigan alumni office. It might be, she could tell me some stories of my Mom and Dad. They met on the Michigan campus, you know."

"I didn't know they went to Michigan," Laurie replied. My dad went there too. Oops!" I slipped up on my Valentine's Day rule."

"So now I know you have a father," Brad responded.

"I sure do. He's the reason I'm so depressed if you must know."

"Is he sick or something?" asked Brad.

"No nothing of that nature, it's just father versus daughter conflicts. That's all I can tell you 'till Valentine's Day. When that day comes, you better be ready, because I'm really going to unload all my problems. In the meantime, please don't probe any deeper."

"I promised not, Laurie. Never fear, I'm keeping my word. You know, this call is special for me. It made a sad day into a happy one."

"Me too. Goodnight, best friend."

"Am I your best friend?" asked Brad. "You sure are my best friend."

Her response was, "Best friend. I like the sound of that. Good night."

Exhausted from the day, Brad tumbled into bed. The meeting with the lawyer was scheduled for tomorrow.

• • •

When he woke in the morning, he sent this quick email to Laurie:

Are you flying back to Columbus Sunday? If you tell me when, I could meet you at the airport. We could drive back to the campus together."

Best Friend.

Mr. Olsen, the attorney, began the meeting Friday morning by explaining that Jay Randall's estate was small enough that it would be settled in a few months. There would be no estate tax. It was mostly a matter of naming Brad as the owner of his Grandfather's checking account, brokerage account, IRA retirement account, house and car. Lots of papers needed signing. When Mr. Olsen asked if Brad planned to sell the house he replied, "Not at the present time. When it's right, I suppose I'll have to sell it, but right now, I need somewhere to call home."

As he left Mr. Olsen's office, Brad asked, "Do you know anyone from town who works for either of the Detroit papers? I'm thinking of becoming a writer. I want to talk to someone regarding the newspaper business."

"No one comes to mind," replied Mr. Olsen, "but let me ask around. Maybe you could have an interview when you return for Christmas vacation."

When Brad got home, he checked his email:

If you promise to hug me lots and kiss me a little, you can meet me outside of baggage claim at the Columbus airport. My flight is supposed to arrive at 2:00 P.M. Sunday.

BF

He emailed back:

I promise to hug you a lot. Can we leave the amount of kissing up for negotiation? BF

Later in the day, he checked again:

As a compromise gesture, I will increase the amount of kissing from a little to some.

BF

• • •

The next morning Laurie appeared bright and early in the kitchen. Their cook Agnes, who had been with the Knowlton's for years, looked up suspiciously. "What you doin' up so early Laurie dear?"

Agnes, you've loved me ever since you came to work here. What was I, about ten when you came?"

"I suspects that's right. You were about ten. And you're right, I been lovin' you ever since. I even remember puttin' a very small serving of broccoli on your plate cause you didn't like it and your father made you eat every bite."

"I need to ask a monster favor."

"Well you kin ask, but I guarantee nothin'."

"I need to learn to cook."

"What'd you say? Did I hear right?"

"Agnes, I need you to teach me to cook. When I leave school, I won't have the money to hire a cook. If I don't learn now, I'll probably just starve."

Agnes was no dummy. She understood people and she knew Laurie very well. "Does your sudden need to cook have something to do with a boy you met at school?"

Laurie tried to stop the blush, but she couldn't. Her cheeks flamed. Agnes laughed and laughed.

"You tell Agnes now. Is this boy special?"

"Oh Agnes, he's very special. And he knows how to cook and I don't."

"Want to start with pancakes?"

"That would be perfect."

"Get you an apron out of the closet and we'll begin."

• • •

Laurie and Shirley had a pleasant time shopping. They went to Bonwit Teller. After trying on about a dozen different formal dresses, they finally decided on a strapless gown in a pale yellow. She thought the yellow would make a good contrast to her long brown hair. Afterwards, at lunch, Shirley started the probing she promised William she would do.

"Tell me, is Brad kind or dominating?"

Laurie had already prepared for this probing. "Mother, you and Dad are reading way too much into this. The Christmas Formal will only be our third date. Brad's three-month period of no personal information will not end until Valentine's Day. If we get that far, it'll be a miracle."

Then Laurie continued, "Mom, could we have a serious talk, something you would keep to yourself? I don't want the discussion to go back to anyone, especially father."

"Why of course dear."

"Mom, we both know father dominates you terribly. I'm reluctant to ask you important stuff because I know he'll worm it out of you. Do you swear to be honest with me and to keep this conversation secret?"

Her Mom thought a minute, "I promise to keep it all secret, even from William."

"Ok, here goes," began Laurie. "How does a person know when they're falling in love? I'm not saying this regarding Brad, but I don't have a clue how falling in love feels."

Shirley Knowlton remained silent a long time. Finally, she admitted, "Well, to tell you the truth, I'm not sure how a person feels when they fall in love. Because, if I'm totally honest, I'm not sure I've ever loved your father."

An astonished Laurie exclaimed, "What did you say?"

"It's a long story. However, now that you're in college, I guess it's time I shared it with you. During my junior year at Michigan, I had several dates with a very nice boy who was a senior. His name was Augie Winchester. If I ever was in love with anyone, it was probably with Augie.

"I was strongly attracted to him. He was in my thoughts constantly. He was truly handsome. I loved kissing him. Back in those days, that's about all we did. Well, maybe a little petting, however, we were very chaste.

"When Augie graduated, he planned to go on a long trip to 'see the world.' Then he would return to get his advanced degree. He wanted to be an accounting professor at a university. I must confess, I dreamed of becoming a professor's wife more than once.

"The sad news is, after Augie left school, he never wrote to me. Not once. Weeks turned into months. I was heartbroken.

"Then your father and I began to date. After we were together a few months, your father decided we should marry. I remember he never asked me to marry him. He just told me he decided we should marry. He offered me an enormous ring.

"I was a senior by then. There were no other prospects for getting my MRS degree. In those days, if you came out of college without an MRS degree, you were pretty much out of it. Everyone would call you an old maid. To this day, I don't understand why I let William put the damn ring on my hand. With the exception of you Laurie, I have literally regretted it all my life."

"Mom, you sound like you really mean that."

"You haven't heard the rest of it yet. There was an announcement in the paper and a wedding date set. A week before the wedding, after all that time, I got a letter from Augie. He began his trip in Africa. There he contacted malaria. He was deathly ill for a very long time. Finally, he recovered enough to write to me. I had to write back to tell him of the upcoming nuptials. It was the hardest letter I've ever written."

Laurie got up, walked around the table and gave her mother a big hug. "Mom, I'm so sorry."

"Well, if I'd married Augie, I'd never have had you, so things eventually work out for the best. Your father always says 'a Knowlton marries with his head, never his heart.' I guess that's the way it has been with us. As the saying goes, 'we walk alone, together.'

"You may not believe this, but in the early years of our marriage I tried to stand up to him. It was no use. He's so strong. Eventually I learned the easy way out was to say 'yes William' and go along with whatever he wanted. He's so self-centered; I don't think he cares about me a bit."

Laurie took out a hankie to dry her mother's eyes. "Well, Mom, you have somebody right here who cares about you a lot." The two women hugged.

Laurie sat back down. "You know Mom; I've been worried about you. Now that I'm in college, have you ever considered getting a job or becoming involved in something that will give you some self-esteem? Living with father all these years, would knock the self - esteem out of any one."

"You're confirming something I've been considering, Laurie. Do you think I could learn to run a computer?"

"Of course, you could. In fact, getting a computer might be a great way to get over your insecurity. Developing computer skills will help you feel self-confident. Right now, you have too much time to think and grieve about the loss of Betty Ann. Getting busy with other things will do wonders for your self-esteem and your outlook on life."

Laurie continued, "You majored in library science, didn't you?"

"Yes, I did. I greatly enjoyed being in the library."

"Maybe you could get a job at a library? It would do wonders for your self-assurance to know you could hold down a job."

"Your father would kill me. It would be bad for his image if his wife took a job."

"Mother, it's time for you to say to hell with father and his damn image! He's demeaned you long enough. You've spent your life taking care of me and allowing him to dominate you.

"I'm away at school. Now's the time to strike out. Be your own person! You're intelligent, you have a fine figure, you face is attractive and you're fun to be around. It's past time for you to reach out so you can achieve your potential!"

Shirley paused, "Maybe you're right. Whatever happens, it'd be fun to torment William for a change."

Laurie figured she was into this now, so she continued. "Mom, how bad is it between you and dad? When he moved into his own room, I thought it was because he snored. Was that really the reason?"

"No, it wasn't Laurie. Frankly, William hasn't come near me ever since he moved out of our bedroom. That's over two years ago, now. I suspect he has some bimbo he's using for sex."

"Have you ever considered a divorce?"

"About once a week ever since Betty Ann and William began to clash. However, I always decided to wait until you were grown up."

"Mom, guess what…I'm grown up now."

"Well if we're having this conversation, I have to agree. You're definitely grown up now." Shirley paused. "Learning the computer and getting a job may well be a first step in restoring my confidence. I feel I need to get my courage up, before I go plunging into a divorce."

"Why don't you tell father you need a computer so we can email each other? Then I can teach you the basics during Christmas vacation. Once you get some computer skills, you're on your way."

"I'll mull it over. I wonder what William would say if I asked for a computer? It'd be fun just to hear him react."

As they were leaving the restaurant, Shirley asked, "If you do fall in love with this Brad or someone else, be sure to let me know how it feels."

They both laughed. Then they headed for home.

That night, as they walked into the dining room for dinner, Laurie slipped a paper into Shirley's hand. "Just hand this to father. Tell him this is what you want for Christmas."

Shirley smiled as she glanced over the paper.

It seemed to take forever but finally, just before dessert, Shirley spoke, "William, I've decided what I want you to give me for Christmas."

"Well that's nice dear, what is it?" a bored William replied.

"This is what I want," announced Shirley handing him the paper.

William stared at the page:

1- Portable Computer with 6 TB ram

1 TB of hard drive

1- 19 inch wide flat monitor

1. HP Deskjet Printer

The request astonished William. "You want a computer? What in heaven's name will you do with a computer?"

Shirley replied, "I plan to join the 21st century. I'll be able to email Laurie as well as all my friends. Maybe I'll take some course work to advance my education."

Laurie added, "I told mother I'd teach her during the Christmas break, so if you can have it here by December 20th we can get her started as soon as I return home."

"This is going to be extremely expensive."

Shirley smiled, "William, just how much does your Country Club cost each year?"

The question silenced William's objection quickly. The rest of the dinner passed in comparative silence.

CHAPTER 13

The night of the Christmas Formal finally arrived. It was accompanied by a cold front from Canada which plunged temperatures down into the teens. The moon was full. Light snow flurries dropped from scattered clouds as they skimmed along the wind whipped sky. Brad arrived at the rendezvous early. He surely didn't want to keep his date waiting in the snowy cold. He abandoned the car to stand at the 'fork in the path' rendezvous.

Laurie arrived on time wrapped tightly in a long coat. Even clad in high heels her long legs quickly shortened the distance between them. She wore a big smile on her face. Her beautiful long brown hair spread over the back of her neck and shoulders. Snowflakes dotted her brown strands.

Brad's eyes filled with joy in anticipation of the evening ahead.

"Have you been waiting long?" Laurie asked. "You look kind of frozen."

"I left the car running so it'd be warm for you. But it's really cold. I guess you'll just have to heat me up after we get to the car."

"I'm sure the heater will do just fine. There'll be no heating up on my part 'till you've seen my new dress. I want you to know Mr. Randall; I bought it just for you."

As they arrived at the dance, Laurie kept herself bundled up in her coat. She went right off to the ladies' room. There she removed her coat, combed her hair and checked herself in the mirror. She thought, *eat your heart out Brad Randall; this is going to be a Christmas Formal you'll never forget.... I hope.*

Brad waited for her at the end of a long hall. There were lots of students around however, he and Laurie only had eyes for each other. One glance told Laurie he was wearing his navy-blue suit. He looked great. The broad shoulders, which topped his six foot three frame, were very sexy. When she got closer, she could see his blue eyes shining. His face was wrapped in a huge smile.

As she approached, Laurie made sure to square her shoulders. She was proud of her height because it made her feel regal. When he saw those bare shoulders, he actually shivered. They looked so wonderful. Next, her long brown hair and the upward tilt to her smiling lips caught his eyes. The pale yellow formal dress completed the picture. It rounded gracefully over her breasts. Then it tapered down her slim figure. At the bottom, the skirt flared outward almost covering her matching pale yellow heels.

His breath caught. He was literally speechless! She reached out her hand to him. With a gentle caress, he lightly took it into his. They both looked into each other's eyes. Finally, Brad got control of his voice. "Miss Lansing, may I have the honor of this dance?"

Laurie glanced around. Then she quipped. "Well, I don't see anyone else around so, I guess you'll have to do."

The band played many old songs from the 40's and 50s. These songs didn't lend themselves to the 'wiggle in front of each other' type of dancing. The way to dance to these slow songs was to hold your partner in your arms.

That began an evening of fun and joy neither of them ever forgot. They danced until their feet hurt. Then they danced some more. He held her close. She relaxed into his arms and allowed her whole body to press against him. They snuck outside a few times to cool off and smooch. The kisses were tender and warm.

Toward the end of the evening, the male singer in the band sang an old song called, 'Always.' For some reason, Laurie and Brad listened closely to the words:

I'll be loving you, always
With a love that's true, always
When the things you've planned
Need a helping hand
I will understand, always.

Days may not be fair, always
That's when I'll be there, always
Not for just an hour
Not for just a day
Not for just a year
But always.

When the song ended, Brad looked into her eyes. "Laurie, those words express exactly how I feel about you."

Laurie smiled, "Then let's call *Always* our special song."

After the dance, they spent a few minutes parked in the warm car by their rendezvous spot. She put her head on his shoulder. In the diffused moonlight, they watched the snow flurries fall gently to the ground.

"I hate to have it end," admitted Brad. "Did I tell you how gorgeous you look in your yellow dress?"

"I think that was the fifteenth time. You did it so often, I started keeping count."

Then she added, "You know, you're much better looking in your blue suit than you were in the tuxedo. I was proud to have you as my date."

"In this snowy cold won't you let me take you to your dorm? I promise not to look where it is."

"How could you drive there if you didn't look?"

"Well you could drive and I'd keep my eyes closed."

"After I left, how would you drive away with your eyes closed?"

The thought rendered Brad silent. Then Laurie spoke again.

"I've a better idea. Let's make out for a few minutes. That'll get me all warmed up. Then I'll need the cold walk to get back to normal."

She began gently kissing his mouth. Then she pressed her lips to his throat. He kissed her throat then her mouth. The kisses deepened. In a few minutes, both were panting.

"I've decided to give you an early Christmas present." Laurie whispered. "Well actually, it's for both of us. Please close your eyes. Don't open them until I say Merry Christmas."

She pulled away from him and positioned herself against the cowling of the car. The snow had stopped. The light from the full moon fell through the windshield. It tumbled over Laurie's shoulders and dress. Eyes shut; Brad listened to any sound Laurie made relating to the Christmas present. He heard her dress rustling, then silence.

He heard her soft voice say, "Merry Christmas, Brad."

He opened his eyes. In total astonishment, his heart contracted at the sight before him. She had pulled down her dress, leaving her breasts bare and open to him. Her soft whiteness was washed in the moonlight streaming through the car windshield.

Brad just stared.

She enjoyed watching Brad stare. Reading his facial expressions told her everything she needed to know. Initially he'd been stunned by what she'd done. In seconds, her unbelievably loving gesture had changed his face into an expression of incredible joy!

If he were looking at a Monet painting for the first time, his face would surely reflect the reverent expression it now held. Shortly, she could read sexual desire come into his eyes. Most importantly, as he continued his open-mouthed stare, his face joyously reflected how much he loved her.

It took at least a minute for him to regain his voice. "I want to remember this view for the rest of my life. I've never seen anything so beautiful…Laurie, this is a first for me. I've never been intimate with anyone before."

"That's nice to hear, Brad, especially because it's a first for me too. You've been so nice regarding my secret past. I feel we've grown close spiritually. It's time to take this next step."

After another pause, she continued, "Brad, this isn't Show and Tell. It's Show and Touch."

"If I touch will I get put in *breast purgatory*?"

Laurie snickered. "No, you silly, this time the rules are reversed. If you don't touch, I'll kill you. Can't you see, Brad, I'm begging you to touch me."

"I'm having trouble deciding whether to touch you with my fingers or my lips."

"Maybe that's why we have two. You can do both. Please remember they're not like bread dough, it's not necessary to knead them. They just want gentle stroking."

Brad reached forward with his right hand. His fingers caressed her shoulders. As they moved down from her shoulders, he gently cupped his hand so his thumb touched the curve under her breast.

At the same time, he bent his face to her other breast. As his lips approached, she shivered with joy. Slowly she felt those lips tenderly circle, then lick her.

"Oh God Brad! I knew it would feel good, but I never dreamed it would feel this good!

"Don't you dare stop," she murmured. "Please Brad, don't ever stop. Whatever you do, keep on loving my breasts, just like you are."

Brad was overcome with her softness. At the same time her hunger for his touch made him feel incredibly desired as well as loved. He felt her hand stroke his head. After an interval, she pulled his hair so he would lift his face for a kiss. When she kissed him, he thought he would explode. Both of his hands were touching her breasts, while her lips and tongue assaulted him.

Suddenly, she broke away, pulling her dress back up covering herself.

"Time out, Brad. Another thirty seconds and I'll be out of control. When I give my whole body to you, it'll not be in a car. I want it to be really special."

Brad took a deep breath. "I know you're right to stop. I sure don't want to, though. What an indescribably beautiful moment. Your breasts are simply magic. Could I touch them just one more time?"

"I truly want to say yes. But because I'm so teased, I simply don't dare. There'll be time next semester."

She kissed him once more. Chastely this time. "Merry Christmas, sweetheart."

She opened the car door, wrapped herself in her coat, and vanished.

Brad sat silently as she faded into the blackness. *It truly was a magical night. I'll never forget what happened.*

CHAPTER 14

On their last date before the Christmas break, they exchanged Christmas gifts.

Laurie gave him a nice pair of leather gloves. Soft fleece lined the inside. When Brad put them on, he found a note inside:

We've made it until Christmas
Can Valentine's Day be far behind?
Thanks for making this fall a very special time in my life.
I'll be thinking of you on Christmas Eve and Christmas morning.
Laurie - Your Best Friend - Always.

When Laurie opened her gift, she found a beautiful jewelry box with a gorgeous white cameo on the cover. When she opened the box, it played a beautiful lilting melody. It was *Always.*

"Now *Always* is seriously our special song," Laurie commented as she kissed him. Then she added, "Remember the Christmas Vacation rules. Email is okay, phone calls are not. Unless I call you."

They kissed again. Then she was gone. It was so strange, Brad realized, not knowing where she went. She was just ...... somewhere.

As he drove toward Michigan that next day, he reflected about decorating a Christmas tree. Somehow, tree trimming all alone seemed pointless. *I guess I'll put off deciding for a few days. One thing is for sure. Grampa taught me to reach out to others so I won't feel sorry for myself. I think I'll buy some little gifts for the Johnson's and maybe for Mr. Olsen, the attorney.*

The first day of vacation, Brad called Mr. Olsen. "I thought I should check in with you, now that I'm home on vacation."

"Glad you did," Mr. Olsen replied. "I've several things to discuss."

"First of all, I found out Chelsea has a resident who works for the Detroit Free Press. His name's Ted Jenkins. He and my son are leaders of the Boy Scout Troop. Right now, they're selling Christmas trees on the lot at the corner of Main Street and Hadlee Road. If you drop by there and meet Jenkins, he can probably steer you in the right direction. Secondly, my wife and I would like to invite you over for Christmas Dinner. My son and his family will be with us of course, so you'll have some people close to your age."

"What a kind offer, Mr. Olsen, I accept. I wasn't looking forward to a Christmas all by myself."

"Good. Now the third thing is, I have a feeler from someone who might want to purchase your house."

Brad didn't even hesitate, "Not interested. I'll probably sell the house someday. But I don't see that day coming 'til after I graduate. I truly need an emotional home base right now."

"I understand, Brad. I think waiting is the right decision. It's simply too soon. Mrs. Olsen told me she is planning Christmas dinner around 2:00 P.M. See you then."

Brad realized he needed to buy some groceries. He delayed his trip to town until late in the day so he would hit the Christmas tree lot after it opened. When he got to the lot, as luck would have it, Don Olsen was on duty with the Scouts, not Ted Jenkins. Don and Brad were acquainted. However, they didn't know each other well. Brad told him he planned to spend Christmas with them at Don's father's house. Without warning, the lot got busy. It did not take long for Brad to begin to assist. He helped the Scouts lift then tie customer's trees to their car tops or stuffed them into trunks and tied down the lids.

As they worked, Don explained that the Scouts were to do the selling. He and Ted Jenkins were on duty to oversee and do the loading. "We need another adult supervisor on the lot tomorrow afternoon because Ted can't get here until after six."

Brad offered to fill in the gap. Don accepted his offer gratefully.

The next day Brad found himself all bundled up with a warm coat, mittens and a hat working on the Christmas tree lot. The boy scouts proved to be nice kids. Brad enjoyed the work. Helping felt good. As he expected, by reaching out, he didn't have time to feel sorry for himself.

When Ted Jenkins arrived, they were quite busy, so Brad just kept on working. When a lull occurred, he and Ted began to talk. Naturally, Ted already had a favorable impression of Brad.

After a few minutes of conversation, Brad opened up. "Mr. Jenkins, I've wanted to talk with you. I'm in my first year in college. My major is writing. Does the Free Press have any programs for summer interns who may be interested in a career in newspaper reporting?"

"It's really not my department Brad, I'm in advertising. However, I think there is a program of some kind. Let me check tomorrow. Maybe I can line you up an appointment with the proper person.

Later, Brad signed up to do regular shifts on the Christmas tree lot. He felt good working in the cold, helping the boy scouts. A few days later, Mr. Jenkins told him an appointment had been scheduled with the Free Press assistant editor for 11:00 A.M. the following Monday. The man's name was Archer Lane. Ted Jenkins told Brad, "When I talked with Archer Lane I gave you a high recommendation."

Brad thanked him profusely.

The following Monday, Brad's interview with Archer Lane went well. Mr. Lane told Brad the Free Press reserved two spots for aspiring reporters during the summer vacation period. He acknowledged, "Usually, we reserve these spots for college juniors, however, in your case, I could make an exception. What you'll be doing mostly is 'gopher' work. Once in a great while there might be something for you to write. When does your semester end?"

Brad looked at his calendar, "Friday May 12th is the last day of school."

All right, replied Archer Lane, "I'll expect you in my office at 8:00 A.M. Monday May 15th. Be ready to run your fanny off, boy. This job is not for the faint of heart. Between now and then, I want you to keep in touch with me. As May 15th approaches, be sure to call to confirm our appointment in case there are any changes.

"I also want to see a copy of your grades. When we enroll a person in our intern program, we keep track of their schoolwork. If your grades slip, we reserve the right to select another intern. Your work for the Free Press will count more than your grades. However, we consider both items when we do our intern reviews. We're seeking people with balance in their lives."

Brad floated out of Archer Lane's office. He returned to work on the Christmas tree lot. The next time he saw Ted Jenkins he told him what had happened and thanked him profusely.

• • •

For Laurie, the Christmas vacation was significantly different than Brad's. She had dates with three young men whom her parents deemed 'eligible males.' She really didn't want to go out with them. However, she knew her parents wouldn't allow her to refuse. It was easier to go out with a clod than to face the wrath of her father. The clods she dated did nothing except to make Brad seem more special.

One thing for sure, she continued her cooking lessons. One night she made a pot roast for the family. Under Agnes' supervision, of course.

She was pleased when Brad's email revealed the news of his summer job at the Free Press. Sometimes she feared her Valentine's Day revelations would ruin things with Brad. Then she would convince herself Brad would still care for her. Her emotions vacillated up and down depending upon which way she was thinking at the moment. After Christmas Eve dinner, before the family went to church, Laurie sneaked off to her room to call him.

"Hi, Merry Christmas!"

"Laurie, I was hoping it would be you. I'm missing you so much! How is your vacation going?"

"You want the truth? I wish we were back at school. I'm tired of dodging around all these young men my parents keep throwing at me."

The remarks caused a pause. Finally, Brad spoke, "I hope you're kidding me."

"I wish I was. Don't worry, sweetheart. All those creeps only make you look better."

"Well I'm glad to hear that. But it worries me when you date other men."

"Brad, dear friend, we are just barely twenty years old. It's necessary to date many people to learn things. Aren't you dating girls up there?"

"There's no point in my doing any dating. I found this girl at school. I'm completely stuck on her."

"You're way too young to be stuck on one girl. However, I do have to admit I'm glad to hear you say it. What'd you decide to do about a Christmas tree?"

"Well, there was one tree left on the Boy Scout lot, so I brought it home. I have it up and the lights are on it. I decided to bag the ornaments, however. Too much work."

"Are you awfully lonely?" asked Laurie.

"You want the truth? The place feels like a morgue with a lighted Christmas tree. However, your call has really lifted my spirits. Maybe I'll go to church to see if I can pick up a hot chick and get some Christmas smooches."

"Don't you dare ...I'm dodging all kissing attempts from my creepy dates. I promise you, I'm kissing no one."

"You just told me I should be dating lots of women at my age."

"Dating is one thing, kissing is way too personal."

"I wish I could kiss you right now."

"I wish you could too, Brad dearest. It's time for church. I have to run. Merry Christmas!"

After the call, Brad sat a long time thinking, as he watched the lighted Christmas tree. *I really miss her. I miss my grandparents too. Guess I may as well go to midnight church. I'll be too lonely if I stay here.*

CHAPTER 15

By the end of Christmas day, Laurie had spent a lot of time with her mother on the computer. Laurie felt it was time for Shirley to send an email message.

"Are you ready to send a message?" she asked her mom.

"Do you think I could?"

"I know you could. Who shall we send it to?"

"Don't I need to know someone's email address to send a message?"

"I bet you don't know one email address, do you?"

"No, I don't know of one."

"Well, you'll have to start asking your friends for their email address. In the meantime, you could send an email to Brad. You remember he's the boy who took me to the Christmas formal. If you send him an email, I bet you'll have an answer tomorrow."

Shirley thought a minute. "Okay, let's try it. What's his email address?"

After they addressed the email, Laurie cautioned her mother not to use their last name. "I don't want to tip him off to anything regarding my family before Valentine's Day."

Shirley wrote:

Dear Brad,

You don't know me, so hello! Laurie has been teaching me to email. She thought you would respond if I sent my first email message to you.

Did you have a good time at the Christmas formal?

Did you like the dress we picked out for Laurie to wear?

Sincerely yours,

Laurie's Mom

As luck would have it, Brad was working on his computer. He quickly picked up the message in his 'in box.' He knew Laurie was teaching her mother the computer. *I can show her the magic of email by responding promptly:*

Hi to Laurie's Mother:

I'm honored your first email came to me.

I had a wonderful time at the Christmas Formal with Laurie. Her yellow dress really set off her soft brown hair. She looked gorgeous. I hope to meet you soon. If you are half as sensitive and kind as your daughter, you must be a very wonderful woman!

Regards,

Brad.

Just as Laurie and her mother were wrapping up the computer lesson, Brad's response arrived. The quick reply really impressed Shirley. "No wonder you want me to learn to email! He's in Michigan and we're in Indiana and we corresponded in seconds! Amazing!" Then she read the message.

Shirley laughed. "He sounds like a nice boy, Laurie."

Laurie then showed her Mom how to put Brad's email address in her address book. It'll be there whenever you want to write to him. Later Laurie emailed Brad and told him his message made a big hit with her Mom.

As New Year's Eve approached, Brad emailed Laurie.

Any chance you could come back to school early so we could be together New Year's Eve?

She replied:

You forget, for valid reasons, my father knows almost nothing about you. He doesn't have a clue as to how important you are in my life. How could I explain my need to go back to school early? Besides there are parties on the 29th and the 31ist which my parents expect me to attend. Maybe next year if we are still together?

Brads response was:

As far as I am concerned, we'll be together next year. Can I pick you up at the airport, as I did after Thanksgiving?

She came back with something truly mystifying.

Thanks for the offer but it won't be necessary. I've made other arrangements to get back to school. I'll probably get to campus before you do, so please call the second you arrive.

When Brad got to school, he parked his car by the dorm so he could unload it. Then he called Laurie. They made a date for dinner at the local coffee shop. When they met at the rendezvous, she threw her arms around him kissing him lovingly. When she did, his concerns regarding 'other men' were somewhat allayed.

Because it was bitter cold, Laurie declined parking the car with Brad and walking back to the place in the path where they parted. Consequently, Brad drove her to the rendezvous spot.

Later, when Brad parked his car at the off-campus house parking lot, he noticed a beautiful yellow Mercedes convertible. When he remarked about the car to the 'student landlord' the reply was, "The car's beautiful, but you should see the girl who parked it here. She's tall and gorgeous! I can hardly wait till she comes back; I'm going to ask her for a date!"

Brad laughed. He thought no more about it.

• • •

January meant a heavy study time on campus. Social events were at a minimum. Mostly Brad and Laurie got together for coffee after studying together at the library until 10:00 P.M.

The first week in February, it snowed six inches! When Laurie came out of the library after it closed, she was disappointed to find Brad wasn't waiting for her. *Maybe it's so cold he's already inside the Union waiting for me.* She headed in that direction.

Wham! Wham! Two snowballs smacked into her coat. She looked up spotting Brad making more snowballs. Laurie's arms were full of books. She was in no position to defend herself. She ran for the Union, dodging a couple of snowballs sent her way. Brad figured the snowball fight was over. He started to follow Laurie inside.

As soon as she was inside, Laurie dumped the books. She stepped back outside quickly making two snowballs. As Brad approached, she threw the first snowball high in the air. Naturally, Brad looked up to watch the flight of the snowball. When he looked up, Laurie calmly fired her second snowball right into Brad's face!

Stunned, he went for more ammunition. A brisk snowball fight followed. Finally, Laurie called to him, "Okay, enough, I'd rather kiss you than throw snowballs at you. Brad immediately held out his arms. She leaped into them.

Brad didn't realize Laurie still had one snowball in her hand. She threw her arms around him so she could deepen the kiss. In seconds, Brad was in 'Lola land.' As she continued to kiss him, Laurie cautiously lifted his jacket, then his shirt, with her left hand. Next, she slipped the snowball down his bare back and mashed it!

EEEOW! screamed Brad as Laurie tore from his grasp and flew into the warmth of the Student Union. She ordered him coffee and waited. It took a long time. When he finally came in from the men's room she greeted him with, "What took you so long?"

"Well, I had to go into the john to remove my jacket and shirt. I had to dry myself off with those stupid paper towels. It's almost impossible to reach a very cold wet back with a paper towel. Now I've put my jacket on without a shirt because the shirt's too wet. Next, I had to deal with my ego. I was totally defeated in a war that I started. You smashed me one in the face and one down my back. Getting trashed by a girl in a snowball fight is a major blow to my self-esteem."

Laurie smiled delightedly. "You still make sexist remarks, Mr. Randall."

As they warmed themselves with coffee Laurie exclaimed, "Guess what? Our next date will be Friday night, which happens to be Valentine's Day. I think we've both been waiting for a long time. Brad, I'm really glad we made it."

"You've no idea how glad I am. Well, I was until tonight's snowball debacle!"

Laurie's grin became wall to wall.

"I suppose I should confess to you Laurie, I've learned a few things about you."

"Oh, what have you learned?"

"I learned you have a father who frustrates you. I also found out you have a mother, because she sent me an email."

"Is that all you've learned?"

"That's all, I swear, Mystery Daughter."

Laurie smiled at him. "As you know, the promise is for me to take you to dinner. Therefore, when you go to the rendezvous Friday night, I want you to walk. No arguments are permitted; just do as you are told. Walk to our special spot. A very puzzled but excited Brad walked back to the dorm.

CHAPTER 16

Thursday evening, the day before the important Valentine's Day date, Brad was in the carrels studying. Laurie walked by and with a big smile, handed him an envelope. "Please read this before tomorrow night. See you at 6:00 sharp."

Before Brad could close his books and follow her, she was gone. He slit the envelope and removed a carefully worded letter:

Dearest Brad:

I know how difficult it has been for you these past months to refrain from probing my past. This letter is to thank you for your patience and also to let you know it has also been difficult for me.

It seems like we grow closer and closer as the days' pass. As this closeness happens, it brings me great joy. But it also makes me feel almost dishonest because I was not allowing all of my life to be open to you.

You are so open and so honest, dear Brad. I needed badly to respond with openness and honesty for you. However, my need to keep my past a secret was so strong, I felt it even more important.

Please know it has not been easy for me. I have wanted to give back to you so badly! Now on Valentine's Day, I can at last open the door and attain the incredible level of honesty with you that you have always given to me.

I only hope and pray that you will still care for me once you know my past and my reason for asking such a difficult thing of you.

Please please dearest Brad, don't throw me away. I am so very much in love with you.

Always,

Your Laurie.

P.S. I used the L word because I truly feel it. I love you!

Brad read the letter three times in the library and once more before he went to bed. Each time the letter warmed his heart. She loves me! I know I'm in love with her. *I wonder what tomorrow will bring?*

• • •

On Valentine's Day, Brad walked to the Rendezvous as he had been instructed to do. After waiting a few minutes, Laurie appeared out of the darkness. She was wearing her shaggy coat and a big smile. When she came up to him, he took her into his arms. As they hugged he admitted, "Laurie, thank you so much for your letter. Thank you for telling me you love me. I've been in love with you since we first met, but now I feel I can tell you. I love you too! They kissed tenderly. The hug continued.

"I'm really scared about tonight," Brad admitted. "I don't know what you could possibly tell me that would change anything between us. I'm in love with you and my love is strong enough to get through anything you say, I'm certain. These last few months have been so special. If you want, we could just keep going without my knowing anything."

"Dearest Brad, I don't want it to change anything between us either. I've been wondering if we could do exactly that. I mean, why do you need to know anything about my background? Then I realized that someday you would find out. Brad, I feel it's far more important that you get the information from me, rather than some distorted version someone else might provide."

"Yeah, I guess you're right."

"So, let's have our special Valentine's out for dinner. It's going to be fun. I promise as far as I'm concerned, my feelings for you will not be altered by tonight's events."

Then she took his hand. "Let's go find where I parked."

She walked up to a gorgeous yellow Mercedes convertible and opened the passenger door. The top was up of course, because it was a cold evening.

"We're going in this?" questioned Brad.

"Why not, I think it's a nice car."

"It's a wonderful car. I think this is the first time I've ever been in a Mercedes. What did you do, rent it for our special night?"

By then Laurie had buckled up and started driving.

"No."

"You borrowed it from a friend?"

"Nope."

"Wait a minute. I remember this car. It was in the same place where I stash my car off campus. I saw it when I came back from Christmas vacation. I remember mentioning the car to the guy who rents the parking spaces. He told me, "The car is gorgeous, but you ought to see the tall brunette who owns it. He said he was going to try to get a date with her. That was you?"

"Bingo.... And... he did ask me out....After a pause she added, "I told him I was involved with someone at the moment."

"Then your parents own this car?" asked Brad. He was obviously confused.

"The car was my Christmas present from my parents. At Thanksgiving, I told my parents how freshmen were getting around the 'no car on campus rule' by parking off campus. So, unbeknownst to me, they decided to give me this car for Christmas. Under the tree was a box with the key. They took me out to garage. There it was, with a great big red bow on the top. It looked just like cars do in the Christmas ads. I decided to drive it back to school and to keep it a secret from you until tonight."

"Wow," Brad exclaimed. "Your parents must be awfully rich to be able to give you a Mercedes convertible."

"Bingo again. Now you've had the first revelation of the evening.

However, I don't want to discuss any more revelations until we get to the restaurant, which is 25 minutes away. So, just sit back and enjoy the ride."

Laurie's reservations were at a very posh restaurant in Columbus. They were given a private booth with a fancy tablecloth. The restaurant carpeting muffled sound, so they could converse without shouting over the noise often heard in restaurants. It was an intimate setting, which is what Laurie wanted for this deep, important conversation.

As she removed her coat, Brad noticed she wore a white blouse with a navy-blue skirt. There were pearls at her throat with matching earrings. Her long brown hair shone in the candle light. It reached well below her shoulders. The skirt ended just above her knees. Her long shapely calves tucked themselves into blue matching heels.

Brad wore his blue suit with a red tie in honor of Valentine's Day. He looked handsome, even sexy, as his tall frame filled out the suit.

After they ordered, she turned to him, "My full name is Laurie Lansing Knowlton."

"Oh," replied Brad, "Is that spelled like Knowlton Dining Hall on campus?"

"Correct," was Laurie's answer. Then she added, "My grandfather gave the money to the university to build Knowlton Dining Hall."

"Oh.......What about the Knowlton dormitory?" asked Brad.

"My Grandfather gave the money to the University to build that building also."

"So, you're really, really rich."

"Well, my parents are. My grandparents were. My grandparents are both deceased."

For several minutes, Brad pondered this information. The longer the silence, the more concerned Laurie became.

CHAPTER 17

She reached across the table, taking his hand in hers. Then she began her story:

"I guess I should begin at the beginning...... My grandfather was a super guy. So was Gram. They were both always very loving and concerned about me...... I miss them dreadfully.

"My grandfather, way back when, decided to open a retail appliance store. He sold stoves, refrigerators and the like. His entire operation was based on service after the sale. His customers simply raved at the way his service technicians could fix their appliances. If someone had a big party scheduled, Grandpa would loan them an extra refrigerator. His men would deliver and pick up the extra fridge at no charge. As his reputation grew, Grandpa started to add more stores.

"Since he started in Indianapolis, Grandpa's first few store additions were in small Indiana towns.

Brad interjected, "Can I ask a question?"

"Sure."

"You never told me where you live. Is Indianapolis a good guess?"

"Actually, my home is in Carmel, Indiana. It's a suburb of Indianapolis."

"Okay. Please continue."

"For some fortunate reason, Grandpa sensed the need to avoid big population centers. He concentrated on small towns where the big cut price competitors would not bother to put stores. His idea proved very profitable, so the business continued to grow.

"Grandpa worked into his eighties. His mind was sharp. He came to work every day. He was controlling, perhaps because he sensed my father, who would take over the presidency of the company, wasn't ready.

"Unlike Grandpa, my father grew up as the son of a rich man. He feels the world has to 'cow tow' to him. Grandpa sensed that Father's 'holier than thou' attitude would be trouble. He felt certain when father took over, it would wreak havoc with the 'sprit de corps' Grandpa had spent his life building among his employees. Consequently, Grandpa kept control right up till he dropped dead at his desk one morning about 10 years ago.

"When Grandpa died, Knowlton's Appliance, Incorporated had grown to about 100 stores. Our stores are located in 8 states. Indiana, Kentucky, Tennessee Illinois, Missouri, Iowa, Nebraska, and Arkansas. You may never have heard of Knowlton's because we have no stores in Michigan or Ohio which is the area you frequent.

"Gram died about a year after Grandpa. I couldn't have asked for more loving, caring people than my father's parents.

"Mom's parents were great too. They were farmers. However, they passed on when I was really small. I have few recollections of them.

"Mother is, with the exception of the handsome man across the table, the most sensitive, loving person I've ever known. However, father is terrible to her. He treats her like she is a servant, not a spouse. I've a lot of baggage that will enter the picture here, Brad so get set for a boatload of 'When the World Turns.'

"When the World Turns?"

"You know the TV soap opera series with all the trauma and family troubles."

"Oh, yeah, I've heard of it. Never watched it though."

"Well, you're going to hear a bunch of it next."

At that propitious moment, the waiter returned with their entrees.

Brad suggested, "Maybe we should eat before we get to your traumatic family issues."

"Good idea, hum… this pasta is delicious!"

After the waiter cleared the dinner they both opted for coffee. Laurie took a sip, then looked at Brad. "Are you still okay? Do you still love me?"

"So far so good. The rich part has me concerned because obviously, our backgrounds are really different. But you need to keep going. Let's get everything out on the table."

Laurie began again. "One thing I don't understand is why a nice loving person like my mother, whose name is Shirley, married my father. Father's name is William, incidentally. All I really know is they were both at the University of Michigan. I think now that father was looking for a hostess to help with his business entertaining. He didn't really want a wife. I guess mother saw a strong man who was financially secure. I've never felt an ounce of love between the two of them. A few weeks ago, my Mom and I had a talk. She confirmed my suspicions about their relationship. Or perhaps I should say the lack of a relationship."

Brad interjected, "That must have made for a strange home life. My grandparents were so loving to each other. They still held hands right up to the end. Can you tell me about your house?"

"I guess that can come next. Not knowing my background must have been difficult for you, Brad. I could always picture exactly where you lived because I'd been there. You've never even had a clue as to where I lived."

"Yes, it was sort of discombobulating at times. I didn't even know what state you were from."

"We have an enormous house with a fence all around the property. It is brick and stone on the outside. There's a swimming pool, a six-car garage, and so many rooms in the house I've never counted them. Ever. Everything in the house is decorated for entertaining. I've never been allowed to have any input on what's on the walls of my own bedroom! If you saw my bedroom you'd think it was the room of a forty-year-old, not a college kid.

"In addition, we have a home on Sanibel Island, which is on the Gulf side of Florida, near Fort Myers. It's also quite posh, with a pool plus the Gulf of Mexico right out the door. I loved my vacations on Sanibel. The beach there is fabulous. But honestly, Brad, all that fancy housing doesn't mean anything to me."

"You know, Laurie, I agree with you. I've never for one instant had the impression you were rich. Usually, I'm uncomfortable around rich kids. They manage to lord it over everyone else. You're just the opposite, down to earth and extremely sensitive."

"I suppose that comes from Mother. It sure doesn't come from father. You may have noticed; I never call him Dad. Calling someone Dad implies warmth and love. Honestly, Brad, my father is a son of a bitch.

"Ouch! I'm so sorry Laurie."

"That makes two of us. Thank goodness, my Mother is the exact opposite. She is soft, sensitive and sweet. Father dominates her terribly. I really feel sorry for her. She's a sponge. She soaks up all the stress my father dumps on us.

"I think her absorption of all that stress may be a major contribution to her illness. She's in a lot of pain. The doctors don't seem to be able to help at all.

She's been much worse since Betty Ann."

"Who's Betty Ann?"

"My late sister. I guess I'm convoluting the story. Betty Ann is a huge part of my troubles. I need to back up and tell that part. My parents had two daughters. Betty Ann was first. She was four years older than I. In our early years, Betty Ann and I were really good pals. She took care of me and we had a lot of fun playing together. She had dark hair, brown eyes and she was an athlete. She loved playing baseball, basketball and field hockey.

"As my sister grew into her teen years, she and father began to clash. I remember one fight really well. Betty Ann wanted to put up posters and pennants to make her room something she liked. Father refused to allow it. He wanted Betty Ann's room to reflect adult taste so when business associates decided to tour our house it would look distinguished.

"One day when Betty Ann was about 12, there was an important baseball game. She pleaded with father to come and watch. He assured her he would. Mother and I went, of course, but father never showed. Betty Ann hit a triple in the last inning and scored the winning run.

"That night at dinner father assured Betty Ann he was in the crowd. "You just missed seeing me," he told her. That night Betty Ann came into my room. She was furious.

Betty Ann declared, "He lied to me. He bold face lied to me. I looked over the crowd. There were only about 25 people there. I know I'd have seen him if he was in that sparse crowd."

I told her, "I looked for him too, Betty Ann. I know he wasn't there. It looks like we can't trust our own father."

"He preaches to us to be honest and then he lies."

"As the years passed, we began to check up on father. By then Betty Ann had a free run of the country club. She spent a lot of time there luring the local boys. She was attractive as well as a good athlete so there were lots of boys around her.

"At night, she would come into my room and share her life with me. I was honored my older sister would be so nice. She told me she often saw father at the club. She began to notice he always seemed to have a young woman with him. She said it seemed to be a different woman every time, but father always had a female for company.

"When Betty Ann got dressed up, she could pass for sixteen when she was really only fourteen. One night she and her date were in a bar. Father came in with a bimbo. Betty Ann told me she had on a skirt so short it barely covered her behind. In addition, her blouse was cut so low it revealed about a mile of cleavage. Betty Ann and her date managed to sneak out the back door of the bar so father never saw her. But Betty Ann knew what our father was doing.

"I clashed with him more than once, too. One Christmas, I guess I was about twelve, I got a crush on one of our cousins who is two years older than I am. He lived in Chicago and was visiting us over the holidays. I really fell for him. Christmas night my cousin caught me under the mistletoe and kissed me! It was my first kiss! I was thrilled to death. Unfortunately, father happened to walk by and see us.

"He grabbed me by the arm so hard he almost broke it. He marched me up to my room and forced me to stay in there until my cousin left the next day. He had my meals sent up. I was not allowed to come out even to say goodbye to my cousin. I had always been angry at father because of the way he treated Betty Ann. After that Christmas, I was angry at him for both of us!

"I think what he did to me was the last straw for Betty Ann because right after that she truly changed into the naughty daughter. My psychology professor would say she was angry at father's infidelity and was screaming for attention. Betty Ann got in with a bunch of drug addicts at school. She began staying out all night.

"As I look back on it, that was when I actually lost my sister. It wasn't ever the same after she got into the drug scene. She stopped coming into my room and she never played with me again. She was a regular teen aged hellion, the prodigal daughter.

"Mother loved the prodigal deeply. She possessed tremendous feelings for Betty Ann. On the other hand, father treated her terribly. As Father imposed more and more restrictions she got more and more wild. Poor mother, the emotional sponge, found herself right in the middle.

"While all this was going on, I played the good daughter role. I played Briar Fox in the Tar Baby story, 'I laid low.'

"One night at dinner during her senior year in high school, Betty Ann announced she was going to Florida for the spring break with one of her sleazy boyfriends.

"Father leaped up screaming, "I absolutely refuse permission for this trip. If you go, I'll cut off your credit card and you won't have any money. It's not proper for a young woman with the Knowlton name to protect, to be seen with such trash. You are forbidden."

"Betty Ann jumped to her feet, glaring at father. 'You're a great one to talk about protecting the Knowlton name. I've seen you with your bimbos and whores all over this town. What you are father, speaks so loud, I cannot hear what you say!"

"She stormed upstairs. When we woke in the morning she was gone.

She must have sneaked out in the night. That house is so big you can go anywhere in the night and no one will hear you.

"With one exception, she never came back, never wrote or let us know where she was. I think father had some private detectives checking on her, but it was never discussed.

"The following August we were seated at dinner, when we heard a motorcycle pull into the driveway. Seconds later, Betty Ann and her boyfriend waltzed into the house. She looked awful. She was thin and pale. Her hair was all stringy. It had no life in it. The guy was all tattoos. He was dirty and smelled terrible. So did my sister, for that matter.

"Betty Ann told us they were passing by and she wanted to stop in to say hi. She ran up to her room and got something. I suspect she had stashed some cash up there. Then she waved goodbye and left on the back of that creep's motorcycle.

"Two months later, the police called. They found her body in a dirty motel. She had overdosed on something."

Brad interjected, "Laurie, I'm so sorry. It must still tear your heart out."

"I get tears every time I think about her. But her behavior and her subsequent death left far more residual damage than just my grief."

"Oh?"

"For one thing, it completely crushed mother. As I think I told you, she has a very loving personality which seems to soaks up other's feelings. If you couple that with her own grief about Betty Ann.... well, she's never recovered. Her physical troubles increased. Her normally cheery disposition drowned in sadness. And like me, she resents the important part Father's treatment of Betty Ann played into the situation.

"If I'm to be completely honest.... Betty Ann's life also fuels my anger at father. If he'd only have been straight with her. If he'd only loved her a little, I'm convinced she never would have gone off the deep end.

"As a consequence of all this, my respect for father is an absolute zero. I have this burning desire to succeed so I can show the SOB I can make it in spite of his lack of love and support.

"What he's done to mother is inexcusable. He's beaten all the self-confidence out of her. She's like a wet sponge with no backbone. I can't understand why she doesn't divorce him. I keep encouraging her to do it, but I think she feels the need to be there when I confront him. Which will be pretty soon I'm sure."

Laurie paused for a swallow of water. After a moment of silence, she said, "I better get back to the story."

Brad interjected, "Let me guess. After Betty Ann died, your father pretended nothing had changed."

"You win a cookie. That's exactly what happened."

Laurie added, "As you know, I've been teaching mother the computer. I'm hoping it will help her gain some self-confidence. I think she needs to get busy. If I can get her to stop grieving, it's my hope she'll become healthy once again."

"What about you, Laurie. How did your sister's death impact you?"

"You know what, Brad; you're the first person who ever asked how I felt."

"She was silent for a long time. Moisture came into her eyes, but tears did not roll down her cheeks. Finally, she admitted, "I had lots of fun with Betty Ann when we were little. I miss my little companion a whole bunch....... It was different when she turned reckless. It was like someone threw a switch. I don't know why; she just became someone else. The Betty Ann I knew and loved just sort of disappeared. Consequently, for me, the person I loved died a year or two before she actually did pass away."

"Now the family dynamic comes roaring down on me. Nothing is ever right with father. If I do exactly as he wishes, he ignores me. If I clash with him he explodes at both me and at mother too. I think he subconsciously realizes I am strong enough to defy him. But he also knows I can't stand to see mother in anguish. He is a master at verbally abusing mother in order to force me to do his will.

"Once again, I need to back up a little......When I was in my early teens I had a problem with my complexion. I had acne. I was also very tall for my age. In the eighth, ninth and tenth grades I wasn't attractive to boys at all. I had to wear flat shoes, no heels.

"At father's command, mother began lining up dates for me from the children of their friends and acquaintances. None of those boys ever wanted to date me. I didn't want to date them. Whenever we were dancing, I had to slouch way down so I wouldn't tower over them. I didn't feel so tall when I did that. It was very awkward

"My father got the firm impression I was an ugly daughter. He still has the same impression. It just sort of stuck in his head.

"Between by sophomore and junior year in high school, my complexion finally cleared up. I began to like myself, so I stood taller and began to square my shoulders when I walked. This made my breasts stick out. Boys discovered I had a figure.

"All of a sudden, several boys started hanging around. They asked me for dates. That's when father seriously entered the picture. He has the impression that no one could possibly be interested in his 'ugly duckling daughter' unless they are after his money. Consequently, he is very nasty to any boy who expresses even a tiny bit of interest in me. As you can imagine, Brad, he was very good at chasing off insecure teenage boys.

The result of this scenario is...... I've never had a serious boyfriend... until you.

"Which leads me to the real reason of why I became the Mystery Daughter. The first night I met you, I had a feeling you were a special person. Then when you stood up, I realized you were actually far taller than me. It was like, wow! As we were walking toward the dorm, I could already tell I was beginning to like you. I made a decision. I would keep my real identity away from you for a while. If it worked out that you liked me, I wanted to be able to do something.

"I wanted to be able to tell my nasty father: *This boy did not become interested in me for* <u>*your*</u> *money. I needed to be able to tell him you didn't even know my last name. Consequently, it was impossible for you to know I was rich. More than anything I wanted to let father know you were attracted to me because of who I was, not because of his money.*

"I know the Mystery Daughter stuff wasn't pleasant for you, Brad. I'm praying you'll find it in your heart to forgive me."

Without a second of hesitation, Brad answered. "There's nothing to forgive, Laurie. What you did is very understandable. Besides, I'm thrilled to hear you liked me right away."

"I've been praying you'd understand, Brad. You are.... Well you're just plain wonderful and every time we're together.... I love you more!"

Laurie slid out from her side of the booth, walked over and kissed him, right in the middle of the restaurant. After a long moment, Laurie sat back down so she could continue.

"If there's some bad news in all this, here's my main concern. In fact, it terrifies me when I think of what might happen. "Father has a mantra, which he pounds at us. *A Knowlton doesn't pick a mate with his heart. He picks a mate with his head.*

"I probably shouldn't share this part with you. But you've been so wonderful to me, I've decided it's something I need to share."

Laurie took a deep breath. She fastened her shining brown eyes on Brad. "Part of me is petrified you and I will fall even deeper in love. If that happens, and we go to my father to talk of marriage, he'll never approve. He'll think you're after his money. If I stand up to him, it'll tear mother apart.

"I can't destroy mother, Brad. I simply can't. Especially after what Betty Ann did.

"So, let me say this to you, Brad dearest. I know I'm in love with you. I seem to fall for you more every day we're together. However, I'm terribly afraid our love affair is going to have to remain strictly a *college romance.*

"When these college years' end, father has it all worked out. I will go to graduate school to get my MBA. I'll start to work for the company. Father, who always seeks to add to his net worth, will find some rich kid for me to marry. *Because a Knowlton does not pick a mate with his heart. He picks a mate with his head.*"

"So please dear Brad, can you manage to just be in love with me a little bit? I don't ever want to hurt you. Don't you see, if you love me too much, I'm deathly afraid, you will be hurt."

A long silence followed. Finally, Brad broke the silence. "It's too late, Laurie. I'm already deeply in love with you. For the record, you can tell your father, I fell in love with you a long time before I knew you were rich."

"Oh Brad. What can we do? We're sliding down a hill. We both know there'll be an awful crash when we get to the bottom."

Brad extended his warmest loving smile. "Then we'll just have to slide slowly. We need to make the most of every day we have together."

Dinner over, they left the restaurant. When they got in the car, he took her gently into his arms. They hugged a long time. Soon they were both crying. After a while Brad whispered, "You know Dearest Laurie, we're still freshmen. We have three and a half years left before we graduate. A lot can happen in three and a half years."

They parked Laurie's car in the off-campus parking spot. For the first time, Brad walked Laurie to her dorm. As they were walking Brad said, "I think you told me you'd answer any questions I asked tonight."

"That's right, I did."

Brad began, "Okay, here goes. The more I'm with you, the more we kiss, the harder it is for me to stop. I want to renew the magic we had after the Christmas dance. I want to become one with you. Have you had any feelings of that nature?"

"Are you kidding? How could I not have feelings like that? I care deeply for you. When you kiss me, I don't want to stop either. Sometimes at night I imagine being naked with you. I often imagine what it would be like to touch you and have you touch me. Frankly, thinking about it is so sexy; I have trouble going to sleep."

"Oh God, Laurie. What are we waiting for?"

"You want the truth? Here goes. We're waiting because you haven't asked! Ever since the Christmas formal, I've been taking the pill. What good has it done? Mr. Brad Randall is too much of gentleman to ask."

"Oh Laurie, believe me I truly wanted to ask. Somehow I felt it would have to wait for the Valentine's Day revelations."

"Well the Valentine's Day revelations are past us now. If we only have three and a half years left to love each other, I say we wait no longer. I need to caution you, however. Since I've never done this, I'll be tender as well as inexperienced."

"That means there'll be two of us who are inexperienced. The most intimate I've ever been with a girl was with you the night of the Christmas formal. You can't imagine how badly I want you, Laurie. Next Friday night, let's go to a motel. We can spend the entire weekend in bed together!"

"I will, on one condition."

"Oh Oh, are we talking about *sex purgatory*?"

Laurie giggled at his joke.

Brad asked, "Okay, what's the condition?"

"Well, we both know I'm rich now, so the one condition is… I get to pay for the room. It'll be our first time together, Brad. I want it to be like a honeymoon for us. I want it to be in a nice hotel suite. And, Oh God, I do want to do it with you!"

"Agreed."

He took her in his arms. They made out for a very long time.

CHAPTER 18

He thought Friday night would never come. When he tried to study, nothing happened. His brain was simply "not available." He kept imagining how it would feel to be in bed with Laurie. He was tense, nervous, excited and frightened all at once.

Laurie's emotions were an image of Brad's. However, she chose to be practical to some degree. She phoned for a reservation at the Columbus Hilton. Realizing she could not pay with her credit card because her parents might see the hotel charge, she withdrew the funds she would need via a check made out to cash. She wanted to cover the cost of the room for two nights plus meals brought up by room service. *We're not going anywhere after they put the 'Do Not Disturb' sign on the hotel door.*

She thought to herself, *if it were an actual honeymoon, I'd have a sexy nightgown. Brad would have some silk pajamas with a robe to match. I'm going shopping.*

On Wednesday after classes, she walked down to her car and took off for the nearest upscale mall. After a few false starts, she found some nice blue silk pajamas for Brad with a matching robe and slippers. She thought he would look great in it, when they had breakfast in the room together. She asked the clerk to please gift-wrap the outfit.

For herself, she found a soft yellow short gown with matching peignoir. Then she toyed with a sexy black number but decided it wouldn't go well with her brown hair. Besides, her feeling for Brad wasn't lustful, it was just plain love. She wanted, in the most tender way, to become one with him.

Having rejected the black number, she settled for a long white gown with another matching peignoir. Then she found some white slippers, which would go well with either gown.

As she drove back to the dorm, she thought to herself, now I'm ready. Then she yelled aloud in the car, "I'm so excited! Is Friday ever gonna get here?"

On Thursday night, as they walked back to Laurie's dorm, they were both bursting with excitement and tension. When they got to a private spot, he threw his arms around her. They kissed deeply. He slid his hand over breast gently touching her. She broke off the kiss and looked at him with a twinkle in her eye. "Young man, you're not supposed to do that until we're on our college honeymoon. Do you want to be put into *feeling purgatory*?"

"Oh God no," Brad responded. "You wouldn't dare do that…Then he looked at her twinkling eyes and added, "Yeah you might, I better behave."

She hugged him. "It's less than 24 hours now. I can hardly wait."

"Me either, I'm going absolutely nuts. Why can't we go now?"

"All things come to those who wait, Darling. Can we take my new fancy car?"

"We might as well. Oh Laurie, I want it to be just as special as it can be."

"Don't worry; it'll be the weekend we'll never forget. I'll pick you up at 5:00. Don't be late."

"Are you kidding? I'll be watching for you out the window from 4:00 o'clock on."

The Friday classes dragged on forever. Finally, the end came. Laurie went back to the dorm, showered and packed a little overnight case. By 4:15 she found herself walking down to get her car.

Brad got out of his last class at 3:00. He went for a jog to relieve his tension, showered, then packed a little suitcase for the weekend. By 4:30 he started looking out the window for the yellow car. It arrived at 4:45, a full fifteen minutes early! He ran down the dorm stairs. Seconds later, their college honeymoon began.

Their eyes locked on each other. She read in his eyes desire, excitement and a great deal of love. He read her eyes and felt tenderness as well as love. He knew he was going to have to curb his need in order to love her properly. He remembered something his grandfather had told him.

"Laurie, I want to remind you of something my grandfather taught me: *True love isn't something you take. It's something you give.*

"I remember your telling me that. It's very profound." Laurie replied. As they drove toward Columbus she asked, "Do you want to stop to get something for dinner?"

"Are you kidding? I don't want to stop for anything."

She reached over and took his hand.

As they rode along she told him, with a twinkle in her eye, "The *feeling purgatory* rules are suspended for the weekend."

He responded by pulling her skirt up, placing his hand on her bare thy, and stroking it gently.

It took forever to check into the hotel and get the bellman out of the room. When he finally left, Brad put the 'Do Not Disturb' sign on the door, then he locked it to be doubly sure.

They looked at each other. "Brad, I'm a little nervous. Maybe we should check out this suite for a minute."

The suite proved to be spacious and lovely. The bedroom featured a king size bed with a large bathroom. The living room had a couch and assorted chairs and tables. As they sat together on the couch, Brad put his arm around her exclaiming, "I could get used to this."

"What the hotel room?"

"No, being rich."

"I will admit being rich has its advantages. But it also has some drawbacks."

"Such as?"

Laurie thought a minute. "For me, the biggest disadvantage comes when people act friendly. You never know if they're friendly because they like you or if they're friendly because they know you're rich."

As Brad pondered that she added, "It doesn't take long to discover the difference, but you have to be very careful knowing whom you can trust."

"Are you saying the Mystery Daughter thing was partly motivated by your own personal desire to know if I was a true friend?"

"I never thought of it in that way, but you might be right. By playing the Mystery Daughter card, it probably did make it easier for me to trust you right from the get go."

She slid her legs down the couch and turned so they could kiss. The kiss went from tender to passionate at lightning speed. "Oh Brad, I am so ready. I want to give you my body right now. Please Brad dearest, take me. Take all of me!

• • •

The next morning, clad in the blue pajamas and robe Laurie had bought for him, Brad tipped the waiter who had brought breakfast into the room. After the waiter left Laurie, clad in her new white gown, swished quietly in from the bedroom.

She began, "I had the most wonderful dream last night."

"Oh?"

"I dreamt I was in a fancy hotel room with the most wonderful man. He began kissing me so tenderly I was immediately aroused. He began undressing me. Everything was going so smoothly until he got to my bra. He had trouble unhooking the darn thing."

"He did? Maybe he lacks practice in that department."

"I'm sure you're right. Anyway, once we were both naked, I felt my body surrender. Our eyes locked. Love shined out. As did desire. I could sense he simply adored me. His eyes were so loving and tender. I never imagined anyone could stroke me as softly and tenderly as he did.

"I'll never forget how we hugged and cried in each other's arms when it was over. We just tenderly held each other, reveling in the incredible closeness we felt."

"Wow.... that was some dream."

"That was just the beginning of the dream."

"There's more?"

"He suggested we take a shower together. I said, 'Naked?' I was stunned by the idea. Then he said, 'I usually am naked when I get into a shower.' He was such fun."

"He must have been a really neat guy."

"Well, up to a point. He wrecked the bath."

"He wrecked it, how?"

"He put a bunch of soap on his fingers and started touching me."

"That wrecked the bath?"

"Well, it materially shortened it. We had to get out, sort of dry off and go back to bed."

"I see."

"Then about two o'clock in the morning I was awakened by his hand on my breast. That led to another extremely wonderful adventure."

"The guy sounds like he was insatiable."

"I don't really know the answer to that. I do know that he stirred me up to the point where I had to wake him this morning and love him all over again."

"I bet he really liked that."

"Yeah, I think he did. The trouble was I woke up. My dream night was over."

"You know Laurie dearest, just talking about it makes me want to go back to bed right now."

"Me too."

"Breakfast'll get cold."

"That's what those silver covers are for. To keep the food hot in case something else gets hot."

• • •

Later, the breakfast was cold, but no one seemed to mind.

"Laurie announced, "We need to eat, especially since we never had dinner last night. I can't have you fading out on me for lack of sustenance."

As the weekend flew by, they both realized what was happening between them was far more than sexual pleasure. It was a spiritual loving of one another. Surely, this was what God intended when sex was created.

On Sunday morning, Laurie wore the yellow nightgown. He couldn't take his eyes off her. After breakfast, they made love one more time. Then it was time to pack up so they could head back to campus.

Just before they left the room, they paused to look around. Their eyes locked. Emotions were running very high. Tears came into Laurie's eyes. She wrapped her arms around him. As she looked into his eyes she whispered, "Brad, I can't express in words how much I love you."

Brad reflected a moment. Then he said, "I guess that's why the sex was so wonderful. When your affection is so strong you can't express it in words, sex becomes God's instrument for communicating the incredible love you feel. I'll never forget you, this room and our time together. Whatever the future holds for us, Laurie, nothing can ever take away this precious college honeymoon, or my love for you."

CHAPTER 19

The emotions involved in first loves are amazing. To experience a first love while attending college together is absolutely incredible! The times together are frequent and filled with pleasure. There are long walks, long talks, and lots of touching. The loving closeness they both felt seemed to grow every day.

Now that the 'Valentine Revelations' were over, Laurie began introducing Brad to her friends. One of her good friends was the dorm advisor Donna Swift, a lanky blonde from Minnesota. She was cute as well as fun. Donna's boyfriend, Ted Sampson, was an old friend of Laurie's from Indianapolis. Their parents knew one another.

It was natural for Donna and Ted to start double dating with Laurie and Brad. They had a lot of happy times together, even though Donna and Ted were both seniors. It turns out the older couple both planned to attend law school at the University of Indiana. They were in love, no doubt about it. Brad and Laurie expected them to be married right after law school, if not before.

To be apart during spring break was tough. As the summer vacation approached, the two lovers became restless and unhappy. The thought of parting for almost three months was extremely painful. However, Laurie insisted on her 'no phone-only email' rule.

After a last wonderful loving night together, they parted ways for the summer. It was a tearful goodbye.

• • •

Now that her freshman year was completed, Laurie's summer meant it was time to start work in her father's office. Her job was to 'swing vacations' for the office staff. She would replace a secretary for a week or two, then the accounts payable clerk, then the purchasing agent. Laurie quickly realized this was a good way to learn the business. In spite of her reservations about working with her father, she could see he was anxious for her to get her feet wet.

She vowed, *I'm going to do my very best. I intend to show that SOB that I can be just as good an executive as he's been, if not better. Actually, I'm not real sure how good he's been. I think I'll do some checking in the financial archives if I get a chance. It'll be interesting to find out just how successful Knowlton Stores Incorporated have been under father's leadership.*

At the end of the day, she would often go into her father's office on the 21st floor of the Knowlton Towers building. She would wait for him to finish up so they could drive home together. Occasionally, he would discuss a business situation and ask her opinion. Then he would critique her answer.

One day, near the end of the vacation, she walked into William's office and found him on the phone. She had time to look around. William's office was an impressive place. The furniture was modern; the bookshelves were warm and extensive. A huge picture window overlooked downtown Indianapolis. An oblong conference table sat on one side of the room. Her father possessed a very large desk with a matching chair.

As he chatted on the phone, he handed Laurie a paper on which he had printed an email message. She read:

I am planning to be in Indianapolis next week and wonder if we could have lunch together. I have something I want to discuss with you. My best day would be either Monday or Tuesday.

Adrian Van Swearington

When her father ended the phone call, he asked Laurie what she thought about the email.

"Who is Adrian Van Swearington? Obviously, I can't imagine what this is about until I know who he is."

Using his 'I am the President of the Company' voice William announced, "We will discuss this as we drive."

As soon as they were under way, her father resumed the conversation. "Adrian Van Swearington is an old friend of mine. I met him years ago, at a business conference. I would guess he is 15 years or so older than I am, but we hit it off rather well. We've shared several meals together over the years.

"He owns a chain of stores similar to Knowlton's except they only have around 40 stores. The thing that interests me greatly is the location of his stores. They are in Oklahoma and Texas. As you know, we have no stores in those two states."

"Do you think he might want to sell you his stores?" asked Laurie. "If he's older than you by 15 years he might be thinking of retirement."

"That's a distinct possibility."

"What's the successor management situation? Does he have family members available to join his team?"

"Great question, Laurie. Now I'm beginning to think you're really getting a feel for the business." He paused for a minute. "As I recall, his son was involved. However, Adrian was very discouraged by his son's performance the last time we talked."

Laurie responded, "My thinking is the addition of 40 stores in states where we have no representation would make a positive impact on our bottom line. We could eliminate all of their office staff and purchasing departments. It would make our buying more effective because we'd be buying larger amounts. Perhaps we could even get bigger discounts from our suppliers."

"Bingo!" exclaimed her father. "Laurie you're truly catching on. I plan to meet with Van Swearington for lunch on Monday. Why don't you wear something nice? I'll see if he would object to your attendance at our meeting."

Laurie was thrilled because she hardly ever obtained her father's approval for anything she did. As she reflected further, she realized she couldn't recall the last time he'd said anything in a positive way about her.

Sure enough, on Monday at 11:45, her father stopped by her desk. "I told Van Swearington we would meet him at the University Club. He was delighted when I asked if you could come. So, let's go."

The University Club décor was the very definition of *old fashioned charm.* On top of a thick carpet, intimate booths lined the walls. Waiters whispered. Even the members spoke in hushed tones. The entire atmosphere was one of warmth and confidentially.

Adrian Van Swearington turned out to be a tall heavyset man with grey hair. His smile and manner were friendly. Laurie noticed a firm grip when they shook hands. She liked him immediately.

After they ordered, Laurie decided it was her job to again play the role of Briar Fox in the Tar Baby story. She would *lay low.* After some preliminary skirmishing, Van Swearington got down to business.

"I asked for this meeting, William, because I need a favor. As you know,

I've not been happy with my son Homer's performance with our company for some time. Well, last month things came to a boiling point. I'm sorry to say my son and I have parted company."

William sympathized, "I remember you were upset about him the last time we talked."

Van Swearington settled back in his chair and let out a deep breath. "Reflecting back, it was a combination of two things. Homer was a rich man's son who just refused to work hard. As you know, you don't get where we are today unless top management works hard and sets a good example. The second thing is, well, he drinks too much. Liquor just gets the best of him."

Laurie could see her father's mouth begin to water. "Doesn't that leave your firm in a bind as to your successor management plan?"

"It does and it doesn't. One thing Homer did right was to marry well. My daughter-in-law is a wonderful, strong woman. Their child, my grandson, Allan Van Swearington, is a real winner. He will complete his MBA at Yale next month. He has super grades. He's a leader on the campus. He also lettered in tennis at Yale, so he understands competition."

Laurie watched her father's face droop for a minute, then he recovered. "Sounds like you are blessed with a real solid grandson, Adrian."

"Well he certainly is. This is where you come in, William. I've been thinking. One of the mistakes I made with Homer, was bringing him into the firm right out of college. He didn't have anything at that point but *book learning*. Everyone knew he obtained his position because he was the son of the boss."

"A tough spot for anyone," empathized William.

Adrian continued, "I've been wondering if you could hire Allan and train him for me. You have a strong organization; it's much larger than ours. Working with you, he could learn a lot in a few years. Then in three to five years, I could pull Allan back into our firm. He would know something besides book learning when he came aboard. In addition, in three to five years, it'll be close to my retirement time."

Laurie could see her father was disappointed Van Swearington didn't make an overture regarding the sale of his company. Then, she saw his wheels begin to turn. She could just hear him thinking, if we get Allan on our side, the sale or merger of Van Swearington's stores could happen in three to five years.

It didn't take long before her father said, "We would be honored to give Allan a position. We'll move him around every six months or so. The training program will give him a great background in chain store operations, purchasing, inventory control, accounting, the works."

"I was hoping you'd agree to do exactly that," remarked Adrian. "Now about Allan's salary."

William cut him off. "There won't be any need to discuss salary, Adrian. If we get an MBA from Yale on our payroll, I'm sure he will more than earn his way. In fact, your biggest worry has to be I might steal him for keeps."

Everyone laughed at that remark. The balance of the luncheon went smoothly. As they left, Adrian told William to expect a call from Allan sometime after he graduated next month.

As they were driving back to the office, William said to Laurie, "I decided to play it big with Van Swearington. If we get our foot in the door with this Allan, who knows what might come out of it?"

Laurie chuckled to herself. She had already figured out what her father had in mind.

CHAPTER 20

Brad's summer opened up a completely new world. It began when he walked into Archer Lane's office at the Free Press promptly at 9:00 A.M. the first Monday after the school semester ended.

"Brad, welcome aboard. Nice to have you with us," Mr. Lane's warm greeting helped Brad relax. "For a while today, why don't you just sit over there and listen to what I do. It might give you a little overview of this crazy business."

Phones rang, people came in and out. Mr. Lane handed out assignments to reporters. He talked with the other co-editors about how the next day's paper would handle certain events.

Around 10:00 A.M., he told Brad to go down and take the plant tour, which was open to the public. "It will give you a real feel for the production side of the business. Then come back here. I'll take you to lunch and we'll discuss the program I have in mind for you."

At lunch, Mr. Lane told Brad he would assign him to different reporters on different days. Brad was to be the 'gopher' for the reporter. He was also to write up the story of the day independently, with no help from anyone. Then he was to give the story to the reporter for his/her critical analysis. Mr. Lane told him the reporters were to hand Brad's work in to him at the end of the day.

"Today you get it really soft, Brad. You get to go to the Tiger game with the sports reporter. Be back in my office tomorrow at 9:00," concluded Mr. Lane.

Brad was thrilled to get *press credentials* and sit in the press box at Comerica Park. Unfortunately, the game lasted a long time. By the time he had written his story, it was after midnight. Now he had to drive an hour to get home to Chelsea. Then an hour back in the morning rush hour traffic. He certainly wasn't going to get much sleep on this job.

As the weeks continued, he found he truly liked the newspaper business. The homicides were awful; however, the human-interest stories were interesting to him. It was a human-interest story that got him the first positive comment on his writing from Mr. Lane.

Although the paper printed seven days a week, Brad was only required to work six. He was off on Sunday. Consequently, Sunday became recovery day. A lengthy email to Laurie was the highlight. His emails to her during the week were necessarily brief.

By July, his body had become used to waking up early. Consequently, even though it was Sunday, he found himself up for an early morning run. When he finished, he stopped on the top of the hill where he had scattered his grandfather's ashes last fall. He remembered the day very clearly. He remembered the hug Laurie gave him when he came down the hill.

As he ate his lonely breakfast, he began to think about writing something. If I'm going to be a writer, I need to start with something in addition to the newspaper stuff. I know that to write successfully, a person has to be himself. He has to write about something he knows. Mr. Lane told me I'm good at writing human-interest stories.

A few moments later he went to his computer and wrote a title:

My Grandfather, Jay Randall

He began to type. *Jan Randall wasn't famous. But he was a really great guy.*

Brad never stopped writing for five hours. The words just seemed to flow from his head. When he tired, he wrote Laurie a long email. He told her about the beginning of his book. Then he waxed poetic:

Laurie in the Rain
I love to walk in the rain with you,
Raindrops in your hair sparkle like the dew
When it catches those first early rays of the sun
I know in my heart my life has begun.

When the rain is warm, you oft take my hand
When you do that, I feel really grand.
If the rain is cold, you snuggle close to my shoulder
My arm comes around you and I feel bolder.

So, I turn you into my loving kiss
And for me, I am then, truly in bliss
So, in the rain, or in the rainbow's glory
Please always remember, I love you Laurie.

It was the first poem he had ever written to her. He wondered what she would say.

Laurie's next email responded:

Your poem, my dearest was really sweet.
In truth, it made me feel really neat.
And if I am to be honest with you,
Brad my darling, I love you too!

The sophomore year at college beckoned.

CHAPTER 21

When Laurie walked into accounting class the first day of her sophomore year, she was surprised to find the Dean of Students standing in the front of the room talking with another man. The class instructor was supposed to be one of the oldest professors on campus. This man did not look old; in fact, he looked rather distinguished. *I wonder what this is all about?*

After the students assembled, the Dean asked for attention. When the room became quiet, he announced, "Today I have some good news and some bad news. First the bad news: Over the summer, Professor Sampleton, who was originally scheduled to teach this class, decided to retire. He is 76 years of age. He has been an institution at Denison for 47 years.

"Dr. Sampleton planned to carry on until he had taught for 50 years. However, his hearing and arthritis have deteriorated to the point he feels he should not continue. He will continue to live here in Granville. I'm sure he'd welcome visits from any of you, should you wish to do so.

"Now, for the good news: The University has always prided itself by hiring faculty members who have actual business experience. Professors who have practical experience in the workplace bring an extra dimension to class discussions and instructions. Your new accounting professor has joined our staff after extensive experience with Sears Roebuck and Company. He worked with Sears for 20 years. His last position was vice president in charge of new store development. He will teach accounting, business ethics, and business management techniques during his stay at Denison.

As the Dean droned on with the introduction, Laurie looked over the new professor. He was tall, about six feet she estimated. His hair was brown and he had a small mustache. His trim body indicated he kept himself in good shape.

The thing that attracted Laurie most, were his warm brown eyes. They reflected a person who cared.

Abruptly she heard the Dean wrap up the introduction, "I'm proud to present to you Dr. Augie Winchester"…Laurie thought, *Augie Winchester…. my mother's college boyfriend! Now I'll really pay attention in class.*

As Augie began the class he appeared confident, even though he was in a new situation. His well-prepared questions evoked an interesting class discussion. The class paid close attention because they could quickly sense they were in the hands of a man who actually had practical experience in the business world.

After class ended, Laurie hung back until all the students left. As she approached, the professor looked at her with those warm brown eyes.

"Dr. Winchester, did the Dean say you did your undergraduate work at the University of Michigan?"

"Yes, that's correct," replied Augie.

"Did you happen to know a girl at Michigan named Shirley Lansing?"

Augie stared…His face actually colored a little. "Yes, I had several dates with a Shirley Lansing. In fact, I was very fond of her."

"Shirley Lansing is my mother. Just the other day we were discussing her college days. She mentioned your name. It stunned me when the Dean introduced you this morning."

Augie smiled warmly. "You are Shirley's daughter?" He looked at her carefully, "Well, you're very pretty just like your mother. However, you're making me feel old. Imagine, having my old girlfriend's daughter in my class. I'm not sure whether I like that or not."

He announced, "I have to walk over to Doane Hall. Have you time to accompany me? When Laurie nodded, he asked, "How's your mother? Is she still full of fun like she was in college?"

Laurie parried with, "Sometimes." She did not want to get into details regarding how low Shirley's self-esteem had become because of William's incessant demeaning treatment.

"How many siblings do you have, Laurie?" asked the professor.

"Laurie replied with her usual honesty, "Mother had two daughters, however my sister died at age 18, so I'm the only one left." Then she turned the conversation around, "How about you Dr. Winchester, have you any children?"

"I have two; a boy and a girl. They are fully grown now, one in college and one in grad school."

Laurie decided her mother would want to know everything, so she said, "It must be quite a change from the business world to become a college professor."

"Yes." Then he hesitated. A few moments later he admitted, "My wife died very suddenly two years ago. It was an aneurism. Somehow, without her support, I just didn't feel the urge to continue in the business rat race. I always wanted to teach at the college level, so I decided to give it a shot. With my resume, I'm sure I could go back into business in any number of situations. However, right now, I'm exactly where I want to be."

"I'm so sorry about your wife. I had no idea."

By then they had reached Doane Hall. Augie turned, "It's not a problem, Laurie. Please give my best to your mother when you talk with her. Tell her she still holds a warm place in my heart. See you in class tomorrow."

Before they parted Laurie asked, "May I have your email address, professor? Perhaps mother would like to send you an email."

Without another word, Augie reached into his pocket removing his card. "My email address is on the card."

When Laurie caught up with Brad at the library, she burst out with the news about Augie Winchester. After relating the story to Brad, she opened her laptop to email her Mom. *I'm so glad I taught her to email.*

As Laurie opened her computer, a message from her Mom appeared. It said:

Hi Laurie: Guess what!! I have a job! I'm working 4 days a week at the library right here in Carmel. I start Monday. I'm excited. I also joined the local fitness club. I've been working out 3 times a week. This old gal is going to get back in shape.

Tell me all about school and Brad!

Love you,

Mom

Within seconds Laurie emailed a reply. *Congratulations on joining the ranks of America's employed! Remember the fitness club only works if you do.*

Then she wrote a separate email:

Mom:

You'll never guess who my new accounting professor is... Are you ready for this...Augie Winchester !!!! Yes, it's the same man you dated in college.

He had a very successful career at Sears Roebuck and Company. He was vice president in charge of store development. Apparently, he decided to get out of the rat race and become a professor.

He's such a good looking man! No wonder you fell for him. I introduced myself to him after class. When I told him I was your daughter, his face got all red.

We walked together over to Doane Hall so we could talk longer. He has two grown children. He told me that two years ago, his wife had an aneurism and died suddenly. He shared with me that without her support he didn't have the heart to stay in the business rat race, so he came back to his initial dream of being a college professor.

I asked for Dr. Winchester's email address in case you wanted to communicate. Without a word, he handed me his card. His email address awinchester@Denison.edu

In my opinion, it would be proper for you to send a note of condolence to your old friend, if you are so inclined.

Love,

Laurie

Laurie read the email over twice. Then she pushed the 'send' button. As she did so she thought, *I wonder what my shy mother will do?*

Back in Carmel, Shirley stared at Laurie's email message a long time. Thoughts whirled round and round in her head... Augie at Denison... Augie now single. Still very handsome according to Laurie. I need a push to start the divorce. Could Augie be the push? No, that wouldn't be proper. It would be for the wrong reason.

Besides, Augie's interest in me will surely have waned. I'll just wait a bit more before I go for the divorce.

I suppose it would be thoughtful to write a letter of condolence to Augie. Yes, that's it. I'll write a thoughtful condolence letter.

She wrote five different emails before she finally settled on this one:

Dear Augie:

I heard from Laurie you are her accounting professor. What a small world! Who would ever dream we would be reconnected this way?

I'm so sorry to hear Laurie's report about your wife's passing. It must have been a major blow to you and your children.

If you have time, I would love to hear about your children and all of the adventures of your life these past 24 years. How can it be 24 years?

Perhaps I shouldn't admit this, but I often find myself fondly remembering our

time together. It was a very special time in my life.

I think writing emails helps keep a person from being lonely.

We were good friends once, Augie. I hope we can become friends again.

Warmest best wishes,

Shirley Lansing Knowlton.

She read it over three times. The old Shirley would never have enough nerve to send it… *Damn it, the new Shirley will.* She pushed the 'send' button. The email message went off into space.

When Augie received Shirley's communication, he smiled. *I have a whole bunch of happy memories of Shirley. I often wondered what would've happened if I hadn't gotten that damn malaria and been unable to write her for so long. I wonder what she looks like now. Probably big, fat and ugly. But, what the heck, I ought to be polite and answer the email.*

He hit the reply button saying:

Shirley:

Nice to hear from you. I also have fond memories of our days together. They were happy days, but oh so long ago.

Getting started teaching three different classes is a bear. If I ever get things organized, I'll send you that longer note you requested.

Augie.

After adding Shirley's email address to his address book, he pushed 'send.'

CHAPTER 22

The fall days of the sophomore year for Laurie and Brad flew by. The trees were in full color. They took many long walks over the hills of Granville. Somehow their feelings for each other grew deeper. They became very close. When they found a way to have sex, it continued to be wonderful and filled with meaning.

One-day Brad asked, "Have you ever played chess?"

"I hardly ever play games, I'm not lucky enough."

"Chess is the one game where there's no luck involved. A person either wins or loses because of his/her skill."

"Well, if there's truly no luck required, I'll let you teach me."

The next day Brad produced a chessboard. The lessons began. It didn't take Laurie long to realize luck is not a factor in chess. Because Brad loved it, Laurie tried hard to learn chess. She enjoyed competing against him. When a game went her way, she was sure Brad allowed it. In a few weeks, confidence in her chess talent began to grow.

One day Laurie saw a notice on the bulletin board in the Union announcing a Chess Club meeting. Without telling Brad, she went to the meeting. Club members played each other, analyzed games and studied the masters. Without telling Brad, Laurie immediately joined the group. This extra effort began to build Laurie's confidence in her chess game. She grinned as she thought, one day Mr. Brad, I'm going to wax you in chess.

When Thanksgiving came, Laurie drove home to Carmel. She was anxious to have a talk with her Mom. However, she found herself so tired she just wanted to crash. When she got home, she emailed Brad of her safe arrival and went to bed.

Thursday filled itself with trouble.

As Laurie came downstairs for the scheduled 1:00 o'clock Thanksgiving dinner, she found her father in the den talking with a rather good-looking young man.

"Laurie, exclaimed William, "Come over here. I want you to meet Allan Van Swearington! You remember Allan's grandfather, don't you? We had lunch with him last summer."

Laurie smiled at Allan. She noticed he was a handsome devil, short blonde hair, blue eyes, nice complexion, and sturdy build. He was short however; she guessed about five feet seven. This meant she towered over him by at least 4 inches.

"Aha," exclaimed Laurie, "You're our Yale trainee. Welcome to Indianapolis."

She extended her hand, which Allan took in a dishrag grip. "So, this is the beautiful Laurie Knowlton. Your father has been bragging of you ever since I came on board last September."

Before Laurie could counter he added, "For once, the package is more beautiful than the advertising."

Laurie thought to herself, *this guy is really smooth. A face man, no doubt... He could charm a monkey, but he's not making an impression on me.*

"Trust me," she countered. "True beauty only occurs when the lady is also intelligent."

As they sat down to the Thanksgiving feast, Laurie found herself sitting right beside Allan Van Swearington. Polite dinner conversation ensued. Allan enjoyed telling Laurie his experiences working with Knowlton and Company. He also managed to tell about what a Big Man on Campus he'd been at Yale. Allan's obvious conceit created an ornery mood in Laurie. She decided to stretch herself to her maximum height. This required Allan to look up whenever he spoke to her. *Sometimes being tall has its advantages.*

It seemed every five minutes Laurie's father kept asking, "How are you two getting along?" Laurie felt William's pressure big time. *Father is as obvious as a tank.*

When dinner ended, Laurie asked Allan, "Do you know how to play chess?"

"Yale men are exceptionally well rounded in all phases of social and business life. Of course, I know how to play chess."

Without another word, Laurie got out her chessboard.

In less than three minutes, Laurie's attack had Allan backed into a corner. Allan's chess proved to be a long way from 'well rounded.' In a very short time, Laurie destroyed him.

She thought to herself, *I just knocked this 'exceptionally well rounded,' conceited Yale man, right on his behind. Boy, am I glad I learned to play chess. Thank you Brad. Thank you, Chess Club.*

When a shaken Allan rose from the chessboard, William suggested he and Laurie go for a walk. The weather was brisk, so they bundled up in warm coats.

"My father must be high on you," Laurie stated as they began to walk.

"Well, I've been able to help him out in several areas. My MBA degree from Yale gives me some good insight on how to help old fashioned executives run their businesses."

"It must be nice to be smart," Laurie commented.

"You know, it really does help. I expect to be moving up the ladder very quickly."

Laurie enjoyed egging him on. It didn't take much to get Allan to brag about himself. As Allan talked, Laurie thought. *I've figured him out now. My first instinct was right. He's a fast crowd, face man, all talk, no substance.*

Finally, as they approached the steps leading back into the house, Allan came out with this. "Laurie, my experience with the fair sex has been very positive. I can't imagine why, but I never seem to have any serious resistance from women. So, I guess I better warn you, I plan to be a big part of your future. As he said this he grasped her shoulders and turned her for a kiss.

Laurie was flabbergasted. Her reaction was to quickly shove him away. Then she stepped up one step on the stairs and stretched herself to her maximum height. Now she really towered over him. From her lofty perch, she glared down.

"Thank you for the warning, Allan. Trust me, if I somehow manage to resist your amazing charm, you can be assured there's a very good reason."

She stormed back into the house closing the door in Allan's astonished face. Dodging William, she went up to her room, quietly closing the door.

Allan stood on the step outside, pondering. *I guess she's just not my type. She's pretty enough. However, she obviously doesn't have enough polish to be a candidate for me.*

The next morning Laurie finally found some time alone with her mother.

"How did you get along with Allan, dear?"

"With the possible exception of father, he is the most self-centered person I've ever met. If I told you what he said to me, you'd never believe it."

"Your father has strong feelings regarding Allan," protested Shirley. He thinks if you two got married, it would be a chinch to merge Allan's grandfather's stores in with Knowlton and Company. Remember, a Knowlton does not marry with their heart. A Knowlton marries with their head."

"Okay Mom, you've given me Father's line. You can make your report to him. Now let's get down to the important stuff. Do you really want me to marry with my head not my heart? Do you want me in the same kind of relationship you have with father?"

"You know I don't. I'm just doing what your father told me to do."

"Honestly, Mom, every boy I compare with Brad comes up so short it's pathetic. I think the world of him. Every day our closeness seems to grow exponentially. I'm absolutely certain that the love we have is for keeps."

Shirley replied, "I've been thinking. Maybe I could come over to Denison for Mother's Day. I'm getting very anxious to meet this Brad."

"That sounds like a great idea to me. Now tell me about you. How's the job going? What did Father say?"

"The job is going great. I really enjoy helping the customers. The people I work with are kind, interesting and helpful. As to what did father say, that too is an interesting question. Let's see, I've been working for over a month, almost seven weeks now. Your father's never found out I have a job."

"You're keeping it a secret?"

"Not at all. You see, he never asks what I do. Consequently, there's been no occasion to tell him."

"Mother, that's incredible. You've been working for seven weeks and he's never asked what you do every day? He is so self-centered it's almost a crime. Now tell me about Augie Winchester. Did you email him?

"I did what you suggested. I sent him a letter of condolences."

"And....come on Mom, what happened?"

"Well, he responded. He told me, when he had a minute, he would write some details of his life and his children."

"Has he done that? Gosh Mom, pulling information out of you is like pulling nails."

"Well, two weeks ago, he wrote a nice long letter. He related information regarding the different places they lived when Sears employed him. He gladly told me about his children and his wife. He was very fond of her. They were happily married for 25 years. Apparently, she had a brain aneurism and just dropped dead."

"Did you answer him?"

"Of course. In fact, I did something I probably never should have done. I told him, "It was nice to hear about a happy marriage, because in my case, with the exception of Laurie, my marriage has been a disaster."

"Did he answer?" Laurie asked in an excited voice.

"Not yet.... I'm afraid... Laurie, do you think I scared him off?"

"I doubt it. Being honest never hurt anyone. At least in the long run. Gee, if you come to visit Mother's Day, maybe you can meet with him."

"Well, meeting him has crossed my mind."

"Mom, you are a devil! Incidentally, you look fabulous! That fitness class is doing wonders for you!"

"I've taken off eight pounds. My dress size is back to a ten. I feel great. You were right, Laurie, working out has really helped."

"Oh Mom, I'm so happy for you. Laurie paused a minute then she asked, "Do you really want to wait till Mother's Day to come to Denison? That's six months away."

"If I lose two pounds a month, I'll be twelve pounds lighter by May. That should mean I can easily get into a size eight! Augie Winchester is going to be impressed with my figure if I have to kill myself."

• • •

That night at dinner, William opened the conversation.

"Well, Laurie dear, how did you and Allan get along last night? I assumed when you went for a walk and never returned, you were together until the wee hours. Hee hee hee."

"Father, Allan is so full of himself it's disgusting. He bored me stiff at dinner. After a twenty-minute walk I shot him down, came back in the house, went up to my room and went to bed."

"You can't be serious!" William exploded. "You need to court Allan so we can acquire those stores his grandfather owns. You knew the importance of this from our meeting with Van Swearington last summer. I can't believe you would let me down in this vital matter."

"I'm sorry for your store acquisition program father, but my courting, as you put it, with Allan Van Swearington, will never happen. I suggest you make some new plans."

"Laurie, you are being impertinent! A Knowlton marries with his head not with his heart! We've always had that as a principal of our family."

"Is marrying with your head the reason you and Mom have such a crummy marriage, Father? Has it been worth all the pain you've put her through?"

Voice rising, William shot back, "What are you referring to, Laurie? Your mother and I have a great marriage."

"Is it really? "Is that why you sleep in separate rooms? Is that why you know absolutely nothing about what your wife does every day?"

"What are you referring to Young Lady?"

"You don't even know Mother's had a job for the past seven weeks! The reason you don't know is because you are so wrapped up in yourself you haven't asked one thing regarding what's going on in her life."

"Mother has a job?" questioned William in an astonished voice.

"Yes dear," Shirley broke in, "I'm working at the Carmel Public Library, four days a week."

"Why are you doing that?" William shouted.

"Because I enjoy working. Now that Laurie's in college, I don't need to sit around the house all day."

"Having you employed will make a bad impression on business. People will say Knowlton's is struggling. You have to quit that job immediately."

Laurie then asked her father, "How have sales been this fall, father?"

"I believe we are up six percent over last year."

"Please explain to me how a six percent increase reflects a negative impact on sales. What do you think mother?"

"Six percent is very good, William. I can remember many years where if we were up one or two percent you jumped for joy," Shirley added in a pleasant voice. "Besides, I'm meeting lots of interesting people at the Library. Rest assured, I've no intention of quitting."

"This is preposterous," bellowed William. "What's wrong with you women? You cannot work without my permission! And you, Laurie, are going to go out with Allan Van Swearington and get him to marry you!"

"Let me put it this way, Father," Laurie replied as she rose to go up to her room, "This Knowlton is going to marry with her heart. She's going to marry someone she loves. She's going to have a happy life. If you don't want to walk me down the aisle to marry the man I select, I will go down that aisle - all - by - my - self!" She stormed from the room.

Shirley quickly followed her daughter. Over her shoulder, she remarked, "In case you need to reach me during my working hours, I'll call my schedule in to your secretary."

William stood with his mouth agape, frustration oozing from every pore. He shouted into the empty room, "I feel like I'm in the middle of a damn revolution." He reached for the whiskey bottle.

CHAPTER 23

Laurie managed to avoid her father for the rest of the Thanksgiving vacation until it was time to say good-bye.

She found William in his den. As she rendered a perfunctory hug she murmured, "I'm sorry I've let you down, father. However, I'm certain my assessment of what kind of a husband Allan would make is correct."

William looked up from his work, "I predict you'll change your mind. Allan's a real catch. Trust me; you won't be able to do any better. You two will make a nice couple."

When Laurie hugged her mother goodbye she reported, "I apologized to father for disappointing him. I didn't back down, however. Father acted as if nothing had happened. He keeps saying 'we will make a nice couple.'

Shirley responded, "Your father is always certain everything will be as he commands."

"Mom, I know I'm right. I won't give up Brad for anything or anyone. Which means father and I are heading for a major clash. I can handle the clash Mom, I know I'm strong enough. But if you get in the middle and get crushed, I don't know what I'll do. You have to promise me you won't get sucked into the middle on this one. I simply cannot be a part of you being all broken up again like you were over Betty Ann.

To her great relief, Laurie saw a confident smile cross her mother's face. "I'm not the vulnerable person I was a few years ago, Laurie. I've just about made up my mind to stick my divorce on William at the same time you and he fight over Brad. My thinking is that I can back you up, and then hit him with the divorce. When my divorce paper smashes him, I'm hoping he'll be so shocked, he'll be distracted to some degree from his upset with you."

"Mom that just might work. They say wealthy, selfish men dread the word divorce because they lose lots of money."

"Well your Father certainly qualifies as a wealthy, selfish man. I think my planned timing is exactly right. I genuinely feel the need to be here to support you."

"You've made my day, Mom. If we girls stick together we can win this encounter. I hope."

A few weeks later Laurie found herself at the Christmas Formal swirling around the dance floor in Brad's arms. She was wearing a pale green strapless dress, which stopped well above her knees. She kept her shoulders square, accenting her figure. Long shapely legs complimented the impression.

Brad beamed. "Have you noticed how many extra glances you're getting from all the boys tonight?"

"Maybe once in a while, however, the only glance I want is from the person who is holding me right now."

"I remember last year all I wanted to do was to pull down your yellow formal and touch you."

"I remember hoping you would.... Then, since you didn't, I had to do it for you."

Brad's eyes were glowing as he said, "That entire night is such a special memory for me."

"For me too."

"Are you still glad you did all that Mystery Daughter stuff so you could convince your father I wasn't interested in your money?"

"Absolutely. In many ways, it was the smartest thing I've ever done. The bad news is dearest Brad; I don't think it'll do much good. Father just hears what he wants to hear. I hate to go home for Christmas because father will surely be pushing Allan Van Swearington at me, big time."

"Why don't you come visit me after Christmas? It would get you away from Allan. We could be together and practice being married."

"Talk about a tempting offer! I'd love to 'play married' with you. But don't you need to work on your book?"

"You've a big term paper due next spring, don't you? You could get started on your paper while I work on my book.

"Let me think about it." Then, right in the middle of the dance floor, she kissed him!

• • •

When Laurie got home, she was relieved to discover Allan had gone home for Christmas. However, he planned to come back sometime between Christmas and New Year's. Sure enough, two days after Christmas, she received a phone call.

"Laurie this is Allan. I'm back in town. I think maybe I got off on the wrong foot with you at Thanksgiving. I want to apologize. I wonder if you would have dinner with me tomorrow night."

Laurie shivered all over thinking about going out with Allan. He really gave her the creeps. *Maybe I should go to please father.* Then she realized *this is going nowhere. It would be better to cut things off right now.*

"Laurie, are you still there?" asked Allan.

"Yes, I'm here, Allan. I've been thinking. Your apology is accepted. Now we can be friends. As far as dinner with you goes... I'm sorry but I have no interest. Your invitation is kind, but the answer is still no thank you."

"Maybe I could just come over to visit?"

"You could come over to visit father or mother. I won't be here. I'm planning to spend the rest of my vacation visiting a friend in Michigan."

Her mind made up, Laurie dashed off an email to Brad and began to pack.

After she stowed the luggage in the car, she went to talk with her mother.

"I'm going to visit a friend in Michigan for the rest of the Christmas break. I'll be working on my term paper. I can do it better up there where I will be away from Father and Allan."

"Will this Michigan friend's name be Brad?"

Laurie blushed as she nodded. Shirley added, "You know you still haven't told me what it feels like to be in love. I'm very curious."

"Oh mother, Brad is so wonderful. He is thoughtful, caring and sweet. He's very handsome. He works extremely hard. I'm sure he'll be a success in life. The main thing is, I just want to be with him all the time.

"If I'm not with him, I find I'm constantly thinking of him. I want him to hold me in his arms and kiss me. I want to sit by a fire and hug. In fact, if you asked me who my best friend is, it would be Brad. It's just wonderful being in love with your best friend. Does that answer your question?"

Shirley hugged her daughter. "I'm so happy for you dearest. I hope you two have a great time. Let me know about Mother's Day weekend. There's someone up there I definitely plan to meet."

"Have you been emailing each other?"

"It's none of your business, but the answer is yes." Shirley blushed. "There have also been several phone calls."

"Oh Mother, that is so exciting!"

• • •

When Brad heard Laurie's car pull into the driveway, he flew out to greet her. After several hugs and kisses, Laurie explained how carefully she'd packed. "I've only one suitcase to go in here, the rest is for school," she told him.

Brad took the suitcase and walked with her to the door. Then he put the suitcase down. He prepared to pick Laurie up so he could carry her over the threshold.

When she realized what Brad was attempting to do, Laurie objected. "Brad you silly, you can't carry me over the threshold. We're not officially married. Besides I'm way too heavy."

Brad chose to ignore her objection, "What do you mean too heavy? You have a gorgeous figure."

"Gorgeous figure or not, when you're five feet nine you weigh a lot."

"Nonsense, I can lift you with ease."

"Brad, I weigh 155 pounds."

"And every pound's in the right place," he replied. Then he stuck his shoulder into her stomach and swept her up in the fireman's carry!

They laughed so hard they barely made it into the house. After he got one step inside the door he sank slowly onto the carpet.

"Oh God, Brad Randall, I'm so in love with you!"

The following four days were filled with love. They ate together, slept together, made love often, and studied together. Every day they worked out to keep in shape. When the studying and writing were over, they went for long walks in the cold and snow.

When the time came to go back to school, a puzzled Brad exclaimed, "I don't understand how I can continue to feel more and more in love with you. I loved you tons when you came. Now I feel my love has grown deeper every day."

Laurie hugged him. "That's exactly the way I feel too! Our love just continues to grow."

• • •

January, February and March flew by. Spring break came. Laurie went to Florida with some girlfriends. Brad went home to continue working on his book. It was getting close to completion. The closer he got to the end, the more anxious he became. He'd made up his mind to share the book with Archer Lane, his boss at the Free Press. Mr. Lane's reaction to his manuscript was going to be important.

School resumed after Spring Break. Spring in Granville is a very special time. Flowering trees dominate the campus. As the days warm, the students devise many ways to enjoy the out of doors. Brad and Laurie loved walking together, studying on the lawns and dancing at the proms. It was a wonderful time to be together and in love. A few days before Mother's Day weekend, Laurie got an email from her mother:

I expect to be in Granville sometime Friday afternoon. I suggest you and Brad plan to have dinner with me at the Granville Inn, say at 7:00 P.M. I'm dying to meet Brad.

Oh, if you happen to mention to Augie we will be dining at that time, maybe he'll drop by to say hello.

Love,
Mom

P.S. If you don't mention it to Augie, I will kill you!

Laurie laughed as she sent this reply:

Are you sure it's Brad you want to meet?

The response:

Well maybe.... both?

The next day after accounting class, Laurie delayed her departure until all the other students left. Then she approached Dr. Winchester.

"Guess what? Mother is coming to visit over the Mother's Day weekend. We're planning to have dinner Friday at the Granville Inn at 7:00 P.M. I know mother would love to see you again. Could you join us for dinner, or are you banned from dining with one of your students?"

"I would ban myself from a dinner with a marginal student, Laurie. He or she might be trying to influence my grade. However, since you are an 'A' student, I might make an exception. If you want the truth, I'm anxious to see your mother. I understand there is a certain Brad person who will also be attending?"

"You know about Brad? How much have you guys been emailing?"

"Emailing the mother of a student?? Whatever gave you that idea? See you Friday."

CHAPTER 24

At 6:45 Friday night, Laurie and Brad found themselves watching Shirley Knowlton walk down the stairs of the Granville Inn.

Anyone could tell Shirley had selected her outfit very carefully. She'd poured herself into a navy-blue dress shamelessly revealing her shapely figure. The V-neck even revealed a tad of cleavage. The skirt was on the short side, exposing gently curving legs. There were grey highlights in her dark hair, which gathered softly around her face. Blue pearl earrings, a matching pearl necklace and some modestly high heels in blue suede, completed the ensemble.

"Mother you look fabulous," Laurie exclaimed. Then she turned and announced, "Brad, this gorgeous creature is my Mother."

Shirley turned to Brad, extending a warm, firm hand. "Before I say anything else, I want to thank you for making my Laurie so happy. She tells me she is completely in love with you. After one look, I can see why. If your personality is as nice as your appearance, and Laurie assures me it is, I can understand why she's in love with you."

Dumbfounded by her directness Brad managed to stammer, "Mrs. Knowlton, you've stunned me with your kind words as well as your attractive appearance. I simply don't know what to say."

Laurie's mother laughed. "Brad I'm sure we'll be great friends, so you have to call me Shirley. This 'misses' stuff is way too formal for my taste."

She turned to Laurie and whispered. "Do you think I overdid it with this dress? I got down to a size eight and I couldn't resist it."

Laurie responded, "Brad's in on all this, Mother, you don't have to whisper. What do you think Brad, did she overdo it a bit with the dress?"

"Are you kidding, she looks fabulous! In fact, I've been thinking she reflects exactly what she is, an attractive mother of a college student."

After a second he continued, "If I know anything about relationships, I know honesty is the foundation. If you came in here looking like something you're not, Dr. Winchester would feel it immediately. Laurie and I have always felt the fast crowd is all about appearance and nothing about substance.

"To me your dress says, "This is me. I'm dressed up because you're important to me. But my code is to always be honest. Therefore, I'm simply showing you that I'm a caring person."

"Wow!" replied Shirley. "No wonder you like this guy!"

"Isn't he wonderful," beamed Laurie, "Ever since our first meeting we've been nothing except honest with each other. It makes such a strong foundation for a relationship."

Shirley smiled. "Honest…That's such a contrast with my friend in Indiana."

A few minutes after they sat down at the table, Augie Winchester made his appearance. He wore a grey suit with a red tie. There was a most enchanting twinkle in his eye. Shirley shocked herself and everyone else at the table, when she rose from her seat, hugged Augie, then kissed him lightly on the cheek. As the kiss ended, Shirley hugged him a second time. She whispered into his ear, "Dearest friend, I'm so sorry I hurt you. I've wanted to hug you and tell you that for a very long time. I hope you can forgive me."

Augie hugged her back, "We'll talk later."

Brad and Augie hit it off right away. Brad opened the conversation in a light tone by saying, "Okay professor, I want to know if Laurie truly got an A in accounting or did she 'pull rank' because you knew her mother."

"If she tried to 'pull rank' with me she probably would have gotten a D or maybe an F. If I have anything going for me as a person, it's my integrity. Back when I was with Sears, everyone knew you never messed with Augie Winchester. Besides, accounting is one subject where there's no gray. You either have it correct or you don't understand the concept. As I recall, Laurie had the highest grade in the class."

"See smarty pants. I told you mine was a legitimate A," burst in Laurie. Then she turned to the others, "Brad and I compete on grades. He got one B last semester, while I pulled straight A's. Which made me the winner. He's still unable to rationalize his defeat."

As he sat down Augie announced, "I need to establish some rules with these young people. When we're together in a social setting like this, I really want to be called Augie. However, when we're on campus, I think you'd better stick with Dr. Winchester. If you think about it, my reasons are pretty obvious. Is that okay with you guys?"

With that beginning, the dinner conversation became fun. After dessert and coffee, Augie asked Shirley to go for a walk. They quickly excused themselves.

A beautiful warm spring night is the perfect setting for a walk. As soon as they were away from the Inn, Augie turned to Shirley, "I truly don't know where to begin. I know when I left you after graduation, it nearly killed me to get on that ship. I was very fond of you, Shirley. If you want to know the truth, I almost asked you to come with me."

"If you had, I'd already decided to say, 'to hell with my parents' I'm going."

"Seriously?"

"Seriously."

"Ouch. That really hurts......But it would have been crazy. We traveled on a cattle boat. I was part of the crew. The boat eventually found its way to Serra Leone. I got off. A day or two day later, the Malaria hit. I became deathly ill. At times, I didn't think I'd make it. Neither did the people who were caring for me. They told me I was completely out of my head for many days.

"After a couple of months, I'd begin to feel somewhat better. Then the Malaria would hit again. If it hadn't been for the missionary hospital some kind people found for me to go into, I'd never have lived through it. Sometimes, I still wonder how I came out alive.

"As soon as I realized I was going to live, I wrote to you. When your letter came, I wished I had died. As a matter of fact, I felt dead inside. It took me years to recover."

"Oh Augie, if you only knew how hard it was to write that letter. I knew in my heart I was still in love with you. But the wedding plans had proceeded so with far with William, I felt there was no turning back. It was the biggest mistake of my life."

"Now you mustn't say that, Shirley. It can't have been all bad if you produced someone as wonderful as Laurie."

"Laurie is the only thing good that ever came from my marriage. Without her, I don't think I'd have had a minute of joy in all these years. William is, well frankly, he's an SOB. That's Laurie's term for him and I agree with it. The only reason I'm sticking around is...Well, I'm certain Laurie will need me when she and her father face off over Brad. There's going to be an awful fight. I need to be there for her. My attorney has already drawn up the divorce papers. All I have to do is serve them on him."

"I'm truly sorry that your life's been so difficult."

"What did you do when you got back from Africa?"

"When I got back to the states, I went to grad school at Stanford. When I graduated with my Doctorate in Economics, Sears made a nice offer. I decided to accept. They started me in Chicago.

"I guess it was about two years later when I met Alice. She was a very wonderful person. We fell in love and married. Alice was a pusher. She wanted nice things, so she pushed me to work my way up the corporate ladder. When I mentioned quitting so I could teach, she wouldn't hear of it. She wanted me to become President of Sears.

"After she passed away, I had no stomach for the rat race. Company politics are awful. Everyone is out for themselves. Each person tries to stab their fellow employees in the back. Once Alice passed, I felt free to go back to my first love, teaching. No, that's my second love. You were my first love, Shirley.

"We have great two kids. Our youngest, Matt, is a sophomore at Wooster College here in Ohio. He's majoring in accounting so he may become a chip off the old block. Our daughter, Loretta is brilliant. She's managed to obtain scholarships where ever she goes. Her undergrad work was at The University of Chicago. Now she's going for her Masters at Johns Hopkins, in Maryland. She plans to be a college professor some day with a major in literature. I guess I've covered that part of my life in our emails."

"Are either of them involved in a romantic way?"

"Well… They don't talk to me much about that stuff. However, I do know Loretta is somewhat interested in a boy she met in one of her classes. I've no idea if anything is serious at this point."

"Are you emotionally ready to have a child marry and become a grandparent Augie?"

"That's a painful question. I can't imagine myself walking Loretta down the aisle. That's the next step to being a grandfather! I'm definitely not ready for that!"

"I'm so glad to hear you had a happy marriage. My situation has been just the opposite. William is impossible to live with. He degrades me terribly. I'm like an instrument for him to maneuver.

"We haven't slept together in years. I'm positive he has bimbos on the side. However, he covers his tracks carefully. Laurie is encouraging me to proceed with the divorce. She despises her father.

"That's unusual," commented Augie. "Usually fathers and daughters get along very well."

"Okay, here's an example. A friend of William has 40 stores in Oklahoma and Texas. The friend sent his grandson to William to get practical training after he completed his MBA at Yale. William has the crazy idea this boy and Laurie should get married so he can arrange a merger and get his hands on those 40 stores. Laurie met the boy and was polite. She knew immediately that he was nothing compared to Brad. Consequently, she shot him down right away. Since then Laurie and her father hardly speak."

Augie responded, "I don't see many boys who come up to Brad. What an outstanding young man."

"Augie, how can you be so sure about Brad? You just met him an hour ago."

"Professors talk, Shirley. When I discovered Laurie was involved, I made a few discrete inquiries. His professors all swear by Brad.

"That's nice to hear, Augie. I'm also enjoying the proprietary feelings you have for my daughter."

What does William think of Brad?"

"William has almost no idea that Brad exists. He has not a shred of interest in his child's desires. It's only about what William wants."

A long silence followed. They approached a dark spot on the sidewalk where some low hanging trees blocked the street light. Shirley turned to Augie, "You never wore a mustache when I knew you in college. I always wondered if you kiss a man with a mustache, does it tickle?"

"There's only one way to find out," Augie replied. He pulled Shirley to him and kissed her.

They kissed just as passionately as they used to when they were in college. Shirley hadn't felt a kiss that intense since…since she couldn't remember. It was probably during her college when Augie was doing the kissing. It shook her to her toes. Her body melted. The kiss awakened feelings she'd totally forgotten were inside her.

When the kiss ended, Augie asked, "Well did it?"

Shirley was pretty dazed. "Did it what?"

"Did my mustache tickle?"

"Oh, Augie, I got so caught up kissing you, I forgot to find out."

"Then we better try again!" He gathered her into his arms once more.

This time the kiss became even more intimate. She tied to think about the mustache a little. No, it didn't tickle she decided.

"Well?"

"It didn't tickle."

"There's no one living at my house except me. Want to go home and have some tea?"

"That's a tempting offer, Augie. You've no idea how badly I want to accept. The way I feel right now we'd have way more than tea.

"However, it's not going to happen. I have to go into the divorce with a clean conscience. I need, for my own integrity, to be able to say I've kept my marriage vows. I just need a few more months.

"Augie, I really want to become your girlfriend once more, if you'll let me."

"I officially declare you to be my girlfriend," Augie announced.

"Oh Augie, you've no idea how thrilled that makes me feel!"

CHAPTER 25

It started at dinner the first night Laurie was home after completing her sophomore year. She and her father got into it again over Allan.

Her father began, “I have had a lot of nice talks with young Van Swearington. He’s a very nice boy, Laurie. When he calls to ask you for a date, I want you to go out with him. This not a request. This is an order!” He glared at her.

Laurie anticipated this conversation with her father. She had decided on her strategy for dealing with the problem on her drive home from school. “Father, I understand how you feel regarding Allan, however, if I encourage him in any way I will be setting him up for a worse hurt down the line. It’s not fair to Allan for me to date him.”

“For heaven’s sake, why not?”

“Because I’m deeply in love with a boy I met at school. He hasn’t asked me yet, but I have every intention of marrying him right after we graduate.”

“Why hasn’t any one told me about this boy?” ragged her father.

“He’s the same boy who asked me to the Christmas formal my freshman year. I remember discussing it with you back then. You haven’t been told more about this boy, because you never ask.”

“You can be sure he’s after my money. Does this boy have a name?”

“His name is the same as it was two years ago, Brad Randall. You probably don’t even remember, so I’ll refresh your memory. When I first met Brad, I was immediately attracted to him. Because I knew you would assume that any boy who became interested in your ugly daughter was after your money, I devised a plan. I didn’t tell Brad my last name until we had been dating for 90 days. By then we were both head over heels in love. There was no way he knew we were rich because he didn’t even know my last name. I know this is hard for you to believe but Brad loves me for me, not for your stupid money."

Before William could respond Shirley added, "I met Brad last spring when I went up to Mother's Day weekend. We spent a lot of time together. He is an outstanding young man. I would be thrilled to death to have him for a son – in -law."

"You stay out of this Shirley," snapped William. "I'll deal with my own daughter." He took out pencil and paper from his pocket. "Write down this Brad person's name and address. I'll have someone check on him. I bet he's as poor as a church mouse."

Laurie complied with the request, then stormed from the room.

The following morning at breakfast Laurie was surprised when her Father offered a compromise.

"If I let you off the hook with Allan for this summer, I'll expect you to honor every one of my subsequent wishes for you. Is that clear?"

Without thinking Laurie replied, "If you keep Allan out of my life, I'll cooperate with you Father."

Because he continued to glare across the table at her she added, "I promise."

The second the words 'I promise' were out of her mouth, she realized she had made a mistake.

A week passed. Nothing came from William that she felt was unfair, so Laurie brushed off her concerns. William's request to 'honor every one of his wishes' apparently simply referred to her summer jobs at the company. She was more than willing to do anything to learn the company ropes.

A few weeks later, she got a big surprise. It was actually the Fourth of July holiday. She entered the dining room for what she thought would be a leisurely breakfast. To her shock, William made an announcement.

"I've made arrangements for you to study in England in the business school at Oxford next year. You'll leave here in mid-August. You will not return until next May."

Laurie was speechless. "But I like Denison. I'm getting an exceptionally good education there."

"You promised to honor my wishes for you, Laurie. I'm holding you to your promise. Besides, a year at Oxford is a real privilege. Thousands of kids would die for the opportunity. You made an agreement with me, I expect you to honor that agreement."

After that blast, he left to go to the country club for his golf game.

Laurie pleaded with her mother. In a few moments, the truth came out.

"Your father feels a year apart from Brad will cool your ardor. Once you have cooled on him, he thinks Allan will fit into the picture very nicely."

"That son of a bitch!" screamed Laurie. "That dirty son of a bitch!" She stormed up to her room.

Laurie called Brad and told him what happened. Strangely enough, he was not as upset as she expected him to be.

"Going to Oxford for a year is a real privilege, Laurie. I don't think you should be so upset. I do feel awful because we won't be together at school. It'll be lonesome as hell. On the other hand, maybe your father has a point. It certainly will be a test for us.

"If our love isn't strong enough to withstand a few months apart, maybe we're not right for each other. Personally, I know my love for you will only get stronger, if that's possible. Besides, we can still email. Maybe we can even talk on the phone once in a while."

"Brad, nothing's going to change the way I feel about you, I'm positive. Maybe, by going along with father this once, he'll relent and be decent to you. Oh, by the way, he's sending someone out to check your credit and your reputation. Don't be surprised if an investigator approaches you or your neighbors for information."

"He's sending someone to investigate me? You know Laurie; I'm beginning to understand why you call him an SOB all the time...... At least we have your mother on our side."

"You're right about that. She told father she would be thrilled to have you as a son-in-law."

"Did she actually say that? I'm so glad. I really like your mom. Do you think you can come up for a few days before you go? I'd love to play house with you again."

"I'll do my best to work that out." Laurie answered before she ended the call.

When Laurie went into work the next day, she met a new girl in the advertising department, Melody Flowers. Melody was from Mississippi. Her southern accent was tremendously obvious. So was her perfume. She was blessed with a most attractive figure which she revealed by wearing a tight sweater with tight slacks. Melody's apparel left absolutely nothing about her shape to the imagination.

"Nice to metcha'al," slurred Melody as she held out a dishrag hand to Laurie. "I understand you're a college girl. Well ah'm one too. I graduated from

Old Miss with a major in advertisin'. I jus' been here a few weeks. It seems like a nice place to work."

Laurie was curious regarding what talent this Bimbo brought to the company. She asked the office manager, "Who hired Melody Flowers?"

"Why your father did," he replied. "The story I got is Melody came in to sell something to your dad. The next thing anyone knew, Melody was working in the advertising department."

Laurie had serious reservations regarding Melody Flowers. However, she decided move cautiously. Someday, perhaps, Melody would come in handy. *Father*, she confided to herself, *'I don't get mad, I get even.'*

Laurie finagled three precious days with Brad in Michigan before she left for England. The parting was truly painful. They were both sobbing. "Dearest Laurie, I know we'll get through this," mumbled Brad over his tears.

"I know we will too, but it really hurts. I guess I never knew how much I loved you until this minute."

They exchanged one last hug and a long last kiss. She climbed into her car and drove from the driveway to the street. Then she stopped, rolling down the window. They looked at each other, each with tears running down their faces. After a minute, she took a deep breath, gave him a wave and headed down the road.

Two days later she left for London.

• • •

A few days after Laurie left, the credit report on Bradley Weatherby Randall landed on William's desk. He studied it carefully. He started with the financials. He was surprised to find a college junior with that much net worth. He owned a $150,000 house with no mortgage. There were several thousand dollars in savings accounts plus an IRA retirement investment.

The retirement account aroused suspicion. How does a college junior have an IRA? He began to examine the personal side of the credit report. There he read:

Bradley Weatherby Randall:

Son of John Randall and Margaret Weatherby (both deceased). Both parents graduated from the University of Michigan. Parents died in automobile wreck when their son Bradley was only one year of age.

Grandparents Jay Randall and Cathy Randall (both deceased) assumed guardianship.

Attended Chelsea High School where he lettered in football for three years. Played starting right end for two years. Honor student. Involved with school newspaper. Elected by fellow students to give the commencement address. Teachers all gave high recommendations as to character and work habits.

At Denison University: made the Dean's list for academic achievement freshman and sophomore years. Writes articles for student newspaper.

In summer works for Detroit Free Press in trainee program. Supervisor Archer Lane expressed high regard for this potential writer. He is apparently writing a book of some sort.

End of Report

William studied the report a second time. This time, the name Margaret Weatherby jumped out at him! He exploded aloud to his empty office, "This kid's mother is Margaret Weatherby! She's the bitch that had the nerve to refuse my marriage offer! There's no way my daughter is going to marry the son of Margaret Weatherby! I knew I didn't like that kid! Now I know why."

CHAPTER 26

Rather than be sad, Laurie decided to make her emails to Brad fun.

She began with this:

Arrived safely. I'm now in my dorm at Oxford. There are tons of handsome guys around here. I had a date with a Duke last night and with an Earl for breakfast this morning.

I understand the prince is on the campus. No doubt, I'll find a way to have a date with him shortly.

I might as well do this English thing right; don't you think?

If I married the duke, I wonder what my title would be?

Lady Laurie Lansing Knowlton Whatshisname.

Sounds pretty cool, doesn't it?

Miss you terribly,

Love,

Your Laurie.

Brad knew he had to come back with something, so he sent this:

You can date all those dukes and all of those earls,
You can let them give you emeralds or pearls.
But if you get serious about one of those guys,
I'll come over there and gouge out his eyes!

That began several months of time apart, a new experience for both of them. It didn't take long to realize, the more they were apart, the greater the need each felt for the other.

Brad worked hard at the Free Press for the balance of the summer. He saved his money. He began to consider flying to London for Christmas. By the middle of October, he knew a trip to see Laurie was mandatory. He simply couldn't stand being without her any longer. Should I surprise her? No, it would be too risky to travel that far as a surprise. Instead, he sent this email:

Laurie dearest:

I have priced round trip tickets to London. I can afford one! Can I come over for a Christmas visit? I just can't stand being away from you any longer. If you want me to come, send me the dates when your vacation starts and ends. I'll see what I can work out on flight times.

Your deal with your dad requires you to be in England. He made no mention regarding my visiting you, did he?

I love you,

B

When Laurie read the email, she went bananas. She dug out the calendar. Then she sent this reply:

I can't tell you how excited your email made me! My vacation is December 17th through January 1. Please book your tickets right away. We'll have a ball being together over here.

The only possible complication could be my parents. One time, they mentioned coming over for a Christmas visit. I've heard nothing further. However, to be sure, I think I'll invent an invitation from the Duke of Cadbury (chocolates) for the Christmas holidays. That will keep mom and dad in the USA.

From now on, you are the Duke of Cadbury.

Lots of love,

L

After she pushed the send button, she got out her calendar so she could start counting the days.

• • •

The greeting at Heathrow Airport was extraordinary! The only thing that exceeded the airport hugs were the airport kisses. Her glowing eyes told him everything he needed to know. She was still in love with him. His tenderness left her breathless. Brad exclaimed, “London with Laurie for fourteen days!”

“No darling, over here it’s called a fort-night.”

“That’s right, I’m now the Duke of Cadbury, aren’t I?”

Laurie joshed, “I assume you own the chocolate company, correct?”

“Hardly, I can barely afford to buy a box.”

“What’s first on the agenda?” Brad asked.

“I’ve rented a car for the fort-night and we’ve a room rented in a modest hotel. I suggest we go there first and get you settled.”

“If we go to the hotel, I’m sure Lord Cadbury will want to go to bed.”

“Why do you think I suggested we start there?”

They made love, slept off Brad’s jet lag, made love, had dinner in the room and made love. In the morning, they had a proper British breakfast in the room and…made love one more time. Finally, they were ready to tour London.

They caught the changing of the guard at Buckingham Palace, then drove out to St. Paul’s Church. Diving on the left side of the road was, to say the least, challenging. They quickly discovered the safest way was to have both of them involved in reminding whoever was driving to stay to the left. An English pub lunch followed. After lunch, it was The Portrait Gallery. They bought a bag of nuts and fed the pigeons at Nelson’s statue. Next it was back to the room to shower and change. That night they went to Simpson’s on the Strand for dinner. At Simpson’s, the waiter brought a cart with roast beef, roast lamb and roast pork to their table. He sliced off each roast whatever they wanted, then added potatoes and vegies. Brad went totally nuts over the food.

The following day they left the car, opting for the tubes. They hit central London. Laurie got kissed in the middle of London Bridge. They snapped photos from the bridge of parliament and Big Ben. Then they walked to Westminster Abbey.

Brad couldn’t get over Westminster Abbey. When they examined the headstones of all the famous people who were buried there, they began to fully grasp the impact that little island has had on the world.

“This is an incredible collection of amazing people! Shakespeare, Shelley, Keats, Faraday, Churchill, Baden Powell, plus all those Kings and Queens! What a great place to be my first overseas trip!”

Laurie said, “I’d like to come back here at 5:00 tonight and go to the evensong service.”

“Sounds like a great idea! I never thought much about traveling. Now I’m really captivated. Just looking at Big Ben is such a thrill."

The next day was Laurie's time to go nuts. They went to see the Crown Jewels at the Tower of London.

"That one diamond in there is a big as a fist!" she exclaimed.

They bought a few Christmas decorations and a tiny two-foot-high tree. The room in their hotel had a small living room which looked very Christmassy when they finished the preparations.

Christmas Eve they went to Westminster Abbey for church. On Christmas morning, they exchanged gifts. Brad gave Laurie a tiny gold Big Ben charm on a gold necklace. Laurie, practical and rich, gave Brad a new portable computer which he badly needed. He was truly appreciative.

One afternoon Laurie bought them a 'high tea' at the Savoy Hotel. 'High tea' was awesome. Cucumber sandwiches, tons of little cakes, plus raspberries and clotted cream! "No wonder the English kings were all fat!" Brad remarked.

On the last day, they took the train to Windsor Castle. Laurie loved the doll house plus all the fancy trappings.

They returned opting to have a pizza in their room. By eight o'clock they were in bed. No one was doing any sleeping.

"The Duke of Cadbury can always sleep on the plane," was the mantra they used as they continued to reawaken each other with soft loving caresses.

The goodbye at Heathrow airport proved to be extremely tough. As Brad gulped down his tears he muttered, "You know Laurie, this separation is proving that we are truly deeply in love."

"Father thought the separation would end it. In actuality, it has strengthened it."

It was a long time after the flight left, before their tears dried.

CHAPTER 27

By the end of spring break, Brad managed to complete the final changes to his book. On Friday, he drove into Detroit, presenting it to Archer Lane.

Archer told him, "Brad, it's highly unusual for someone as young as you to write a book. Just getting it completed is sufficient for congratulations to be in order for you. I'll read it over and give you my frank opinion. Whatever happens, don't get your hopes up as to getting it published. It's almost impossible for a beginning author to get a book published."

Brad left happy because he knew he'd done a good job with the book.

A few weeks later Archer Lane called Brad. "I really enjoyed your book, Brad. In fact, I liked it so much I took it over to a literary agent named Michael Sweeney who's a friend of mine.

"It seems Sweeney liked it too. He's willing to represent you to see if he can get a publisher for your book. He's going to email you some forms to sign to make sure he gets a commission for his work if it happens to publish. If he can't find a publisher, it won't cost you anything."

"Wow," responded Brad. "That's really good news. Thanks so much for your help Mr. Lane."

When the forms came from Michael Sweeney, there was a note of caution:

"Don't spend your money yet, kid. Out of every 1,150 manuscripts, only one gets published. Rest assured however, I'll give it my best shot."

Regards,
Michael

• • •

Miracle of miracles! In early May, Brad received a call from Michael Sweeney:

"We got lucky, kid. We've a publisher! There'll probably be a lot of revising, but it'll definitely be worth it. Congratulations!"

"Really?" exclaimed Brad. "I can't believe it! Thank you, thank you!"

Sweeney continued, "This is a small publisher. He hopes to have it ready to go on the street in early fall. If you have a dedication, Brad, please email it up to me. I'll get them to put it in the front of the book."

After the call, Brad floated around for a couple of days. He told no one. He decided he would wait until he saw a printed copy before he even told Laurie. Then he would surprise her!

He seriously considered the dedication page. It was a place to say something extremely personal and he wanted to get it right.

When nothing came to his mind after a few days, he decided to go for a walk in the woods. He remembered a nearby hiking trail which led down to a small lake. He hopped into his car and drove over.

The spring flowers were just coming into bloom. Growing close to the ground, they made a beautiful contrast to the dark damp spring ground. Brad's soul became very peaceful as he walked. When he got to the lake, no one was around. He stripped off his clothes and took a quick skinny dip. As he dried out in the warm sun, the words he was seeking for his dedication came to him.

When he got back home, he typed them out. After a series of minor revisions, he emailed them to Michael Sweeney.

• • •

Laurie thought the spring in England would never end. Oh, Oxford was wonderful. England in the spring was beautiful. However, her heart remained with Brad. She found herself counting the days until the semester ended in mid-May so she could return.

She decided to surprise Brad by flying directly to Detroit. She knew he'd be working at the Free Press now that the summer vacation at Denison had begun. The length of the commute from Detroit to Chelsea assured Laurie he wouldn't get home until well after 6:00P.M.

Her plane landed on time at 2:30 P.M. She cleared customs. A taxi all the way from Metro airport to Brad's house in Chelsea was expensive. Laurie was past caring. When she arrived at Brad's house, she went next door to his neighbor, Mary Sue Johnson.

After receiving Mary Sue's warm greeting, Laurie explained, "I need the key to Brad's house. He thinks I'm still in England. I'm going to surprise him."

Mary Sue was delighted to help in the surprise. "You know Laurie, I felt from the first minute that you and Brad were destined to be together. You've given him a great lift. Every time he comes over for dinner, he raves about you. We're so happy for you guys!"

The first thing Laurie did when she was alone in Brad's house was bathe. She felt grungy after all those hours on the plane. After a long hot soak, she wrapped herself in a towel. She needed to cool down for a minute, so she found her favorite rocking chair in the living room. She planned to get up to dress.... then the jet lag hit her.... she drifted off to sleep.

By the time she wakened, darkness had set in. Humm, she thought to herself, maybe I'll just wait here wrapped in the towel. If I know Brad, he won't want me to be dressed for very long.

About 7:30, she heard the key in the door. In walked a disgruntled Brad. He felt tired. He hated coming home to an empty house. Suddenly he heard Laurie's gentle voice say, "You look tired young man. Want to go to bed?" With a twinkle in her eye, she stood up allowing the towel to drop the floor.

"Laurie!" He ran across the room, throwing his arms around her and kissing her passionately. He kissed her again. And again. His hands gently caressed her. Laurie's skin flushed, she found herself as ready as Brad.

"This has to be the greatest surprise of my entire life! When did you.... Oh, the hell with the questions, let's get into bed! We can talk later."

He knew he had to curb his excitement so he could be certain Laurie had a satisfying experience. It didn't happen. They had been apart for such a long time, the need to complete things came in a fierce rush. When it ended, they found themselves wrapped in an incredible closeness.

"You know Brad; the sex for me is always a pathway to a wonderful closeness with you. It's been that way from the very beginning. We touch each other; we love each other; we explode into each other. Then suddenly we are hugging with a simply magic closeness. I just feel like I want to stay right here in your arms forever."

"You expressed it very well, Laurie. The closeness that comes after the sex is, in many ways, the best part of the whole thing."

"Are you hungry?" asked Laurie.

"For more of you," replied Brad as he began again stoking her breast.

"Not till later, sorry, I'm starving." She rose from the bed, heading for the kitchen.

Brad asked, "How'd you get into the house?"

"Mary Sue let me in. She thinks we're made for each other."

After they ate, they made love again. Then sleep overcame everything else. Jet lag is tough for those who don't travel a lot.

Brad called the Free Press Saturday morning. He begged off work because he was sick. He wasn't exactly sick; however, he did spend most of the day in bed. With the exception of one walk in the afternoon, they only got up to eat.

On Sunday, Brad drove Laurie home to Carmel, outside of Indianapolis. He hoped to meet Laurie's father, but it was not to be. William was at a convention in Chicago.

However, he did get his first look at Laurie's house. "Holy smoke, you guys really are rich," muttered Brad as he toured the many rooms, the fancy fenced in yard and the swimming pool.

Shirley knocked herself out to be kind to Brad. She had Agnes, the cook, prepare a special midafternoon dinner for the three of them. At the dinner, she told Brad the history of the house as well as the construction details. Late in the afternoon, Brad left for the six-hour drive back to Chelsea. His work began early on Mondays.

After Brad left, Laurie and her mother shared a cup of tea. Laurie began:

"I've missed you Mom. Start talking. We've got lots of catching up to do."

"Laurie, are you ever going to learn proper English? We *have* lots of catching up to do. We've got is...well it doesn't reflect well on your education."

"Oh Mom, no wonder I love you so much. No matter how old I get, you're still Mom. She walked around the coffee table hugging her soundly.

Shirley smiled. "I'm sorry... I digressed and I'm anxious to get caught up. But aren't you tired from your jet lag?"

"Laurie grinned. "Don't tell Dad, but I've been home for three days. I flew into Detroit and spent the weekend with Brad. The jet lag is pretty well behind me now, and I want to get caught up. What's with you and Augie?"

"I'm dying to tell you. But you talk first. You never said much about your Christmas with the Duke of Cadbury. Did you have a good time?"

"Confession time. The Duke of Cadbury was someone I invented so you and Dad wouldn't come to London at Christmas. Brad flew over and we spent the fort-night together. We....well we basically had a honeymoon in London. It was a fabulous time. I'm so in love with him, I can hardly wait till we get married."

"I'm really glad to hear your love withstood your father's imposed space gap. Brad is truly a winner in my book. Augie really likes him too. Has he asked you yet?"

"Not in so many words, but we talk about being married all the time. Our plan is for me to go to the U of M for grad school so we can be together when he starts his full-time job with the Detroit Free Press.

"I've been thinking.... If he doesn't ask me pretty soon, I may ask him. We need to get the confrontation with father behind us."

"Oh Laurie, I agree. Augie has been so patient. We want to move forward too."

"OK, your turn, let's hear about Augie."

A besotted expression swept across Shirley's face. Her eyes lit up and she tipped her head back shaking out her lose long brown hair.

"Laurie...... it's almost as if we were still in college. We email every day....... wonderful long letters. I'm afraid to let him call me, so I call him... often. We've even managed to have a couple of weekends together when your father had a trip. We've had separate bedrooms, of course. I've ruled out anything else until I file for the divorce. But we both really want to get things moving."

• • •

When Laurie went in to work Monday morning, her father's secretary approached. "I've a paper that needs your dad's signature today. I can't fax it, because the company requires an original signature. Would you drive up to Chicago and get it signed? He's staying at the Hilton down in the loop. It'll give you a chance to visit with him. He is at the 'Chain Store Owners' convention."

Laurie's summer job at the company had always required her to fill in wherever she was needed. Without a word, she took the paper, smiled cheerfully and headed for Chicago in her yellow Mercedes.

The drive took five hours. Because she started after 9:00, she missed the worst of the Chicago traffic. When she arrived at the Hilton, she went to the front desk. "May I please have the room number of William Knowlton?"

"We don't give out the room numbers of our guests," replied the rather stuffy young man behind the counter. "I'll call the room for you. Please pick up the house phone over there." He indicated a bank of house phones on a table adjacent to the check-in-counter.

William answered the phone, "Knowlton."

"Hi dad, it's Laurie."

"Laurie, how nice of you to call. You're back from Oxford, are you?"

"Yes, I came in yesterday. Dad, when I came in to work this morning your secretary gave me a paper you need to sign today. She couldn't fax it because they need an original signature. She sent me up to get your signature. Maybe we have time for a brief chat.

"You're here in Chicago?"

"Yes, I'm in the hotel lobby. What's your room number?"

William reacted without thinking, "My room number is 1150. Please give me a minute Laurie; I just got out of the shower....click... he hung up.

William whirled around. There, draped all over the coach in a thin negligee, was Melody Flowers. "Leave at once," William snapped. "That was Laurie on the phone. She's on her way up with a paper for me to sign. Hurry hurry!"

Melody was no fool. She grabbed her full-length raincoat from the closet and dashed from the room up to the next floor of the hotel.

A few seconds after Melody left, Laurie knocked on the door. "Father, I'm so glad to see you." They gave each other a friendly hug.

After a few minutes of chit chat, Laurie sensed her father was uncharacteristically nervous. Thinking he was in a hurry, she handed over the paper for his signature. Then she slipped into the bathroom for a pit stop.

As she sat on the toilet, she looked up. A brassiere and a pair of ladies' panties were hanging from the shower curtain rod. *Father, you son of a bitch,* thought Laurie. *You are planking some bimbo. She's staying right here in the hotel with you. How does he dare do that in the middle of a convention? Surely, someone he knows will see them together.*

As she sat there staring, Laurie realized her cell phone had a camera. Like everyone these days, the cell phone was always in her purse. In a few seconds, she snapped a picture of the offending, incriminating garments.

Calming her anger, she returned to the main room of the suite. She smiled wistfully at her father, "Do you have a convention meeting soon?"

"Ah, the convention is meeting over at the Palmer House, not in this hotel. Yes, I have to get over there shortly."

"Then I best be going. It'll be dark by the time I get back to Carmel."

Laurie bid William good-bye, then left the room. Once in the hall, she looked for a hiding place. A few doors from her father's room, she found an alcove where the ice machine for guests was located. Laurie ducked in and waited. In a few minutes, she heard a door open. She peeked quickly around the corner. A glimpse of Melody Flowers entering her father's room clad in a rain coat confirmed Laurie's suspicions.

A rain coat? It's a beautiful day. I bet I spooked the Hell out of them! Poor Melody, she didn't have time to dress.

Damn, I wish I'd taken a picture of Melody, but she was too quick. What can I do to get more proof?

When Laurie returned to the lobby, she noticed a nice young woman had replaced the stuffy man at the reception desk.

Laurie approached, "Can you tell me what room Mrs. Knowlton is in?" The clerk looked at the registration screen. She answered, "We're not allowed to give out guest room numbers, however, I can call on the house phone and you can talk to Mrs. Knowlton."

Laurie knew then her hunch was correct. Melody Flowers was posing as her mother. "That won't be necessary. Then Laurie reached into her pocket. She took out a $100 bill, covering most of it with her hand laying it on the counter.

"Don't people have to sign a card when they resister at the hotel?" whispered Laurie.

"Yes of course," replied the clerk.

"I need a big favor," Laurie asked, as she moved the $100 bill toward the clerk. "My father is planking a bimbo up there. They're claiming the bimbo's my mother. My mother is home in Indianapolis. Would you make a photo copy of their registration for me?"

The clerk looked around. No one was close by. Then she spoke, "I could never do that, it would be against the rules." As she announced this, she picked a card from the file, walked over to the copy machine where she made a copy handing it to Laurie. As the clerk pocketed the hundred, she murmured, "I hate guys that step out on their wives." Laurie fled.

However, she didn't return directly to Indianapolis. Instead, she went to the Palmer House Hotel. She found a sign board that listed the daily schedule of events in the hotel. As Laurie had guessed, there was nothing to indicate a meeting of the Chain Store Owners Convention.

Laurie went to the concierge and secured a printed copy of the hotel's agenda. She now had paper evidence that there was no Chain Store Convention at that hotel. Then she headed back home.

With the photos she took, plus the incorrect hotel registration, plus the Palmer House schedule of events, Laurie knew she possessed extremely damaging evidence which her Mom could use when she filed for divorce.

As Laurie neared Indianapolis on the return trip, she put in a phone call to Knowlton Company. "May I speak to Melody Flowers?"

The operator reported, "Melody's called in sick. She's not expected back until Wednesday at the earliest."

"Bingo," cheered Laurie.

As soon as Laurie arrived home, she went into a huddle with her mother. Shirley didn't feel the least bit surprised. "I was virtually certain he was being unfaithful. Now at last, we have concrete proof."

Then she thought a minute. "You know, Laurie, I've been hanging back on the divorce only because I thought you might need my assistance when you confront your father over Brad. I'm sure he's going to be very nasty."

"I expect he will be, Mom. The truth is I don't give a damn. However, you need to get moving. You've given me too many precious years. Augie is a saint for being so patient with you. He deserves better."

"The legal papers have been finished for some time. I promise to see the lawyer tomorrow and pick them up." promised Shirley.

Shirley hurried to her room to email Augie:

Finally, a real break has occurred! Laurie caught William being unfaithful. She even obtained third party evidence of what she discovered. I'm talking with the attorney again tomorrow.

Thank you for being so patient with me. I'll keep you posted, Sweetheart.

Love, Shirley.

CHAPTER 28

When Brad returned from delivering Laurie to Carmel, he went back to work. This was his third summer at the Free Press. Archer Lane continued to be impressed with his work. He assured Brad a position would be ready for him next June, after his graduation.

As a consequence, Brad felt financially secure as he drove home one Friday in late June. When he got home, he opened the mail. He found a letter from Michael Sweeney, his agent, along with a large check. Michael wrote:

Here you are kid, a check from the publisher as advanced commissions for your book. Congratulations again. Looks like the book will be out in late September. Don't spend it all at once.

MS.

Wow! Thought Brad. I know exactly what I'm going to do with this check!

• • •

In the fall, their senior year of college started. Brad and Laurie were filled with mixed emotions. They were thrilled to be back together again. Their joy was somewhat tempered by the realization that their college years were drawing to a close. They knew when they reached graduation day next May, it would be the end of some wonderful happy times. The song, *Gaudeamus Igitur* from the *Student Prince* expressed their feelings.... "*While we are young, let us rejoice.*"

Every day that fall Brad watched for the mail. He was excited about his upcoming surprise for Laurie. One day in early October, a large package came to his dorm. Brad opened it when his roommate was absent. He immediately called Laurie.

"We have to meet tonight at the bench by the library where we first met," he breathlessly explained.

She replied, "We've agreed not to date during the week. This is not permitted by our rules."

"Laurie, for once in your life, forget your damn rules. Just meet me at the bench at 8:00."

"Well, because it's you and you're so special, I'll relent. What's the occasion?"

"See you at 8:00," Brad replied mysteriously.

By October, in Ohio, it is dark well before 8:00. Wisely, Brad remembered to bring a flashlight. When Laurie arrived at the bench, she found Brad anxiously waiting, flashlight in hand. A large package rested on the bench beside him. As she sat down, she could see in the glow of the flashlight, that his eyes were shining at her.

"Okay big guy, what's up?"

Without a word, Brad handed her the package. She knew immediately he had given her a book. She read the title, *The Grandfather by Bradley W. Randall.* "Brad," she screamed "your book! It's published? Incredible! Wonderful! Oh sweetheart, I'm so proud of you!"

She hugged him hard. She kissed him then hugged him again. A few moments later, she assumed a haughty disgruntled expression. "And exactly why was I not informed about this extremely important thing going on in your life?"

"I wanted to surprise you."

"Well, it's an awfully big thing to keep secret. But maybe I'll forgive you this once."

"Before you get too mad, why don't you read the dedication page?" Brad suggested.

Laurie found the page:

"To my grandparents, Cathy and Jay Randall,
Who became my parents
When mom and dad died in an accident
When I was just a one-year-old.

And to Laurie, whose love and tenderness carried me over the rough spots when I was all alone."

"Oh Brad, I'm ……." Her tears were soon flowing, choking back the words she wanted to say. Brad hugged her until her tears stopped.

"Now I've something else important to discuss," announced Brad as he sat her back down on the bench. He put his arm around her. He looked directly into her eyes. "This book means I'm not as poor as a 'church mouse' anymore. The Free Press has guaranteed me a job next June when I graduate. As a consequence, I feel I'm now in a fairly strong financial position."

He continued, "You know I love you more than anything, Laurie. So, with all my heart, I'm asking you to marry me."

"You're being serious, aren't you? You're truly asking me to marry you?"

"Not only am I serious, but, on the assumption you would say yes, I already bought your engagement ring." He took a small box from his pocket. As he opened the box, he turned the flashlight so it would shine on the ring.

It sparkled and dazzled. Laurie could feel her heart raging with joy! "Oh Brad!" She hugged him so hard he thought he might not be able to breathe.

To his surprise, she got up from the bench and began pacing. After a minute to formulate her words, she stepped in front of him. Taking his hands in hers she whispered, "You've no idea how badly I want to say 'yes' and put on that ring.

"But what will we do about father? That SOB is going to give us an extremely hard time. If we come to him as fact accomplished, meaning already engaged, I fear it will be even tougher."

Brad countered, "Now that your dad's been caught with the bimbo and your mom is getting ready to file for divorce, what's there to save? It's time to be honest with yourself, Laurie. You have no relationship with your father."

Laurie thought a minute. Then she said, "Perhaps it's just my own integrity. Whatever he's done, he's still my father. I need to feel, in my own heart, I did the right thing until he simply went 'over the top'. I know this, Brad, if he's as nasty to you as I expect, that'll be over the top."

"Well," replied Brad, "I anticipated this might be a problem, so I bought this for you." He handed her a thin jewelry store box. Puzzled, Laurie opened the box. In it, she found a thin gold chain for around her neck.

Brad explained, "Maybe you could accept the ring and just wear it around your neck for a few weeks, until we get down to Indianapolis and face the father problem."

"I've a better idea. I'll put on this ring and wear it whenever you and I are alone. Only when I'm with someone else will I put it on the necklace and hide it under my blouse. Will that work for you, Sweetheart?"

"Sure, it works for me."

Laurie paused for a minute. "OK, under those conditions, Mr. Bradley Weatherby Randall, with all my heart, I joyfully accept your proposal of marriage. You've made me so happy I can't express my love for you in words. I'm just going to kiss you till your ears fall off." Which she did.

They stayed on the bench a long time. She kept turning on the flashlight to look at her diamond ring. They talked of a June wedding. They discussed renting an apartment somewhere in between Ann Arbor and Detroit or, living in Brad's house in Chelsea.

When it was time to go back to the dorm, Laurie declared, "I think you should go home with me for Thanksgiving. I want to wear my engagement ring too badly to wait any longer. I'm virtually certain it'll be a disaster, so we might as well get the confrontation behind us."

Thanksgiving was only a few weeks away. Finally, it became so late they knew the time had come to say goodnight. "This bench is becoming a very special part of our lives, isn't it?" asked Laurie, as they stood to begin the walk back to her dorm.

"It sure is."

They were desperately in love. Their love had grown stronger over the three plus years they had spent together. Both knew Laurie's father was a powerful man who was used to having his way. They were certain, however, that nothing would ever drive them apart.

CHAPTER 29

William Knowlton loved the fall weather. He loved the brisk autumn wind and the cool dry air as it descended upon Indianapolis. Consequently, on this mid - October day of Laurie's senior year, he was in a good mood. He had no idea that the precious business marriage he dreamed about for his daughter had been shattered by that upstart Brad Randall the night before.

As was his custom upon reaching his desk, he glanced at his 'in' box. He found a strange envelope market 'personal and confidential.' The envelope had not been opened by his secretary because William had instructed her never to open anything marked personal or confidential.

Dear Mr. Knowlton:

I have spent my life serving wealthy executives in a unique manner. Perhaps you could call what I do 'Industrial Espionage.'

I can be your 'eyes and ears' anywhere, anytime. Your employees, associates, competition or family members never have to know I work for you.

I have successfully posed as a laborer, an office worker, a butler or a lab technician. In short, I can be whatever you need... where ever you need me.

If you think I could render a service to you, please my call cell phone 468 638 4562. Sincerely,

C. Smythe

William almost tossed the letter. Then, for some reason, he read it a second time. A sly expression crossed his face. *Shirley and Laurie are slowly creating a revolution in my home. Maybe this Smythe could be hired as a butler. He could be my eyes and ears at home when I'm out.......* He dialed the number. He and Smythe arranged to meet at an 'out of the way' restaurant that afternoon.

William entered the restaurant requesting a booth in the back where he would not be noticed. After the waiter served him a cocktail, a slight skinny man sidled up to the table.

"Knowlton?"

When William nodded, the man muttered, "Smythe."

"Sit down."

Smythe slithered into the booth. There was something incredibly slippery about this man. William was pleased with his first impression. This guy could be nosey. He could *ease drop* on conversations and generally keep William posted regarding the situation in his home.

"Tell me about yourself, Smythe," William directed.

"I growed up in London. Me folks weren't too well off so I went out on the streets at a young age. You ever heard of Speaker's Corner in Hyde Park?"

"Yes, I have actually been there. It's that place in a London park where anyone can get up and speak on any topic."

"Spot on, Sir. Well, I used to make my living there."

"You got paid to speak there?"

"No no Sir, I.... well I guess you could say I made my livin' by lifting the wallets of the people listening in the audience."

"I see."

"I got pretty good at it, sir. Then one day I reached into a Bobbie's pocket by mistake. Cost me two years in the pen it did. When I got out, I decided to come to America and try my luck here. But I upgraded my practice into Industrial Espionage. This is much safer for me. Pays better too."

"Tell me about your last few jobs, Smythe."

"Well, my last job was a corker. I gots meself hired by a man who thought his wife was cheatin on im. Turns out he was right. Got some photos of her and her lover in bed together. I recon it saved 'me client a ton in the divorce settlement, cause he gave me a big bonus!

"Job fore that? I posed as a laborer in a factory the union was tryin to organize. I was able to tip off management as to which of their people were pushin the union. Guess that worked out all right, cause the union lost the election."

William made the decision to proceed with Smythe. He said, "In my home my daughter and my wife seem to be plotting things against me. I think it would be helpful if I knew what they were up to. If I agreed to hire you, how would you proceed?"

"Could you get me hired on as a butler? I done two or three butlers in me time so I know how to wait table and such. Butlers can hear a lot of stuff if they stay in the background or if they hang around a keyhole, if you know what I mean."

"Do you have a cell phone?"

"Yes sir."

"This may take several months. Are you willing, if the job takes that long?"

"I'm willin if you're paying my monthly fee."

In a few minutes, they had agreed to the financial arrangements.

William thought for a minute. He told Smythe, "We're planning a party next Friday evening. Come to my house at 5:00 P.M. I'll tell my wife I've hired you for the night to help out. We hire temporary help for parties often, so she won't suspect a thing. Then I'll suggest we hire you permanently and allow you to live in the servant's bedroom on the third floor. If you ever have information for me, call my cell phone."

"Mr. Knowlton sir, you got a deal."

The night before the party the following week, William announced to Shirley, "I've hired a butler named Smythe to help… 'what's her name' the cook, for the party tomorrow."

"William, Agnes has been with us since Laurie was a little girl. Surely you know her name."

"Of course, I know her name. I simply forgot. You know Shirley, there are so many important people in my life I cannot be involved with the unimportant people."

"What an interesting comment, William. I was always under the impression that God thinks all people are important."

Smythe proved to be an excellent butler. He kept his mouth shut and was respectful of his employer's guests. It was easy for William to complete the arrangements to have him living in the house full time. The servant's bedroom on the third floor hadn't been used since Agnes moved out into her own place several years earlier.

• • •

The news that a Denison student authored a published book spread rapidly across the campus. Teachers and students alike offered Brad congratulations. Brad enjoyed his brief moment in the spotlight. Laurie, filled with pride for him, savored every moment.

One-day Brad found himself in front of the library waiting for Laurie to meet with him, so he could walk her to her dorm. Just as Laurie came out of the library, a good looking first year student approached Brad.

"Are you Brad Randall?"

"Yes."

"I read your book. It's wonderful! Would you autograph it for me?"

As she handed him his book to sign she batted her long lashes at him. "If you ever need an escort to a dance or anything, I'd love to be able to say I had a date with a real author."

By then Laurie was on the scene. "Hands off young lady, he's already mine." Laurie flashed her ring in front of the astonished woman as she took Brad's arm possessively.

"Woops! I'm so sorry," exclaimed the girl as she faded from view.

They hadn't taken ten steps when another girl confronted Brad. "Will you autograph my copy of your book?"

As Brad signed, Laurie moaned. "How am I going to be able to live with you with all this adulation? If you get a big head Brad Randall, I'll skin you alive!"

Brad's book shipment was actually 50 books. Apparently, he could either sell them or give them away. Brad autographed several copies and presented them to friends. When he gave the book to his writing professor, it was a poignant moment. The Professor actually got tears in her eyes.

Brad's agent, Michael Sweeney insisted Brad have a web site ready to go when the book hit the stores. Sure enough, the emails to the web site proved exciting to read. Both Laurie and Brad spent time together answering the emails from his fans.

One night, while monitoring the website, Brad came across this interesting note:

Brad:

You don't know me but I was your mother's roommate at U of M. We were very good friends. In fact, I was one of her bridesmaids.

When she and your father had that tragic accident, I had already moved to California so I couldn't come back for the funeral. Then I lost track of how to reach you. I always wondered how you turned out. It appears you are doing very well.

If you get a minute, drop me a note and tell me about yourself. I loved your book. Your grandfather must have been a great guy.

Affectionately,

Joanne Dartforth (Warren)

Box 7232

San Diego, California.92128

"Mother's roommate! What a lucky break," exclaimed Brad. He sat down and wrote a long informative email telling her about his life.

Then he went to his dresser. He started digging through in search of a photo. After a few minutes, he found the photo of his mother with another boy who was not his dad. Brad had found the photo back when he cleaned out grandfather's dresser after Jay passed away. He murmured to himself, 'I always wondered what the story was regarding this picture. Maybe this Joanne Dartforth Warren can tell me.'

He scanned the photo, adding it to his email.

Then he added this as a PS:

P.S. I found this picture in my grandfather's things after his death. I've no idea who is in the picture with my mother. I'm hoping you can tell me.

Having almost no information about my parents is difficult. I'll be truly grateful for anything you can share with me.

Regards,

Brad Randall

Right before Brad and Laurie left for the fateful Thanksgiving visit to her home, he checked his email. He found a response from Mrs. Dartforth (Warren.) Brad was in a rush; but he took the time to print the email. As it came off the printer, something caught his eye. In a heartbeat, he stopped right where he was so he could read the entire message.

"Holy smoke," exclaimed Brad, "I wonder if he knows." He decided to say nothing to Laurie 'til he found out the answer.

CHAPTER 30

They drove to Carmel in Laurie's yellow Mercedes. Driving that car was always a fun adventure for both of them. Laurie wore her engagement ring all the way. They kept looking at it, as they smiled at one another.

"I think what I should do is approach your father in the old-fashioned way," Brad observed. "He may respect me more if I do. I'll talk to him a while. Then I'll simply ask him if it would be all right if we got married."

Laurie thought a minute, "My guess is whatever approach we try will fail. Please don't be shocked if it does. He should be home when we arrive. What I'll do is go upstairs to unpack and talk with mother, while you go to the guillotine. She removed her ring sliding it onto the gold necklace, so it would be hidden beneath her blouse when they entered the house.

Laurie squeezed his hand. "Don't worry, Darling. Whatever happens we're going to get married in June with or without father."

When Laurie pushed open the door she was approached by a short slim man wearing a butler uniform.

"You must be Miss Laurie," he exclaimed as he approached to take her suitcase.

Somewhat taken aback, Laurie asked, "Who are you and why are you here?"

"Smythe ma'am. I be the new butler. I think your father hired me because the house needed more attention now that Mrs. Knowlton is a....shall we say.... employed?"

"Oh, I see. How long have you been here Mr. Smythe?"

"It's just Smythe Ma'am. In England, where I was trained, servants are addressed by the surname name only. I've been here just a few weeks, Ma'am.

"Well Smythe, this is Mr. Brad Randall."

"Nice to meet you Smythe." Brad extended his hand. Somewhat taken aback that Brad would shake hands with a servant, Smythe responded with a soft grip.

"Is my father here, Smythe?"

"He be in his office, Ma'am."

Smythe gathered both Laurie and Brad's suitcases. He quickly disappeared up the stairs. As he went up, he had to make way for Shirley who rushed down to hug her daughter and Brad.

William never even came out to say hello.

After they each got a hug from Shirley, Laurie and Brad looked at each other. Brad smiled grimly, "Point me to his office. I want to get this over with as soon as possible."

Laurie grabbed her mother's hand. They followed Brad as he approached the study. They saw Brad pause outside the study door. He took a deep breath. Then he knocked.

"Come in," a forceful voice declared. Brad entered. Before he could close the door completely, he heard an angry snarl. "What do you want?"

Laurie and Shirley walked quietly to the study door so they could listen. They had no compunction eavesdropping. Fortunately, the partially open door assured that they could hear clearly.

Brad looked around. The study was a wonderful room. Bookshelves lined one wall. A big picture window was located behind the desk. The view showed the incredible garden and spacious lawn, which made up Laurie's back yard.

There were some paintings on the opposite wall. They were somber paintings but the small lights shining down on them helped. A vase of fresh flowers rested beside the desk.

Mr. Knowlton sat stiffly on a large, leather covered desk chair, at an enormous desk. He still wore a tie. William's suit coat rested on the leather couch. His face wore a monstrous scowl.

Brad confronted the scowl with a smile. "My name is Brad Randall." He approached the desk extending his hand.

William made no move to rise or extend his hand. He simply stared at this young upstart.

"I know who you are, Randall," he snapped. "In fact, I know all about you. You're after Laurie's money. Furthermore, I know Laurie doesn't really care for you. She simply feels sorry for you. Laurie knows Knowlton's don't marry with what they feel in their hearts, they marry for what they know in their heads."

Suddenly William stood. He rose up to his full height. His voice exploded.

"You're not welcome in this house. Since it's my house, I'll give you one minute to get out or…. I'll call the police. They'll arrest you for trespassing."

Brad expected trouble. But this unwarranted explosion seemed beyond normal reason. "You can't be serious, Mr. Knowlton. In addition, you are badly mistaken. Laurie and I are very much in love. In fact, I came in here today to ask you for Laurie's hand in marriage."

"You'll never be allowed to marry my daughter," snarled Knowlton. "Laurie's going to marry Allan Van Swearington. Now get out of this house before I call the police."

The door burst open. Shirley and Laurie came in. From the corner of his eye, Brad noticed Laurie sliding the ring on her third left finger.

"Not so fast William," announced Shirley. "You've no right to be so nasty with Brad. You didn't even allow him to say hello. You ought to be ashamed of yourself."

"You stay out of this Shirley. What were you doing out there, eavesdropping? I'll deal with this upstart gold digger my own way!" roared William.

"Father," yelled Laurie, "Sit down and shut up. If you ever want me to speak to you again, sit down and shut up!"

A stunned William paused in his outburst. His daughter had never spoken to him in that tone. His fury built up another notch.

The exchange between the members of the Knowlton family gave Brad a minute to think. As William paused in his ranting Brad quietly spoke up. "I think I know what the problem is folks. I received this email today just before I left my room. I decided to wait to tell Laurie 'till I found out if Mr. Knowlton knows. By the way he's behaving, I'm sure he does.

"Knows what?" asked a befuddled Laurie.

William bellowed, "What are you trying to imply, you inscrutable kid?"

Brad took a paper from his pocket. "If I read this aloud everyone will understand. It's from my mother's college roommate Joanne Dartforth. Do you remember her, Mr. Knowlton?"

Laurie's Father's face paled.

Then without waiting for an answer, Brad started reading:

Brad:

The picture you sent of your mother with that other boy was taken early in her freshman year. The boy's name was William 'something or other' I can't remember his last name. He was really rich. His parents owned a bunch of chain stores or something.

Anyway, Margaret dated him about five or six times. It seemed his mother knew Margaret's mother so she felt forced to go out with William. When she came back to school after spring break, she told me she planned to break it off with William. Things were going nowhere because she simply didn't like him.

"I'm not going to sit here and listen to this drivel," interrupted William.

"Then I suggest you leave," countered Shirley. "You can stay at your 'Bimbo's' apartment. Brad please continue."

Shirley's statement stunned William. The reference to the Bimbo's apartment terrified him. How much did Shirley know about Melody? Momentarily, he froze into silence. Brad continued.

Well, about an hour after she left for the 'shoot down William' dinner date, Margaret stormed back into the room hopping mad. I remember it as if it were yesterday, because it was so funny.

Your mother blurted out, "That pompous ass asked me to marry him! No, he didn't really do that, he simply announced that HE decided we should marry. Then he shoved this big diamond ring at me as if he needed to buy my consent. It never occurred to him I might want to have some input in selecting the man I plan to marry. I was so angry I called him self-centered goat! Next, I shoved the ring back in his face, told him never to call me again and walked out. I took a taxi back. How anyone can be as self-centered as that nincompoop is beyond my comprehension! Apparently, he told Margaret something about a person should decide to marry with their head not their hearts!"

By the time Margaret unloaded, I was laughing so hard I was almost crying. Margaret looked at me and then she started laughing too. It was simply hysterical.

I think we laughed about it for several weeks.

I'll try to remember some more stories about your Mom, Brad. I'll send them along when I can.

Affectionately,

Joanne Dartforth (Warren)

A long silence gripped the room. Finally, Laurie found her voice. "You're taking it out on Brad because his mother refused to marry you! Father, his mother died when Brad was a one-year-old! She refused you before Brad was even born! How can Brad in any way be responsible for what his mother did years before he was born?"

Then Shirley chimed in, "William you ought to be ashamed. These two children are deeply in love. We should support them all we can."

Shaking with anger, William found his voice, "Knowlton's marry with their heads not their hearts. Laurie will marry Allan Van Swearington."

Laurie stepped forward thrusting her left hand into her father's face. "Do you see my engagement ring father? Brad and I have promised each other to marry! We're planning a June wedding. Right now, I seriously doubt you'll be invited. I'd rather walk down the aisle by myself, than with you!"

"As long as we've come to this family impasse, it's time for my news," announced Shirley in a loud voice. She stepped up to William's desk, staring at him. "I'm filing for a divorce. It's impossible to live with you!"

She continued, "Here are my wedding and engagement rings. I don't want them because, with the exception of Laurie, nothing has ever been happy in our marriage. I'm hereby serving you with an official copy of the divorce action. Tomorrow, my attorney will file copies of these documents at the courthouse.

William stood up. He walked around the desk confronting Shirley. "How dare you attempt to divorce me, you Bitch."

Brad anticipated what was coming. He started moving. However, he was clear across the room. William drew back his hand preparing to smash Shirley across the face.

Out of the corner of his eye, Brad saw Shirley raise her arm to ward off the pending blow. Brad couldn't reach William's arm before it swung, so he dived. His shoulder caught William right in the stomach. Brad never made a better flying tackle in his entire high school football career! William crumpled to the carpet with Brad on top of him. William's intended blow landed harmlessly on Brad's back.

A badly shaken Shirley, turned as pale as a swan. However, she managed to take a deep breath and gather herself. In a firm voice, laden with undertones, Shirley announced, "I'll handle this, Brad." She placed her hand on Brad's shoulder restraining him from any further assault against her husband.

"William, the time is now 6:15. If you're not out of this house by 6:45, I'll call the police to have you forcibly removed. The knowledge that William Knowlton is a wife beater, will look great in all the papers."

As Brad climbed off, William came up sputtering. "You can't do this to me!"

Shirley countered, "William, I just did. Now get out of this house. You have thirty minutes."

"You forget Shirley. This house is in joint name. I have just as much right to be here as you! So, if you want a divorce, you can leave."

"Where would you have me go? It'd be silly for me to go to your Bimbo's apartment. Somehow, I don't think she'd want to share a bed with me. Besides, it's really your apartment, isn't it? My understanding is that the company is paying the rent!"

As William's jaw dropped, she added, "Please remember, the more you fight the divorce, the more I'll demand for my financial share of the settlement."

She went to the door and called for Smythe. "Please go help Mr. Knowlton pack his bags. He's leaving this house."

A badly shaken William stood, staring around the room. Losing his dream of Laurie marrying Van Swearington infuriated him. However, Shirley's actions frightened him. He knew the old Chinese proverb:

Wealthy man who divorce - no longer wealthy man.

The fact that Shirley knew about Melody gave William real concern. Her grounds for divorce would be very strong. He decided to retreat. He would fight another day.

Without another word, he walked upstairs and began packing.

Shirley followed him out into the hall. She called after his retreating form, "William, you better give the Bimbo a call to tell her you're coming. You never know, a girl like Melody may be entertaining someone else tonight."

Shirley then returned to the den and asked Agnes to bring champagne. The toasts began.

Some thirty minutes later, William opened the door. In an instant, dead silence descended on the room.

"I am leaving now."

Shirley snapped, "Good, take Smythe with you."

"Smythe stays. You forget, Shirley, I own half of this house. Smythe will remain here and keep track of my things."

"Just leave. Smythe is a non-issue."

"Not till I say one thing to my ugly duckling daughter. Laurie, if you allow yourself to be engaged to THAT person you are just plain stupid. Stupid, stupid, stupid!"

Laurie blanched. She coldly glared at her father. "Well, William, that makes three strikes. You hurt my mother, you hurt my fiancé, and you hurt me. Three strikes means, you're out! From now on, I call you William, not father. My father has ceased to exist!"

She slammed the door in his face.

Then she opened it again so she could yell at him as he walked down the hall.

"For your information William, your STUPID daughter has made the Dean's list every year in college. She was just informed last week she has qualified for the scholastic honorary Phi Beta Kappa!" The door slammed a second time.

A second later, she opened the door and shouted, "I hope you realize, William the man your STUPID daughter is engaged to marry, just saved you a bunch of money. If he hadn't stopped you from hitting mother, it would have cost you a bundle!" The door slammed for the third time.

Laurie turned her back against the door leaning against it. Everyone could see the terrible hurt on her face as she slowly slid down to the floor. Then she burst into tears. Shirley moved to comfort her daughter. Brad moved faster. He sat on the floor next to her, hugging as hard as he could. Shirley joined them. They both spent several minutes on the floor comforting Laurie.

As her tears stopped, Laurie turned to her mother. "Mom, you picked a really lousy husband."

"I think everyone here agrees," Shirley acknowledged. "But… I'll bet you'll like my next one!"

Then she smiled as she spoke to Brad. "You've been a prince. I'm so embarrassed you were subject to all our family squabbling. Thank goodness, you and Laurie have each other. I know your lives will be filled with joy."

Then Shirley added, "Brad, I'm old but I'm not old fashioned. I told Smythe to put your suitcase in the guest room. Where you sleep, is none of my business."

Laurie grinned at her mother. "Mom you're great. The three of us are going to have lots of fun together."

Shirley astonished them with her response, "I'm hoping it will be four of us having fun. Which reminds me, I need to make a phone call to your accounting professor."

When Augie came to the phone, Shirley spoke, "Happy Thanksgiving tomorrow. Have your children arrived yet?"

"No, but I expect them at any minute."

"Are they staying all weekend?"

No, they have to go back on Friday. Too many activities to spend an entire weekend with father. Why the phone call, Shirley? You usually email."

"Well, now that I know your children are leaving Friday, would you enjoy a visitor on Saturday?"

"Would the visitor be a beautiful brunette with a gorgeous figure who answers to the name of Shirley?"

"The brunette might have a few grey strands. I choose not to comment about the figure. Augie, I finally did it. I gave William the divorce papers. I returned his rings to him and kicked him out of the house."

"What happened?" asked Augie.

Shirley related the entire incident. She concluded, "I knew there would be an explosion when Brad and Laurie made their intentions known to William. That's the reason why I have been so slow with the divorce action. I just knew it was necessary that I be on hand. I was right, Augie. It was a terrible fight. However, it's finally over. You have been wonderfully patient.

I have conducted myself in such a manner that I can say under oath, I was faithful to William right up to the time I filed for divorce."

There was a pause, then Shirley added; "Now I feel free to do as I wish. Augie, more than anything, I wish to visit you!"

Augie replied, "If you and I are alone in my house, I cannot promise to be a gentleman."

"If you are a gentleman, I'll kill you. I should be in before suppertime. I can hardly wait."

"I'll have a warm dinner waiting for you."

"Don't bother with the warm dinner, Augie, it'll just get cold. We can eat afterwards." Then she hung up.

She thought, the *old Shirley would never have imagined those things. However, new Shirley did. I'm beginning to enjoy new Shirley. She seems to be a real fun gal!'*

After Shirley went to bed that night, Brad and Laurie found their way to the living room couch. Head on Brad's shoulder, Laurie let her tears flow. She knew now there would be no reconcilement with William. Her father was lost to her forever.

After a while, she began to think of Brad. "It must have been terrible for you watching all that horrible fighting."

Brad nodded. You know, Laurie, the sad part is I never had a father, only a grandfather. I was truly hoping William and I could become pals. He's going to miss out on a lot, especially if we have children."

After a long silence, Brad decided to try to lighten the mood. "I've learned one thing is for sure, Laurie."

"Oh?"

"When it comes to picking husbands, my mother was smarter than your mother."

"There'll be no argument from me on that issue."

Then Laurie added, "I'm going to change one rule regarding you and me. From now on, I will not become 100% naked when we go to bed."

"What!!! How can you dare say that?"

"Well, I have this beautiful engagement ring a wonderful man gave to me. I've no intention of taking it off, even when we go to bed!"

Hugs and laughter proved to be wonderful medicine.

CHAPTER 31

Thanksgiving Day in Carmel, Indiana dawned bright, cold and clear. Laurie and Brad, after a night of lovemaking, appeared in the dining room together, holding hands. It made Shirley beam with joy, especially when she saw the elation in the eyes of her daughter.

Shirley felt a freedom in her heart she hadn't felt in years. She was bright and cheerful. She informed the children, "I'm going to Granville to visit Augie tomorrow."

Laurie hugged her mother at the news. "Mom, if anyone ever deserved a good break it's you. We wish you the best!"

"I hope you have a sexy night gown," quipped Brad.

"Brad!" admonished Laurie.

"It's all right, I can take a little ribbing," smiled Shirley. Then she added, "Goodness, you two sound like you've been married for years!"

"Well, if you think about it Mom, this is the end of the third year we've been together. So, in a sense, we have been married for years."

Laurie gave an adoring look across the table at her fiancé. "You, Mr. Randall, are becoming a very comfortable old shoe."

When the relatives arrived for Thanksgiving dinner, Shirley called for everyone's attention. The room fell silent, as Shirley addressed the gathering.

"I have two happy announcements. First of all, I've decided to divorce William. He's not here today because he moved out last night. As I'm sure many of you suspected, William and I have been unhappy for many years. Because I've read so many stories of how a divorce is difficult for children, I elected to wait until our daughter was fully grown. I'm certain now that Laurie is emotionally ready to handle the divorce. In fact, she's been encouraging me.

"My other news is very exciting. I wish to announce the engagement of my daughter Laurie, to her classmate at Denison, Bradley Weatherby Randall. Laurie and Brad have been in love since their freshman year. When you get to know Brad, I'm sure you'll all like him as much as we do. I feel virtually certain this marriage will be an especially loving happy one. My joy in making this announcement cannot be expressed in words."

The group broke into loud applause.

Then Laurie spoke up. "My fiancé' has already had a book published. We brought some along to sell, so if you want an autographed copy, just let us know."

Everyone crowded around to shake Brad's hand and to ogle Laurie's engagement ring. A beaming Laurie enjoyed showing it off, as she introduced Brad to her relatives.

Brad was pleasantly surprised when he sold several books. He decided, *Laurie's relatives are rich enough. They can buy their own copy. I've already given away too many.*

No one appeared to be upset when they heard William and Shirley had called it quits. In fact, most of Shirley's relatives congratulated her on the divorce move. Their attitude confirmed what Shirley expected. Everyone who knew her well understood it had been an unhappy marriage. It quickly became apparent that William's absence created a positive influence on the festive holiday atmosphere.

Then the doorbell rang. Smythe was in the kitchen, so Laurie opened it. There stood Allan Van Swearington.

Allan's appearance stunned Laurie for a second. She quickly realized her father must have asked Allan to the Thanksgiving gathering some time ago. She smiled at him, took his coat and invited him into the living room.

Taking Allan by the arm she exclaimed, "Come over here Allan, there's someone I want you to meet."

They walked up to Brad. Laurie performed the introduction.

"Allan, I'd like you to meet my fiancé, Brad Randall. Brad this is Allan Van Swearington."

Brad gave Allan a strong handshake. Allan responded with a dishrag grip. Laurie snuggled up to Brad. With a subtle gesture, she brought her ring well into Allan's view. "We're talking about a June wedding, aren't we Dear?"

"We certainly are," replied Brad. "Tell me Allan, how are things going at Knowlton Company?"

The three of them made small talk for a minute. Allan inquired as to

William's whereabouts.

Laurie chose to answer. "Mother and William have decided to divorce. Consequently, he's not here today."

Allan was obviously stunned by that news. He retreated into the crowd. Soon after the dinner, he made his excuses and departed.

After he left, Laurie twinkled at Brad. "That was kind of fun, wasn't it?"

On Friday morning, Shirley left for Granville. After Shirley left, Laurie got out her yellow Mercedes. She told Brad she wanted to go shopping. Within a few minutes, Brad determined that the real purpose of the trip was so Laurie could introduce Brad to her former school mates and show off her ring. Laurie would drop in on a friend, stay for 10 or 15 minutes, and then hurry on to another house. Brad understood. He was so proud to be Laurie's fiancé; he rather enjoyed the entire process. The only problem was that Laurie gave away several of his autographed books.

"I enjoy autographing the books Laurie. It's really a high. However, if you have a special person you want to have a book, you better hold back 'til we get there. I'm almost out."

"Will do."

About noon, they found themselves in downtown Indianapolis. "Come on," exclaimed Laurie, "I want you to meet Joan Wright. Bring her our last book. She's the special one."

"Who's Joan Wright?" asked Brad, as Laurie tugged his arm to get him into the elevator of a tall office building.

She used to be my piano teacher. We became extremely good friends. One day she decided piano teaching didn't pay enough. She's a single woman, so she needs money to keep afloat.

Joan went back to school and became a legal secretary. Right now, she works for Caspar Silenski, who's the Knowlton Company attorney. I guess she runs the place. By all reports, she's a major player in the law firm's operations.

Silenski's office reflected a distinctive atmosphere. Heavy leather furniture, fancy artwork, book shelves filled with handsome hard covers and of course, a vase of flowers at the reception desk.

Laurie asked the receptionist if they could see Joan Wright. In a minute, a friendly middle-aged woman walked into the reception room. As Laurie and Joan hugged, Brad observed a tastefully dressed woman with her hair drawn back in a ponytail. She'd wrapped the tail in a pretty ribbon, which created a perky look.

Joan greeted Brad with a warm handshake coupled with an enthusiastic smile. Brad felt affection for her immediately.

As Laurie introduced Brad, she flashed the diamond ring under Joan's nose. Her technique at showing off the ring without seeming too obvious was improving.

"You're engaged!" exclaimed Joan in an excited voice. "Oh Laurie, I'm so happy for you!" She gave Laurie a second hug. Then she hugged Brad warmly.

As she hugged Brad, she murmured in his ear, "You are one lucky guy, Mister. I want you to remember, if you hurt my Laurie, I'll kill you with my bare hands."

"Don't worry; I could never hurt Laurie. I'm too much in love with her."

"Well, this calls for a celebration. Give me a minute to clear my desk. I'll take you to lunch," declared Joan.

Once they were seated, the first subject that came up was Shirley and William's pending divorce. Joan, like many who knew them both, remarked, "It's about time."

As they neared the end of the meal, Joan put on a serious face. "Laurie, I've been meaning to talk with you for several months regarding something important. Today's the perfect time. I assume you two have no secrets from each other?"

"No secrets, unless a surprise is in the offing. Then secrets are legal," replied Laurie. She continued, "For instance, that rascal never told me his book was being published until he put the printed copy in my hand!"

"Joan responded, "I bet you were surprised, big time. I'm anxious to read this Brad."

Laurie whispered to Joan, "He used his first check from the book to buy my ring!"

"He must be a real romantic," was Joan's whispered reply. Brad could hear all of it, but he remained silently smiling.

Joan then turned serious. "First I have to ask, if anyone ever told you of the Trust your grandfather left for you?"

"Trust? I never heard of any trust," Laurie replied.

Joan continued, "I had a suspicion that was the case. Well, here's the story.

"Several years ago, Mr. Silenski acquired the files of an old law firm in town called Mason and Smith. Mason was your grandfather's attorney, Laurie. Smith was the oldest partner. Smith died first, leaving only Mason. When Mason died, there was no one to look after their files. Silenski agreed to acquire the files.

Apparently, your grandfather died before Mason, so he knew nothing of what happened.

When Silenski acquired these files, no one wanted or had time to review them… except yours truly. One day while I was doing this, I came across copies of the two trusts your grandfather set up for the benefit of his two grandchildren."

"Two grandchildren?" questioned Laurie.

"Oh yes, this trust was completed way before Betty Ann… went off the deep end."

"What's in the trust?" asked Brad.

"Shares of Knowlton Company stock. Giving stock to grandchildren is a way of avoiding the estate tax. They call this type of trust a Generation Skipping Trust. Your grandfather knew if he placed stock in a Generation Skipping Trust, those shares would not be subject to the estate tax when his son, William, died. That means the estate tax on those shares in the trust would skip a generation, hence the name, Generation Skipping Trust.

"Before your grandfather died, he placed 10 shares of Knowlton stock in each trust. After his death, your father inherited the remaining 80 shares of the company.

"As you may know, I've been doing all the Knowlton legal work for the past several years. Actually, Mr. Silenski does the tricky work, but I do tons of paper work, filing, etc. I've learned Knowlton is a closely held company with only 100 shares outstanding. Your father owns 80 shares, which makes him the majority shareholder.

"There's an important reason I want to be sure you know this Laurie. I think Mr. Silenski and your father are keeping knowledge of these trusts to themselves. With the divorce and the pending property settlement, I think you should be aware of what's in those trusts.

"The problem is……. if you ask Silenski for a copy of the trust, he might fire me. I'm sure I'm breaching all kinds of ethics by even mentioning this to you."

There was silence for a long minute. Then Brad asked, "Laurie, aren't you taking business law this semester?

"Yes, why?"

"Why don't you casually drop in on Mr. Silenski? Tell him you vaguely remember your grandfather telling you something about a trust. Then tell him your business law professor made a class assignment that requires each student to bring in all the trust instruments and other legal papers they could find. The professor would then review the legal issues involved with the class."

"Sounds like something I could pull off," acknowledged Laurie. "What do you think, Joan?"

"An approach like that would at least keep me out of the middle. Tell you what; Silenski has an opening at 2:30 this afternoon. Why don't you drop in then? In the interim, I'll make copies of the trusts, so you can read them at your leisure."

At 2:30, Laurie just happened to drop by Mr. Silenski's office. "Why Mr. Silenski how nice to see you," she exclaimed, pausing at his office door.

Silenski looked up. There stood Laurie, wrapped in glowing beauty. "Laurie, you look wonderful."

After introducing her fiancé and some chitchat Laurie declared, "I need a favor. My business law professor wants all students to bring to class next week all the trusts, wills and stuff we can find. He wants to review them with the class before the finals, which will occur right before Christmas break. I seem to remember my grandfather telling me about a trust a long time ago. I think father told me you had a copy. Could you make me a copy so I could take it to class?"

"Silenski paused, "I'll ask Joan to mail it to you. When you leave, please give Joan your school address. Then he poked a button on his intercom. "Joan, please make a copy of the trust Laurie's grandfather created. She needs it for business law class. She'll give you the school address so you can mail it to her."

"Will do," Joan's voice echoed over the inter com.

Joan gave Laurie a thick envelope when she came out. "I can save postage by handing it to you."

"Funny he didn't mention the divorce," mentioned Laurie.

"I don't think he's talked to William today. Mr. Silenski's been gone all morning. He's just now begun to return his calls. Please go quickly before he changes his mind. The women exchanged a brief hug. Laurie and Brad disappeared.

Later that afternoon Mr. Silenski stopped by Joan's desk. "Joan, I think you should disregard my earlier instruction regarding mailing the trust document to Laurie. I want to get Mr. Knowlton's permission before we mail it.

"Yes sir," Joan replied. "I will not mail it."

CHAPTER 32

Shirley started on the road to Granville with a joy filled heart. As the trip progressed, however, she began to become afraid. She was certain she wanted Augie badly.

The trouble was, Shirley's past sex life had been a disaster. In her heart, she felt the problem belonged to William's extreme selfishness. However, there was always a nagging guilt. Has our sexual incompatibility been my fault?

Shirley pulled into Granville stopping at a gas station to freshen up. She combed out her long hair, applied fresh lipstick and a touch of blush. She wore a sheer blouse with a grey skirt. A suit jacket covered the blouse, well almost covered it. Some cleavage was visible under the jacket.

Shirley's heart almost stopped as she drove into Augie's driveway. He came out of the house in an instant. He gave her a hug, and then picked up her suitcase. They rushed inside. Once the door shut, they threw their arms around each other hugging. A gentle, tender kiss followed.

Without a word, Shirley pulled Augie over so they could sit together on the living room couch. Then she simply blurted out what was in her heart.

"Oh Augie, I'm so scared. I want you badly. You cannot know how many times I have imagined our being in bed together. However, my sex life with William has been a complete disaster.

Augie, I'm not sure if I've ever had an orgasm. William was a sexual taker, not a giver. He never tried to please me. Not one time. He only had sex for himself. I keep wondering if it was my fault that our sex life was so terrible. Augie, I don't want to fail you. I want to be a wonderful sex partner for you. Please help me."

"Based on what you've told me of William, he's the most selfish person I've ever encountered. It doesn't surprise me your sex life has been a disaster."

He paused in an effort to get the words correctly. "Shirley, loving sex is not taking, it's giving. If I love you in a gentle tender manner, your response will create sensational sex for me. If you touch me tenderly, you will find arousing me will also you arouse you. There's a total difference between selfish, me first sex, and loving sex. The most important difference is… I'm terribly fond of you."

Oh Augie, I'm so glad you told me because I feel the same way about you."

Augie continued, "We're going to bed to love each other in a sexual way. I know it'll work out wonderfully."

Besides, we have all weekend to be together. The first time, may be a little awkward. Trust me. It won't take long for each of us to learn how to love the other. By the end of the weekend, I'm sure we'll be able to work everything out, just the way you dreamed it would be."

"Thank you, sweet Augie. You're helping my confidence more than you know," Shirley's replied.

He kissed her. The kiss quickly deepened. Soon they were both panting. Shirley melted. Everything in her body began to scream for Augie. It was easy for Augie to read what she wanted. Without a word, he turned Shirley towards the stairway. The bedroom was at the top of the stairs.

When the bedroom door shut, Shirley sat on the edge of the bed. Augie slowly removed her jacket, then her blouse. He gasped as he saw her clad only in her bra. His obvious joy gave Shirley lots of confidence. She stood up, kissed him, then unbuttoned and removed Augie's shirt.

"A hug half naked is only great if your bra is off."

Shirley turned so he could unfasten the bra. She took a step back as she turned to face him. This gave him a good look at her beautiful, well-formed breasts. For a wonderful moment, he stared at her while she observed his strong, hairy torso. As they came together into a huge hug, he crushed her breasts into his naked chest.

Then he released her enough to bury his face into her softness. It feels so good, Shirley thought, I hope he never stops.

Augie thought he was just getting started but things moved way faster than he expected. Intoxicated by desire, Shirley pleaded for him. The climax shattered them both. When it ended, the tears began. Shirley couldn't help it, all her pent-up emotions flooded out in the form of tears. It began as a trickle. Seconds later Augie's chest was wet with her tears. He stroked her back as he tried to calm her down. As the tears subsided, they cuddled together. She'd never felt so complete in her entire life.

Shirley found her voice. "Augie, I've dreamed of making love with you ever since college. You were incredible. Thank you so much."

Augie replied, "A love like we just experienced makes me feel very close to you."

"Feeling close may be the best part of loving." Shirley continued, "You know something, Augie. I'm certain now. That was my first real orgasm. William is many horrible things. Now I'm beginning to realize that SOB's bedroom manners are the nastiest part about him."

"Let's not go there; it's just too nice being here together."

There was silence for a minute. Then Shirley asked, "Do you think we could do it again?"

"Now?"

"Now!"

"Well if I die trying, it'll be a great way to go." He reached for her breast. Shirley moaned joyously.

• • •

Brad and Laurie spent the evening reading the trust documents. When Laurie got to the beneficiary section, she was surprised to see her late sister, Betty Ann, was the beneficiary of her trust. "I'll have to change the beneficiary," she told Brad.

He responded, "Wait a minute. If your trust has Betty Ann as beneficiary, maybe Betty Ann's trust has you as her beneficiary."

They examined Betty Ann's trust. Sure enough, Betty Ann's beneficiary was Laurie Lansing Knowlton. "You are the owner of 20 shares," Brad announced. "If there are only 100 shares issued, you own 20% of the company."

"I agree. However, it says here I only get access to one third of the assets at age 23. Then I get another third at age 26 and another third at age 30. I guess grandpa didn't trust his granddaughters to handle money at young ages."

"Have you talked to our Denison friend, Donna Swift lately?" asked Brad. She was planning on law school. She lives in Indianapolis. She must have graduated by now. I think we need to talk to her or with some lawyer."

Laurie looked at her watch. "It's too late to call Donna now, but we should be able to get an appointment tomorrow."

When they tumbled into bed, their naked bodies touched. As they stroked each other Laurie asked, "I wonder how mother got along today?"

The next day, Laurie and Brad went to visit their old double date friend, Donna Swift. Donna resided in an unpretentious office located in a suburb of Indianapolis.

She explained, "Ted Samson, my boyfriend from Denison, is taking a special tax course. We're living together. After he graduates next June, we'll get married.

She didn't have a diamond yet. She turned only slightly green when she saw the beautiful ring Laurie flashed casually around the office.

"I'm so happy for you guys," she exclaimed. It was easy to tell, in spite of her lack of a ring, she truly meant it.

Laurie acknowledged, "It seems crazy for us to be engaged at the same time my parents are in the middle of a divorce.

"I don't think it's crazy at all. I knew you guys were deeply in love way back in your freshman year."

When they got down to business, Donna read the trust documents carefully. She acknowledged their correct interpretation of the clause that prevented Laurie from access to the money until she was 23. She explained that those one third/ one third/ one third clauses were standard estate planning ideas.

Then Donna read something interesting. "Laurie, your father is the trustee of the trusts. It is therefore true you have no access to the trust assets. However, at age 21, you do have the right to hire and fire the trustee. You have the legal right to fire your father and name yourself trustee of your own trust. That means you would be able to vote the Knowlton shares, even though you don't actually have possession of them."

"I would love to fire my trustee father. How do we go about it?" asked Laurie.

"Let me do some research. Then let's get together at Christmas.

After a few minutes' reflection, Donna explained, "You know, the financial fact when dealing with the owner of a closely held company is that the ownership of the corporation usually represents somewhere between 80% and 90% of their net worth. Consequently, your mother's divorce settlement will have to involve the transfer of a significant amount of Knowlton Company shares."

As she soaked up this information, Laurie had a thought, which she expressed out loud. "Suppose Mother inveigles at least 31 shares in the divorce settlement. I have 20 shares. 31 plus 20 = 51 shares. Since the Knowlton stock issue is only 100 shares, there could be some extremely interesting situations possible."

As Laurie pondered what she had just said, a strange expression crossed her face. To Brad, who knew her well, it was easy to see what she was thinking. D*on't get mad, get even!*

They made a date for a meeting on Saturday morning December 23rd, at Laurie's house. Laurie assured Donna her mother would attend.

When they drove back to school on Sunday, Laurie was uncharacteristically silent. "A penny for your thoughts," offered Brad.

"I'm thinking about owning shares of Knowlton stock. I'm also thinking about William calling me stupid. You know me, Brad, I would love to get revenge on that SOB."

• • •

At the same time as Laurie and Brad drove back to school after Thanksgiving, Shirley and Augie were intensely enjoying each other's company. They went out for walks. They dined in casual restaurants in nearby towns. They spent a lot of time together in bed.

"Can you stay over Monday?" asked Augie. "I've only three classes tomorrow. I can be home early."

"I'm supposed to work at the library Tuesday. I'll call tomorrow and switch a day with someone. I'm so happy with you Augie; I truly don't want to leave."

As Augie prepared to leave Monday morning, Shirley chided him, "Now professor, keep your mind on the subject, not on those pretty coeds."

Augie smiled, "It might be easier today. During my 'chaste' period there have been days when looking at those pretty college coeds with their tight sweaters and short skirts became more than a little distracting."

"Why Augie, you sound like a dirty old man."

"I am a dirty old man. Hasn't this weekend has proven that to you?"

After Augie left, Shirley called to make the necessary arrangements at the library. Then some devilment snuck into her happy mood. Off she went to look for a shopping mall which featured a Victoria's Secret shop. When she found one, a twinkle came into her eyes. After some pondering, she purchased a red brassiere with matching red panties. Then she bought a red garter belt plus some long red stockings. An adjacent shoe store provided a pair of matching red high heels.

As the time approached for Augie to return, Shirley slipped into the red lingerie. Then she wrapped herself in her robe so she could stay warm. She waited in the living room. When she heard Augie's car, she slipped off the robe. Clad only in the red lingerie, she draped herself over the banister leading upstairs in an extremely provocative manner.

When Augie came in, he his jaw dropped. He froze in stupefied silence!

Shirley smiled, "Hi professor. I thought this outfit would help you keep your mind on the subject!"

Augie just stood there stammering.

Shirley turned. With a provocative wiggle, she walked up the stairs. Needless to say, Augie followed her closely. Very closely.

Much later, Augie found himself in a shower. He was sexually depleted. However, every minute of the encounter with the lady in the red lingerie was etched in his memory. Suddenly, the glass shower door opened. Shirley threw a glass of cold water on him.

"EEOW, what was that for?"

"You are taking too long. I want you back in bed."

Augie reached out, grabbing Shirley. He pulled her into the shower.

"Shirley Lansing, I adore you," he murmured as they played with each other under the shower.

"You know, Augie, the old Shirley would never have done that. But the new Shirley is enjoying it immensely."

"Well I certainly like the new Shirley."

"That makes two of us!"

Chapter 33

For the Christmas formal, their senior year, Laurie picked a pale blue chiffon dress, which reached nearly to the floor. It had spaghetti straps and fit tightly around her bodice. Her spectacular figure looked even better in the dress. Most beautiful of all were her eyes. The way her love shined out as she looked at Brad, left him almost speechless. He considered himself the luckiest man in the world.

They held each other close, dancing almost every dance. Many of their friends had heard about the engagement. However, they hadn't seen the ring. Consequently, the dancing was stopped many times as friends offered congratulations.

The memory of that warm, cozy night remained with them forever.

• • •

Laurie decided Brad would go home with her for Christmas. She refused to allow him to be alone any longer. Brad looked forward to having company when he opened presents by the tree.

He decided to do his Christmas shopping at Victoria's Secret. He bought fancy lingerie for both Shirley and Laurie. He figured a big laugh would result.

When they got to Laurie's home, they found Augie had arrived just ahead of them. Augie planned to spend the time before Christmas with Shirley. Then he would leave Christmas Eve day to be with his own children for the balance of the holidays.

"Mom," asked Laurie, "We've an important meeting tomorrow. I'm concerned about secrecy. I think you should give Smythe the day off. In fact, you can terminate him permanently as far as I'm concerned. For some reason the guy gives me the creeps."

"When William left, I tried to let him go. If you recall, William insisted Smythe stay here to watch his *property interests*. I was so anxious to get William out of the house, I caved and let Smythe stay."

"Can you find a way to get him out of here tomorrow?"

Shirley scratched her head. "I know, I'll order a Christmas present from some town away from Carmel and ask him to go pick it up. He loves driving my fancy car. That should keep him away long enough."

A total of six attended the meeting on December 23rd. Laurie and Brad, Shirley, Augie, Donna Swift, the attorney, and Joan Wright, the legal assistant to Caspar Silenski were all invited. (Joan had been invited because she was Laurie's friend, not at the request of her employer.)

Laurie took charge from the start. "I've called this meeting for several reasons. As you know, thanks to Joan here, we've discovered two trusts grandfather gave to my late sister Betty Ann and to me. The trustee of these trusts is William. He's been keeping the knowledge of these trusts to himself.

"Each trust holds 10 shares of Knowlton stock. Since there are only 100 shares of this closely held company, the two trusts represent a 20% interest. Joan has a hunch William has no knowledge of the fact that Betty Ann's trust names my trust as beneficiary. Which means, as of right now, the trustee of my trust, William, has the legal power to vote my 20 shares of Knowlton stock.

"The first object of our meeting today is to discuss this trust situation.

"The second object is to talk about the upcoming property settlement in mother's divorce proceedings.

"The third object is to protect Joan's job. Joan is badly needed at her firm. Unfortunately, she has truly 'walked an ethical high wire' by telling us about these trusts.

"Joan, why don't you begin by filling in the others with the history of these trusts?"

Joan began by explaining how, when Grandfather Knowlton's attorney passed away, the records came to her firm. "I'm almost positive no one except me has ever opened those dead files."

"One of my responsibilities at Silenski has been to cover all the paper work for Knowlton Company. To my knowledge, the trusts have never been mentioned in any minutes or proceedings. My hunch is Mr. Knowlton either doesn't know about these trusts, or he's forgotten Betty Ann was given a trust. He could also think the corporation reacquired the shares in Betty Ann's trust as treasury stock. As you all know, treasury stock has no vote."

Laurie spoke, "Thank you Joan. Now I want to turn the floor over to my good friend and attorney, Donna Swift. Donna is a young attorney. However, her practice is doing well because she's smart, honest and articulate. She's also an attorney who cares about people. As you all know, there aren't many attorneys who truly care about their clients."

Donna smiled. "Actually, Laurie, it is my opinion that Betty Ann's trust ceased to be a legal entity after her passing. The only asset in her trust was the 10 shares of Knowlton stock which should now be in your trust. I suggest from this point forward; we should only assume one trust with 20 Shares of stock.

"Now, let's get into the details of Laurie's trust. First of all, the trust stipulates that Laurie has no access to the assets until she reaches age 23. She gets one third of the assets at that time, one third more when she turns 26 and the balance of trust assets become hers when she turns 30.

"This clause seems to preclude any voting rights for Laurie at this time because she's just 21 years old. However, I did find a clause in the trust that gives the trust beneficiary, (Laurie) once she attains age 21, the right to hire and fire the trustee of her trust.

"It's my opinion that Laurie has the power to fire the current trustee, William, and name herself trustee. If she were the trustee, she could vote the 20 shares held by her trust. "Laurie asked me to research how she could actually replace Mr. Knowlton as trustee. The answer is a simple letter informing the existing trustee he has been replaced, must be filed at the courthouse."

Laurie spoke up. "Let me get this straight. Are you saying it would be possible for me to walk into a board meeting, and hand my father a document replacing him as trustee? Then I could become my own trustee?"

"That's correct, and he could do nothing about it," replied Donna. Then she added, "Providing the document has been filed at the courthouse prior to the meeting and that the county clerk stamps the document certifying the change in trustees."

Laurie then addressed the group. "Okay people, I've been thinking about this a lot since we discovered the existence of these trusts at Thanksgiving. Maybe this is crazy, but since William called me 'stupid' I've been very angry. I'm deeply hurt and I'm committed to prove him wrong.

"Hear my pipe dream. When the time comes to decide the property settlement, mother (or her attorney) shows William and Selinski the very damaging photographs which prove William has a bimbo. Because William has been unfaithful, Mother's position in the divorce property settlement should be very strong.

"She demands 60% of William's assets in the divorce settlement right down the line. She demands 60% of both houses, 60% of the retirement plan, 60% of the investments and 60% of the Knowlton shares.

"William owns 80 shares of Knowlton stock, so mother is asking for 60% of 80 shares which is 48 shares. William will fight giving away 60% of the company tooth and nail.

Eventually, very reluctantly, mother agrees to accept 40% of the shares of Knowlton stock in exchange for 100% of this house and 100% of the house in Florida. This reluctant compromise will leave mother 40% of 80 shares or 32 shares of the Knowlton stock. She makes this offer contingent on a speedy end to the divorce.

"William does the math. He realizes that 80 minus 32 will leave him 48 shares. I think William will snap up the offer because he will think he still holds majority. Even if he has knowledge of my 10 shares, 32 plus 10 is only 42 and William has 48. So, hopefully William agrees. The divorce settles quickly before Shirley changes her mind.

"After the divorce is final, Shirley requests a board meeting. When the meeting starts, I show up with the paper replacing William as trustee. Then we nominate Mother to be Chairman of the Board. In the process of voting, William discovers I own 20 shares. 20 plus 32 is 52 shares. Mother and I control the company.

"We can then fire William. We can kick his behind right out of the building!"

"Slow down Laurie," inserted Augie. If you fire William you're going to bite the hand that feeds you. Shirley has no knowledge of running the business."

Laurie looked at Augie. "You are absolutely correct, Augie. But Mother has a new boyfriend who could run Knowlton's in his sleep."

"Hold on young lady……. don't get me involved in this."

"Why not Augie? If we pull this off, we need you to step in and run the company. It'd just be for a few years. As soon as I get my MBA and a little experience under your guidance, I promise to take over and you can go back to teaching."

"I need a little time to think about that," replied Augie. Then he muttered loud enough so everyone could hear, "That's the first time in my life I've been offered a job by a college kid." Everyone snickered.

Laurie continued, "Now, while Augie thinks, we have one other issue and that is Joan's job security. Here's what I'm thinking as I dream this dream.

"Donna is doing well in her law practice. Suppose we throw her the Knowlton legal account? This extra business will mean she needs a really good assistant. Suppose Donna hires Joan? Joan gives notice to Silenski two weeks before the board meeting. She should get off cleanly because she won't be there when the recriminations begin."

Donna and Joan looked at each other. Before they could say anything, Shirley spoke up, "Donna, I'm not happy with my divorce lawyer. He's a nice man, but I have the feeling William has some kind of a connection with him. Could you handle my divorce for me? That will give you some extra funds to use to hire Joan, wouldn't it? Besides, since you're in on this strategy, you're the perfect person to handle the property settlement, aren't you?"

Donna turned to Joan. "I've been dreaming of working with someone with your experience, Joan. I just haven't been able to find the money. With the fees from Shirley's divorce and perhaps the Knowlton legal account, I'm sure we could find the money to keep you happy. Working with you would be a total joy."

Joan responded, "I'm sure I've violated something by informing Laurie of the existence of these trusts. That being true, if Silenski fired me, I would wind up with a bad recommendation. Making a move ahead of the legal confrontation at the board meeting makes incredible sense. Besides, Silenski's right on the edge of being a crook. I've wanted to leave him for some time. Perhaps I've reached the time."

She continued, "Oh Laurie, I forgot to tell you what happened after you left the office at Thanksgiving. Remember when Silenski asked me to mail you the trust over the intercom? As you know, I had them all photocopied so I gave them to you to save postage. After you left, Silenski came out and told me not to mail them to you. He told me he didn't think Mr. Knowlton wanted you to have them just yet. I replied, *Okay, I won't mail them.*"

A long silence followed Joan's presentation. Augie broke the quiet. "You know, I've been sitting here listening as an outsider. At least until a minute ago, I thought I was an outsider. Here's what I've been thinking. What William and Silenski are up to doesn't pass the smell test. In fact, I think it stinks. Donna, doesn't a trustee have to act in a certain manner? Doesn't a trustee have to act in the best interest of the trust beneficiary?

"He sure does," replied Donna. "In fact, he may be criminally liable for the way he's acted as a trustee."

Augie continued, "Would you research that please, Donna? In addition, I want Laurie to go into Knowlton next week and make copies of William's expense accounts. That trip to the 'Chain Store Owners' convention at company expense could easily be construed as an effort to short change the 20% minority shareholders. I've never heard of the 'Chain Store Owners' group. Brad, you know how to drive a computer, maybe you could do an on-line search and see what you find out. If there is such an organization, they will surely have a web site."

Then Augie took a deep breath. "Laurie, if you truly feel you need me to run Knowlton's for a few years, I guess I can go along with you. Please understand however, I'll only do it until you're ready to take over. I'd much rather remain a college professor."

As everyone clapped, Shirley jumped up kissing Augie right on the mouth!

With a big smile at Augie, Laurie took over the meeting again. "I think we recognize all of this could easily fall apart.

"I'd like to poll the group now to see how everyone feels regarding the plan. Let's start with Shirley."

Shirley smiled as she thought for a minute. "William's been so cruel; I think the possibility of firing him from Knowlton makes the risk worth taking."

"Brad?"

"What's our alternative? If we don't try this, William continues to run roughshod over you and Shirley as he's always done. I vote go."

"Donna?"

"I favor the plan for several reasons. First of all, if the divorce settlement doesn't work out as we hope, we've lost nothing. We can just stonewall the settlement. We haven't informed William of your potential 20 voting shares. That can remain secret. Of course, the longer we wait, the greater the possibility he'll find out about your 20% interest, so speed will remain essential.

"Secondly, I'm absolutely thrilled with the possibility of representing Knowlton Company. That's a big plumb for me, as is Shirley's divorce responsibility. I'm deeply grateful for the chance. I can promise I'll do my utmost to be worthy of the trust you place in me. I also need to say that I'm smart enough to get help if I get into some legal matter which is over my head."

"Third, I'm totally delighted to work with Joan. I feel we would make a great team."

"Joan?"

"I think we have a shot at pulling this off. I'm also delighted to get away from Silenski. He's a really slippery person. Working with Donna should be a joy for both of us."

"Augie?"

"I'll be honest. I hate giving up my teaching job. However, for Shirley I'd do just about anything. As I'm sure you all suspect, she's become a very important part of my life. As to the plan, I feel good about the element where if the settlement doesn't go as planned, we can just stonewall and come up with something else. It's always wise to have an alternative strategy. I say we try to pull it off."

Laurie took over again. "It appears the vote is unanimous. Great! Thank you all so much. As of right now, this plan is on go. Remember, it all hinges on the property settlement. Nothing happens until that is secure and unchangeable. So please keep all this extremely confidential. Mother and Donna, the ball's in your court. Please move as quickly as possible. Good luck."

The meeting ended with coffee and rolls.

The next day, December 24th, Augie planned to leave to be with his children for Christmas. He and Shirley enjoyed a 6:00 o'clock breakfast so Augie could get an early start.

Augie asked, "Where're Brad and Laurie?

Shirley replied, "They're still asleep....No, perhaps I should rephrase. They may be asleep or they may not be asleep. The proper answer is they have not yet made their appearance this morning. I think it's highly likely they are doing exactly what you and I were doing a few minutes ago.

Augie grinned. Then he reached across squeezing Shirley's hand.

Shirley looked at his eyes, "Augie, I need to say something and I don't need you to respond. In fact, I'd prefer that you not respond. Just reflect on what I'm going to say.

"A few years ago, I think Laurie was a freshman, she asked me what it felt like to fall in love. I told her I truly didn't know, because I never loved William. Later in the conversation, I asked her if she ever fell in love to tell me what it felt like.

"One day she told me how she felt about Brad. She told me she thought of him constantly, she wanted to be with him to the exclusion of everyone else. If she was not with him she found herself wondering what she could do to make him happy the next time they were together."

Shirley continued, "If that's the definition of love, Augie, I'm experiencing the identical symptoms. Which means... I'm in love with you."

Augie smiled at her, "You didn't need to tell me Shirley. Every time I look in your eyes, I can read how you feel. However, it is exciting to hear the words."

Then he asked, "Spring break at school is the last week in March this year. Do you think you could arrange with the library to have that time off? I want to take a trip with you to meet my children. I need their approval for something I want very much to do."

"Consider it done," beamed Shirley.

He hugged her one last time before he got into the car. "Ah Shirley, when you pack for the trip to meet my children, maybe you better leave the red lingerie outfit home. I wouldn't want them to get the wrong impression. I want you to wear that outfit often, but only when it's just the two of us."

Shirley laughed. With a last wave, he drove away.

• • •

The day after a happy Christmas, Laurie wandered into Knowlton's offices very early in the morning. She'd been a filing clerk during one of her vacation shifts last summer, so she knew exactly where to go.

Quickly locating the proper filing cabinet, she pulled out three years of her father's expense accounts. At the copy machine, she copied each month, stuffing each page into her purse. Then she replaced the originals in the files. She was virtually certain no one had seen her.

As she left the building, she walked smack into Melody Flowers just coming in to work.

"Laurie darlin', I hear congratulations are in order," she oozed. "Do let me see yo'alls ring. Oh, that is so precious. I'm happy for you!"

Laurie politely nodded, "Thank you, Melody."

Then Melody whispered in her ear in a conspiratorial voice, "Darlin', Iah've been thinkin'. When the divorce is over, ah might become your stepmother! Now wouldn't that be somthin'!"

Laurie thought a minute. "Melody, when mother gets through taking William to the financial cleaners, you'll probably have to find a new fish. William will no longer be rich enough to be in your league."

As Melody's jaw dropped, Laurie walked away.

CHAPTER 34

Donna Swift was no fool. The potential acquisition of the legal business from Knowlton Company presented an incredible opportunity. She knew it all depended on whether or not *Operation Laurie's Dream* would come to fruition.

Because her part in the plan was extremely significant, she wanted to do it correctly. This meant she needed time to *do her legal homework.*

A day into the New Year, Joan Wright received a terse phone call from Donna. "We need to talk; can we meet for lunch?"

"Name the time and the place."

"Maria's Tea Room on 12th street, at 1:30 tomorrow."

"I know where it is. I'll see you then."

When the two women met for the second time, there was a confirmation of the instant warmth they had each felt during their first meeting. Joan and Donna were both very fond of Laurie. It was natural they would begin to like each other right away.

They chatted amicably about Laurie until the food arrived. Then Donna began explaining her dilemma.

"Joan, I've a ton of research to do in order to make sure I do my part properly in *Operation Laurie's Dream.*"

"*Operation Laurie's Dream.* Is that what we're calling it?

"Well, I thought it sounded kind of sexy, what do you think?"

"Works for me, in fact I kind of like it."

Donna then blurted out her problem. "Here's my dilemma. I need you on board right away, however I can't afford you full time until the Knowlton business comes in. Would you mind working some Saturdays and Sundays for me?

"I got a big advance from Mrs. Knowlton for the divorce work. That'll allow me to pay you for your weekends. I'm certain you could free up enough time for me to do the research I need to do. I have to be sure everything is in apple pie order when we come up to bat."

Joan thought a moment. "Weekends are kind of boring for a single lady my age. This is so important; I understand where you're coming from. My answer is, count me in. I'll be at your office Saturday morning at nine."

"Laurie told me you were wonderful," replied Donna. "I'm deeply grateful."

It didn't take long for Joan to impress Donna by the work plus the knowledge she brought to her little one-person firm. She and Joan did a lot of thinking together as to how to manage the upcoming divorce negotiations.

The first thing they did was prepare two letters for Shirley's signature. One letter was to Shirley's current divorce attorney informing him that he had been replaced. The second was a notice to William and Silenski informing them that Donna Swift had replaced Shirley's original legal counsel.

• • •

When Silenski received the official notice of change in counsel, he immediately did some research on Donna Swift. After he researched her inexperience, he called William.

"I don't know why your wife tossed away a competent attorney, but she gave us a real break. A child now represents her, just two years out of law school. I promise William, I'll eat her for breakfast."

"Sounds good to me, Caspar. We need all the help we can get. I want to keep as much of my net worth as possible."

Silenski continued, "Her name's Donna Swift. Here's her resume. Indiana Law School, did well there, undergraduate work at Denison, where she made Phi Beta Kappa. It appears she's smart but with no experience. In fact, I wouldn't be surprised it this is her first divorce case."

"Undergrad at Denison. I bet she's one of Laurie's friends. Laurie must have talked Shirley into helping her friend. Big mistake."

• • •

As planned, Shirley and Augie made a spring vacation trip. It gave Shirley a chance to meet Augie's two adult children. His children were more than polite to Shirley. They knew and felt their father's sadness over losing his wife. Both expressed happiness over his new love.

The minute they returned from their spring vacation trip, Donna met with Shirley to prepare strategy. When she felt fully prepared, Donna called Silenski.

"We're ready to discuss the property settlement."

Silenski wanted the meeting to be held in his office. Donna held out for a neutral site. She felt Silenski's fancy office would be too intimidating.

They agreed on two conference rooms at a local hotel. Donna wanted to keep Shirley close by, but not in the same room with William. Both Laurie and Joan had warned Donna about how dominating William could be.

The meeting began with William, Silenski and Donna in one room. Shirley was located in an adjacent room. Donna opened the negotiations by speaking frankly.

"My client wants to settle this matter as soon as possible. She feels there's no point in dragging it out. There is also the adverse publicity issue for Knowlton and Company."

Silenski asked, "Adverse publicity issue?"

"Yes," Donna replied. "We don't think it's in the best interest of the company to have these photographs in the local paper. What do you think Mr. Knowlton?"

As she said this, she spread the photos and other incriminating documents Laurie had secured last May in Chicago on the table. Silenski was flabbergasted! William was thunderstruck!

Donna continued, "My client has a strong desire to send these photos to all the papers." Here she paused to let the idea sink in. Then she added, "I've been trying to persuade her that hurting the company image with the public will be counterproductive. It will bite the hand that feeds her, so to speak.

"She's reluctantly agreed to withhold releasing the photos in exchange for my assurance that we will get a quick settlement and move the divorce proceedings forward. That is my object here this morning. If we can work out the property settlement today, Mrs. Knowlton will agree to sit on the photos as far as the press is concerned."

Seeing the two stunned faces across the table, Donna added, "I have the feeling these photos were unknown to you, Mr. Silenski. Would you like a few minutes alone with your client?"

"That would be very helpful."

"I'll step outside while you two talk."

When Donna left, Silenski whirled on William. "It appears you got caught with your *you know what* in the cookie jar."

"So what," growled William.

"So, you are now going to get your clock cleaned. With those photos, Shirley can kill you in the property settlement. These photos really strengthen their case. If I'd have known about them, I probably wouldn't have agreed to represent you."

"Silenski.... you've gotten so much business from us, you wouldn't dare not represent me. Now quit bluffing and figure out what to do."

Silenski thought for a few minutes. The silence was deadly. "I guess our best strategy is to see what she wants and then haggle for better terms. Sound all right to you?'

"I guess, let's see what they're offering."

Silenski went to the room next door asking Donna to return. Donna gave Shirley a big wink as she left.

In a few minutes, Donna laid a typed paper onto the table. As she did this she announced, "Since we've agreed Shirley is the injured party, this is what she wants:

Assets of William and Shirley with the percentage of same going to Shirley
Residence Carmel, Ind. To be sold 60%
Florida Residence. To be sold 60%
Retirement Plan 60%
Brokerage account 60%
Knowlton Stock 60% (48 Shares)

Silenski and William laughed. They pretended it was a big joke.

"Ok," replied Donna, "make us a counter offer. I'll be in the next room with Shirley."

When the parties got back together, William's list offered 40% of each of the items except none of the Knowlton shares.

After considerable haggling, Donna suggested, "Why don't the three of us work up a reasonable offer. Then let me present it to Shirley. She really doesn't want to drag this out. More delay means more bitterness."

She continued, "You're going to have to include some Knowlton shares. They are by far your most valuable asset and a significant percentage of your net worth. Come on people, let's get realistic."

Silenski wrote some numbers on a paper. Handing it to William he asked, "How about this?"

Carmel Residence 60%
Florida Residence 50%
Retirement Plan 50%
Brokerage account 50%
Knowlton Stock 30% (24 shares)

After a few minutes of discussion William announced, "Okay present it to her. Try hard to sell it."

After a long time, Donna came back:

"Shirley insists on more Knowlton stock. 50% of Knowlton is mandatory. I explained to her the importance of William maintaining majority control of the company. I told her you would never relinquish the majority portion. Then I asked if she was interested in a management position in the company?

"It turns out that was a key question. She obviously knows nothing regarding the operations of the company. So, after considerable thinking she agreed to this:

Carmel Residence 100%
Sanibel Residence 100%
Retirement plan 0%
Brokerage Account 100%
Knowlton shares 40% (32 shares)
This offer is good for today only.

"In other words, she is taking 100% of the real estate and the securities. She allows you to keep 100% of your retirement plan. She also allows you to continue your control of the corporation. If I were you guys, I would snap up this offer in a heartbeat."

They asked Donna to step out of the room so they could talk privately.

When Donna left, William turned to his attorney, "This is a pretty good offer. I get to keep my majority position. Shirley's 32 shares will not be a problem because I'll be able to decide if dividends are to be paid. You can bet your boots Knowlton's will never pay a dividend."

"I hate to take advantage of a young attorney," Silenski acknowledged with a twinkle in his eye. However, business is business. I knew when your wife hired an inexperienced lawyer we'd come out on top. I say we grab this offer. We settle the whole damn divorce right now."

William thought for a minute. "You know there's the trust from my father to Laurie. She holds 10 shares in that trust. She can't get at the shares for some time, however."

William continued to speculate out loud. "Suppose years from now Laurie and Shirley gang up on me. They have Laurie's 10 plus Shirley's 32 shares. That is only 42 shares. I hold 48. I say we grab this right now. I promise you, Knowlton will never pay a dividend. This lady lawyer is a chump."

Silenski laid the paper with the offer in front of William. "If you sign this, the divorce is 90% complete."

William signed with a flourish!

• • •

That night Donna sent an email to all the participants of the December 23rd meeting:

Operation Laurie's Dream is still on go. Property settlement negotiations are over. Shirley is to receive 100% of both houses, 100% of the marketable securities and 32 Shares of Knowlton stock! William keeps 100% of his retirement plan and 48 shares of Knowlton stock. Just as Laurie predicted, when William realized he would maintain majority ownership, he jumped at the deal. I suspect his motivation for the quick acceptance is he never plans to pay a dividend to the minority shareholders.

The divorce is now 90% complete. We should have it finalized in about two weeks!

Joan has really helped me.

Donna

A short time later Laurie responded to everyone involved with this email.

Great news! Well done Donna, Joan and Mother!

One thing just occurred to me. When the divorce proceedings are before the judge, ask him to require William to hold regular board meetings. Try to get one scheduled on a Friday as soon as possible. (Brad and I don't have many classes on Friday)

Once the divorce is final, and the board meeting date scheduled, we have to watch our timing carefully:

1. Joan must give Silenski notice two weeks before the board meeting.

2. Donna must have the 'trustee replacement' papers prepared and filed at the courthouse the morning of the board meeting.

3. Donna: please draft a document threatening to charge William for not acting in the interest of the 20% shareholders. Don't spend too much time on it Donna, I don't plan to file it. I just want to hold it over William's head as a threat.

There is an old saying from a Chess Master, "The threat is more powerful than the execution."

If I have in my hand the threat of a possible jail term for William, it should keep him in line when this is over.

Mother, it would be wonderful to have Augie at the meeting. Can you talk him into coming? Maybe we three could ride over together.

I think this is going to work people. Please, all of you, keep hoping and be sure to keep everything extremely confidential. A leak could be fatal.

Deepest thanks to all.

Laurie

• • •

At the final divorce hearing, just before the judge made everything official, Shirley spoke up. "Your honor, I have a request."

The judge replied, "I'm listening."

"I've allowed William to continue as majority shareholder at our company. However, I have interest in the proceedings. Could you to require William to have regular board meetings which will be open to all shareholders?"

The judge replied, "The request seems reasonable to me. I'll add to the decree a requirement that quarterly board meetings are scheduled. The first meeting will be (he looked at his calendar) April 23rd at 10:00 A.M. in the Knowlton conference room. Is that date all right with all of the parties?"

Shirley asked, "I prefer a Friday. Is the 23rd a Friday?"

The judge replied, "No but the 24th is a Friday. Is that date all right with you Mr. Knowlton?" William nodded. Then the judge said, "Friday the 24th then. So ordered. This marriage is officially terminated."

Shirley and Donna hugged each other warmly.

CHAPTER 35

On April 10th, Joan Wright handed her letter of resignation to Caspar Silenski. She gave him two weeks' notice, which meant April 24th would be her last day.

The resignation stunned Caspar. "Joan, you can't do this. We need you here. Surely you're joking."

"I'm not joking. Someone wants me badly. They are willing to pay to get me."

Then Caspar parried, "Joan we'll increase your salary by 20%. Will that keep you?"

"Mr. Silenski, if you had offered to pay me that much some time ago, I wouldn't have been looking. However, I can't use my new job offer as a lever to get more money from you. It would be ethically improper. I've made my commitment to them. I intend to keep my word."

Silenski fumbled around the desk. Then he looked at his calendar. Your last day will be the day of the Knowlton board meeting. Joan, you know everything regarding Knowlton, including how to do the minutes. Will you please get me through the board meeting before you leave?"

"You've been a good employer. Of course, I'll stay for the Knowlton board meeting."

As she retreated to her desk, she muttered to herself. *Wouldn't miss it for the world!*

• • •

Laurie, Augie and Brad drove together from Denison to Carmel on Thursday the 23rd. On the way, Augie discussed a problem with Laurie.

"I'm planning to ask your mother to marry me, Laurie. I want to be able to tell her that I have asked you, and received your permission."

"You're asking me for permission to marry my mother?"

"Well, there's no one else to ask."

"Boy, I wish I was still in your accounting class. I'd really have you over a barrel."

Augie and Brad grinned at her riposte.

Laurie continued in a very stern deep voice, "Will you support her in the manner to which she is accustomed?"

"She's so damn rich, I don't see how I can on a professor's salary. However, my love will make up for any financial shortage we incur."

"Time to stop kidding," cried Laurie. "Augie, I'm thrilled to death for you and mother. As you know, her life's been pretty tragic until now. She deserves the love of someone wonderful like you. Rest assured, you have my blessing as well as my approval to propose to my mother."

"Thank you, Laurie."

"Do you have the ring with you?"

"Yes."

"How exciting! Can you show it to me?"

"Isn't that bad luck or something? What if she says no?"

"Augie there's not a chance in the world mother will say no. However, I don't want to create any bad luck, so I'll wait to see the ring."

After a pause, she asked, "Will I have to call you father after you are married, or can I still call you Augie?"

"I've no intention of replacing your father. I want to be your friend. Augie is, and will remain, just fine with me."

"When will you ask her?"

"As soon as we can be alone. I see no reason to wait."

Laurie sped up so they could get home faster.

They arrived at 5:00, which gave them some time before dinner. Augie asked Shirley to go for a walk with him on this beautiful spring day.

Right after they left, Donna and Joan dropped by on the way home from work.

"We just thought we should check in before tomorrow's meeting," Donna exclaimed, as they were welcomed with big hugs.

Laurie's living room was huge. It ran from the front to the back of the house. Large picture windows dominated the walls at each end of the room.

Suddenly Brad called out. "Come here people, there's a major happening in the back yard."

The three women joined him at the window. A huge oak tree grew in the center of the yard. A bench, with Shirley sitting on it, rested under the oak. Augie was on one knee staring into Shirley's eyes. They were holding hands.

"Don't get to close to the glass," Brad whispered. "They might see us."

Outside, Augie was making a little speech. "Shirley, I think you know how much I'm in love with you. We have so much fun together. The sex is great, but that's such a small part of what we have together. I simply don't want to be alone anymore. When we're together, I feel complete. Shirley, will you marry me?"

"Oh Augie, I want to accept right now. However, my divorce has only been final for two weeks. I should talk to Laurie before I commit, don't you think?"

"I already talked to Laurie. She gave me her blessing and her permission."

"You asked my daughter for permission to marry me?"

"Who else is there to ask?"

"Augie, I've wanted to be your wife for so long I can't see any reason to wait. I accept your proposal with incredible joy!"

Augie reached in his pocket for the ring. As he brought it out, he explained, "This is my mother's diamond. It's not a real large stone, so I asked them glop it up with some other stuff."

"Glop it up! Men! Those are beautiful blue sapphires! This ring is simply gorgeous. Now get off your knees so you can put this on my finger and get kissed."

They stood together under the oak as Augie slid the ring onto Shirley's hand. They kissed for a long time. Then, as Shirley started to say, "Let's go in the house and tell"….the back door burst open! The four watchers ran into the yard yelling and screaming congratulations!

After everyone settled down, Laurie told about the view from the window. "Oh mother, it was like a silent movie. We could see what was going on but couldn't hear a sound. It was so romantic!"

They persuaded Donna and Joan to stay for dinner. A real engagement celebration followed. However, Donna cautioned everyone to go easy on the champagne because of the important meeting tomorrow.

After dinner, Laurie suggested they go into the den so they could review everyone's part in the upcoming meeting.

As they settled into the room Brad thought he heard a strange sound. Was it static? He looked around for a radio that had been left on. Nothing. Then he stuck his head under the conference table which William had placed in the room years earlier.

Laurie thought Brad had lost him mind. "What are you?"

Brad cut her off exclaiming in a loud voice. "It sure is nice weather out there." At the same time, he raised his hand putting a finger to his lips calling for silence. He put his head back under the table for a second, then gestured to Augie to look.

The room became silent. Brad grabbed a paper and wrote on it 'make idle conversation.'

"It certainly has been a lovely day. A great day to become engaged." Shirley announced.

"I hear it's supposed to rain tomorrow." added Donna.

By now Brad had gestured Laurie and Shirley to look under the table. There was a microphone under the table. It was nothing fancy, just one of those devices that allows a mother to monitor a baby from a different room.

Augie, Brad Shirley and Laurie stepped out of the room. Donna and Joan kept up a banal conversation.

In the hall, Shirley was incensed! "Who would plant a microphone in there?"

Brad and Laurie said in unison, "Smythe?"

"Has to be," acknowledged Shirley."

Brad whispered, "Where's his room?"

"I'll take you," Laurie offered. "Mom, go back in and make conversation.

Augie and Brad followed Laurie as she quickly darted up the two flights of stairs to the butler's room.

Without knocking, they burst into the room! They caught Smythe red handed! He had the listening end of the monitor at his side and a pad of paper on which to take notes. They could hear the girls in the den discussing wedding plans for Shirley's wedding as clearly as if they were in the same room. In seconds, Brad had locked his arm around Smyth's neck, holding him tightly.

"I don't think he heard much, but you can never be sure." Laurie murmured.

"I'm guessing he at least knows we're up to something." Brad added.

After a moment of reflection Augie suggested, "Let's remove this monitor and his cell phone. Then we lock him in the room until tomorrow noon. We can let him go after lunch. The important thing is to keep him from making contact with William until after… you know."

Brad asked, "Is there a way to lock this door, Laurie?"

"It's a key lock and the key locks it from either direction, so yes."

In a few minutes, they had stripped all communication equipment and even paper from Smythe's room. Augie went to the window and looked down. Three floors up and no roof on which to climb out. "I don't think he would try to get out this way."

They took Smythe's key, locking the door from the outside.

As they went downstairs Brad said, "I'm not comfortable with that door lock. Can we go to the hardware and get a good padlock and hasp?

"Yes, I agree," said Laurie. "I'll explain to the girls. We can wait until you get back and a better lock is installed."

Augie looked at Brad. "You're a lot bigger than I am Brad. You stay here on guard in case Smythe tries to force his way out. I'll make the hardware run. Laurie, we'll need a drill and a screw driver when I get back."

"I'll get them from the shop as soon as I alert the others as to what's going on."

Brad hustled back upstairs to the hall outside of Smythe's door. Smythe was picking at the lock with a pencil. Then the pencil snapped. Brad heard Smythe curse. Then he heard him lie down on the bed.

In a few minutes, a strong padlock and hasp were installed, which both men were certain would keep Smythe locked up until tomorrow noon.

Secure from spies, Laurie began the meeting. She omitted not one detail. She informed everyone she was going to go into the office early because she wanted to invite two employees to the board meeting. Then she reminded Donna about recording the trustee change before the meeting. Donna just laughed.

"Do you think I'd forget that? Not a chance."

As Laurie was about to end the meeting, Augie asked for the floor. He began, "There are two women involved in this caper and I want to ask you each a question." As he said this, all eyes turned to Shirley and Laurie.

"I think we have a good chance of pulling this off. If we do, and we literally throw William out of his office, what's going to happen one or two years from now? Are either of you going to be besieged with doubts or guilt over what we've done? Revenge is a strong motive, but it can carry with it serious emotional repercussions. It goes without saying, you are both very sensitive women."

There was a profound silence in the room. Laurie looked at her mother.

Shirley looked at her daughter. Shirley nodded, indicating that Laurie should speak first. After reflecting a moment, Laurie answered.

"Last Thanksgiving, after William called me stupid and trashed Brad, I was really mad. I wanted revenge. But that was November. Now it's April. My anger has dissipated, as has my desire for revenge. What we are about to do, in my opinion is to strike a blow for doing the right thing. William has been unfair and very selfish.

"He was a major contributor to Betty Ann's revolt which, without a doubt, led to her death. He has treated my mother with distain and damaged her emotionally to the point where she was physically ill for a long time. How much damage William has done to me is impossible to measure, but it's a lot, I can assure you. Augie's question is very thoughtful, but this is not about revenge, it's about justice!"

Shirley added, "You have it exactly right, Laurie. Augie's question is very discerning because, as he said, we are both sensitive women. But this isn't about revenge. It's about justice, just like Laurie said. I promise you, two or five years from now I will have no guilts about giving this ugly man exactly what he deserves."

The next morning before she left the house, Shirley gave Agnes instructions to let Smythe out at 1:00 o'clock.

CHAPTER 36

The central object in the conference room at Knowlton Company was an oval shaped table surrounded by high backed comfortable chairs. The window reflected a view of downtown Indianapolis. The walls had books lining one side and tasteful paintings on the other.

The meeting was scheduled to begin at 10:00. At 9:55 Laurie's cell phone rang.

"Miss Laurie! I'm so glad I caught you."

"Agnes! What's wrong?"

"That Smythe. After you left, he began calling and yelling something awful. I went up there. He claimed he was starving. He said he never got dinner last night. He begged me for some breakfast. Foolishly, I brought something up for him. When I unlocked the door, he shoved me onto to the floor and ran away. Good thing you took his cell phone last night. I expect he's hunting up a pay phone right this minute. I'm so sorry Miss Laurie."

"Agnes, are you hurt?"

"I expect I'll have a big bruise on my tail, but I'll be alright in a day or two."

"Don't worry, I'll think of something."

Laurie immediately went into a whispered conversation with Donna.

Promptly at 10:00 A.M. William, Caspar Silenski, and Joan Wright strode into the conference room.

Immediately Donna stood. "This is an important meeting. I suggest we all turn off our cell phones."

Laurie watched. As she had hoped, everyone behaved like a robot and turned off their phones. People are so used to being told to turn off their phones they don't think anything about it.

"What are all these people doing here?" William bellowed as he replaced his phone in the holder on his belt and seated himself at one end of the table. "This meeting is for stockholders only. All non-shareholders will have to leave."

As he said this, he banged the gavel on the table to announce to the audience that he was in charge.

Laurie spoke up, "Is Mr. Silenski a shareholder?"

William muttered, "No, but he's my legal advisor."

"What about Joan Wright?"

"She takes the minutes," growled William.

Laurie spoke again in a controlled tone. "Well, if you get to have an advisor, and your advisor gets to have an assistant, shouldn't the other shareholders get to have advisors and assistants?"

William looked at Silenski. Silenski shrugged his shoulders as if to say, she has a point.

William growled, "Who's the man next to Shirley."

Laurie countered, "This is Augie Winchester. He's mother's advisor.

My advisor is Donna Swift, whom you know. My assistant is my fiancé Brad Randall, whom you also know."

"The two employees you both know. Macho O'Hara, head of security, and Sally Ryan, who is in charge of public relations."

"Humph," growled William. "Those last two will have to go. I'm willing to accept the others."

Without another word, Laurie walked over to Macho and Sally. She spoke to them quietly. Then the three of them left the room. When they got outside Laurie whispered, "I'm sorry. Please stay close. I hope to have you back inside in a few minutes."

"Laurie, what's going on?" asked Sally.

"You'll know in about 15 minutes," Laurie replied as she reentered the conference room.

When Laurie sat down, William bellowed out, "The meeting will come to order. Is there any new business?"

Laurie interrupted. "William, I think the first item, according to Roberts Rules of Order, is the reading of the minutes of the last meeting, is it not?"

William flushed, paused a minute. Then he growled. "Joan, please read the minutes."

After they were read and approved Laurie called out, "Mr. Chairman, isn't the election of officers the next item? I believe the first officer to be elected should be the Chairman of the Board."

"This is a farce," exclaimed William.

Donna weighed in, "Please remember Mr. Knowlton, part of the divorce settlement was quarterly board meetings.

William glared over at Silenski who nodded, indicating that Donna had a point.

All right," replied William. "The nominations for chairman of the board are now in order."

Silenski spoke up, "I nominate William Knowlton."

Laurie leaped to her feet. "Mr. Chairman, since Mr. Silenski owns no stock I don't think he can vote or make any motions. We studied all this in my business law course so I'm quite sure I'm correct."

"All right," grumbled William, "since you are insisting we go on with this fiasco, I nominate myself for the post of Chairman of the Board."

"And I," responded Laurie who remained on her feet, "nominate Shirley Lansing for Chairman of the Board."

"This is ridiculous, William growled. "Are there any more nominations?"

He looked around the room. There were no other nominations.

William announced, "I cast 48 votes for William Knowlton."

Shirley announced, "I cast 32 votes for Shirley Lansing."

Laurie announced, "I cast 20 votes for Shirley Lansing."

William exploded, "What are you talking about young woman? You don't own any shares in this company. Now that I think about it, you don't even belong in this room because you're not a shareholder. Now get out!"

Laurie retorted, "William, have you forgotten your father's generation skipping trust?"

"No I haven't forgotten. You get no trust assets until you are 23 years old. Besides your trust only has 10 shares which you cannot vote until you are 30."

Donna stood up. "Mr. Knowlton, if you recall, right before this meeting, I delivered some documents to you. It's obvious you haven't had time to review them. If I could explain these documents, it will help everyone and save considerable time."

William snorted. "Documents? Oh yes, I thought they related to the divorce."

"No," countered Donna, "they related to the two trusts your father made before he died. As you may know, he left 10 shares of Knowlton stock to each of his granddaughters. You are correct, Mr. Knowlton, Laurie attains one third of the trust assets at age 23, one third at age 26 and the balance of the trust assets at 30."

"However," and here Donna let forth a huge smile, "the trust documents do allow Laurie to name the trustee of her trust once she reaches age 21. One of the documents I gave you this morning informs you of your replacement as the trustee of Laurie's trust.

"Laurie has named herself trustee. I recorded this document at the county clerk's office this morning. I'm sure Mr. Silenski will agree that the stamp of the county clerk, which is attached to these documents, means they are binding as well as enforceable."

A long pause ensued while Silenski and William reviewed the documents.

After a long time, William announced, "Silenski agrees with you. Apparently, these documents are proper. This means Laurie has the right to vote the 10 shares in her trust."

Donna continued, "I'm glad that we are in agreement. Now, as to the trust your father established for Betty Ann Knowlton (deceased)"

William snapped, "We put Betty Ann's stock back into the company as treasury stock."

Donna replied, "My information is different. There is a beneficiary arrangement in Betty Ann's trust. The beneficiary arrangement precludes the refund of the stock to the company. If the stock was made into treasury stock, it was done improperly. My guess is it was never done, because I could find no documentation supporting your contention."

Donna continued, "The beneficiary of Betty Ann's trust is her sister's trust. Consequently, Laurie has 20 shares that she can vote. Her statement of 20 votes for Shirley Lansing for Chairman of the Board is quite proper."

At that point, Augie whispered to Shirley. "The gavel is the symbol of power. Go get it."

All this time, timid Shirley Lansing had quietly remained seated at the opposite end of the conference table. When William turned to talk with Silenski, Shirley, with a nod from Augie, gathered her courage. She quietly advanced to the end of the table. William had his back turned as he conferred with Silenski. Shirley reached over William's shoulder seizing the gavel!

Gavel in hand, Shirley returned to her end of the table and spoke in a commanding voice, "William, sit down. Please watch your manners. During my administration, there will be politeness among the board members."

At that point, Brad could not contain himself any longer. He jumped up exclaiming, "Let's have a round of applause for the new chairman of the Board,

Shirley Lansing."

Everyone clapped except William, Silenski and Joan. (Joan kept a straight face because she was still Silenski's employee.) William snapped at Brad. "You sit down! You're nothing but an impertinent young whippersnapper!"

Shirley exclaimed, "William, one more outburst like that and I'll find you out of order and force you to leave."

To show his disdain for Shirley, William remained standing, his beet red face in shock. Shirley paid no heed. She turned to Laurie.

"Would you please ask Sally and Macho to return to the meeting?"

William's face flushed with anger! This caused Shirley to add, "During my administration all shareholders will be courteous to all employees."

While Laurie went to the door for Sally and Macho, William and Silenski continued meticulously examining the documents Donna had given them.

Outside, Laurie whispered to Macho, "Your job is to keep William from striking mother. He almost did the other night, however Brad intervened. It was a narrow escape. If William approaches mother, or me for that matter, please protect us."

"Yes ma'am," muttered a shocked Macho.

When Macho and Sally were seated, Shirley announced, "The board has elected me Chairman. As a consequence, things will be different around here."

Chairman Shirley then called out, "The next order of business will be the election of the president and chief operating officer of Knowlton Company. As we all know, William Knowlton has held the position for many years."

For the first time, William smiled. He was sure timid Shirley would nominate him to this important position once again.

At that point, Laurie stood again. "Madame Chairman, I have some information to bring to the attention of the board which will have great bearing on the election of President and CEO."

"The chair recognizes shareholder Laurie Lansing Knowlton," replied Shirley.

"I plan to make three points," began Laurie.

"First: I submit for the board to examine, copies of William's expenses for the last three years. There have been several times when William has gone to conventions at company expense when in fact there have been no conventions. There are three different expenditures totaling $15,000 each year for a convention of 'Chain Store Owners.' To our knowledge, there's no such group as the Chain Store Owners.

"Second: The company history reveals that William has taken enormous cash bonuses every year. This is the normal pattern for someone who owns 100% of a closely held company. However, William knew that Knowlton had minority shareholders. Twenty percent of the bonus money he took belongs to the minority shareholders. This has gone on since shortly after my grandfather created the trusts, which is over 15 years ago.

If the 20% minority shareholder share averages $100,000 per year, it is my calculation (assuming 6% interest) that William owes my trust $2,467,252. I submit that William's conduct has been both unethical and criminal.

"Third: Up until today, the trustee of my trust has been William. It is obvious he has not acted in the best interest of the trust beneficiary. This is also a criminal offence, which could possibly include prison time. I have yet to decide whether to file this claim with the proper authorities. However, if I do, and William winds up behind bars, it will be very bad publicity for Knowlton Company."

She concluded, "As a consequence of these offenses I move that William Knowlton be removed at once from the position as President and CEO of Knowlton Company without severance pay. Furthermore, I cast my 20 votes for that motion."

William jumped to his feet. He screamed at the top of his lungs, "You can't do that to me!"

Shirley announced, "I cast my 32 votes in support of this motion. William, you may think we can't do that to you, <u>but we just did</u>."

As William strode down the room toward Shirley, Macho got up following him closely. Brad, who was between William and Shirley, also rose to his feet. Observing two very large men surrounding him, William paused half way down the room.

Shirley glared at William. Then she announced, "You have a decision to make William. As a shareholder, you're entitled to stay for the balance of the meeting. If you wish to leave now, that will be understood under the circumstances."

William glared at Silenski. Next, he glared at Shirley. Finally, he gave Laurie the finger! Then he sat down. His red face revealed intense anger.

Shirley then turned to Macho. "Macho, when this meeting is over I want you to escort Mr. Knowlton from the building. Do not allow him to return to his former office."

Then, turning to her ex-husband she added, "We will forward any personal items left in your office to you later on, William. Shall we send them to the Bimbo's address?"

"She's not a Bimbo. Her name is Melody Flowers."

Shirley ignored this comment.

Sally, I want a notice that William has been deposed circulated to all the employees immediately. If you do that, I'm sure there will be many of our employees who will want to thank William for his kindnesses to them over the years. There will be many who will want to wish him well. I envision a hall of well-wishers ready to bestow their heartwarming affection for William as he leaves the building. I estimate that this meeting will be over in about 20 minutes. Sally left on her mission. In a few minutes, she returned.

Shirley then turned to the room of people. "Does the board have a suggestion for a successor to William for the office of President and CEO?"

Laurie stood, "Madame Chairman I nominate August Winchester for that position." She proceeded to rattle off Augie's extensive credentials. After a three-minute nominating speech, she concluded by announcing her 20 votes for Augie.

Shirley announced, "I add my 32 votes. William, do you want to make it unanimous?"

"No, 48 votes against," growled William.

"Motion carried by a vote of 52 to 48," announced Shirley. Most of the people in the room applauded.

Laurie stood again. "Madame Chairman, I think Augie should have a new legal team. Mr. Silenski has been too much in William's pocket. Consequently, I move we remove Mr. Silenski as company legal counsel. I nominate Donna Swift to be Legal counsel for Knowlton Company. Please cast my 20 votes for Donna Swift."

Shirley replied, "I cast my 32 votes for Donna Swift....... William, do you want to make it unanimous?"

William glared at his attorney for a second. Then he growled, "Hell yes, 48 votes to remove Silenski."

Everyone laughed at that.

Shirley then admonished Silenski, "Mr. Silenski, your final pay from Knowlton Company will be as of 1:00 today. Please be sure your personal work for William isn't included in the invoice to the company. The legal work surrounding William's divorce is definitely not a company expense."

Laurie stood to address her father. "Before we adjourn, I want to warn

William that I have a document to initiate criminal action for his improper trusteeship right here in my hand. (She held up a legal document.) If I were a smart daughter, I would probably go ahead and bring in the authorities.

"My understanding is the legal penalty for violation of trustee fiduciary responsibilities is somewhere between five and fifteen years. However, because I am a stupid daughter, I'm going to hang on to this for a while. If you step one-step out of line, William, I'll file it so fast you'll feel like a train hit you."

Shirley then handed another paper to Macho. "After you escort William from the building, please take this paper to Melody Flowers. She will read that she is also terminated. Then you will please escort Melody from the premises."

Sally, "Will you handle the press notices on all of these changes?"

"With pleasure Madame Chairman," Sally smiled.

"Now I call this meeting to a close. William I hope you enjoy your walk of best wishes from all of your grateful employees."

As William walked past Shirley, he growled. "I don't see how you managed to do this to me."

"I didn't have anything to do with it, William. It was the daughter you called stupid who planned the entire thing.

"Oh, William...... if the daughter you call stupid, tossed you out of your job, what does that make you? Stupider than stupid? Or, how about, more stupid than stupid? Or, maybe stupidest?"

Laughter exploded throughout the room. William couldn't speak. He simply followed Macho out of the room.

The conference room exploded with joy. Augie came up to Laurie, hugging her and acknowledging, "For a stupid daughter, you run one hell of a meeting!"

When William and Macho walked out, they found...nothing. The halls were empty. People were going about their jobs however, no one, not one person, stepped forward to shake William's hand.

After William left the main office room, a great cheer went up from the employees. Macho was sure William heard it. A few minutes later, a second cheer occurred as Melody Flowers found herself escorted from the building.

As William was climbing into his car, a taxi pulled up in front of the building. A breathless Smythe got out. Spying William, he rushed over.

"Mr. Knowlton, sir I've been trying to phone you for an hour! When I couldn't get your phone to answer, I caught a cab. I'm not sure what those people at your house are plannin' but it's gonna be trouble for you."

"Smythe your warning's too late. It's already happened."

William entered his car, then seeing the astonished look on Smythe's face he rolled down the window bellowing, "You're fired!"

• • •

William spent the afternoon at the club going over Donna Swift's legal documents again and again. He searched for a loophole. He knew Caspar had been searching also, so around 3:30 he called.

"Have you discovered anything? When do we file whatever it is we need to file?"

Caspar replied. "It appears iron clad to me. The decisive factor is the potential criminal indictment against you. If Laurie decides to take that to the authorities, you are in for a minimum of eight years, maybe as much as fifteen. If I were you, I'd quietly steal away, William. I'd never risk a jail term, especially when you are culpable as hell."

"But what am I going to live on?"

"Well, you have your IRA but if you take money from that before you are 59 ½ years old, you pay a 10% penalty on whatever you take out. You are 52 now so I suggest you leave your IRA alone for at least 7 years. That leaves you with two choices. You can get a job."

"A job, what do you mean get a job?"

"You know work, flip hamburgers, mow lawns, clerk in a department store."

"What's my other choice?"

"In a couple of months maybe you could call Augie Westchester or Winchester or whatever his name is, and ask him to buy your minority interest in Knowlton Company. He'll discount it like hell, and maybe subtract what he figures you owe Laurie's trust, but you might get some cash to live on."

William ended the call. He had another drink. Around 5:00 P.M., he gave up. He went home to Melody Flower's furnished apartment where he'd been staying since Shirley made him leave their house.

As soon as he walked in the door, he sensed something different. In just a moment, he figured it out. Melody had packed up and left.

She didn't even leave a note.

William sat down in a straight chair at the dining room table. He stared for hours at the blank wall opposite.

Finally, he announced to the empty room, "The dumbest thing I ever did in my whole life was tell Laurie she was stupid."

Then he recalled how the employees had cheered when he walked out. That was another blow. Unexpectedly, something his father had tried to teach him, which he had ignored, came into his head.

"*You better make a few friends on the way up, William, or you won't have any on the way down.*"

His head fell into his hands. He remained in that position for a long time. As the sun set, the room darkened. He never bothered to get up and turn on a light.

EPILOGUE

On May 1st Augie Winchester and Shirley Lansing married. It was a small wedding with only family members present. The couple enjoyed a one-week honeymoon cruise in the Caribbean. They could only be gone for a week because Augie was reluctant to leave his new job as President of Knowlton Company and Shirley was very involved planning her daughter's wedding.

• • •

The wedding nuptials for Laurie Lansing Knowlton and Bradley Weatherby Randall took place on June 15th. Donna Swift and Joan Wright were the attendants. Well-wishers filled the church and enjoyed a large reception.

Augie offered to walk Laurie up the aisle. After careful consideration, she turned him down.

"I want everyone to realize, that for me, William has ceased to exist."

Laurie's gown was spectacular. Every girl dreams of a bridal dress like this one. It was traditional white satin, which covered her shoulders and tapered around her narrow hips. Then it flowed into a slim skirt which accented her striking figure and long legs.

It only took a minute for the guests to realize the dress was a minor part of the pageant. As the bridal march began, some were shocked to see the bride walking up the aisle, all alone.

Laurie squared her shoulders as she stretched into her full five feet nine inches. With the added height of her three inch heels, she became a towering Goddess.

Her carriage amazed everyone. A person could read what she felt by her body language and expression as she walked up the aisle.

Nobody was giving this bride away.

She was her own person, walking up the aisle to Brad, whom she adored. The glow in Laurie's eyes reflected the deep love she felt for the man who waited.

If a guest managed to glance away from Laurie to look at the groom, they could bask in the incredible loving look Brad radiated to his bride as she walked toward him.

When they joined hands at the altar Laurie whispered, "I had to marry you to see you in a tux that fits."

Brad giggled at the memory of the too small tuxedo he'd borrowed to get himself out of *kissing purgatory* four years earlier.

Laurie added, "It was worth the wait."

Brad replied, "Laurie dearest, you are far above the bride of my dreams. I love you so much!"

This conversation took so long the minister finally spoke. "If you two are ready… we can begin." Everyone laughed. This created a great atmosphere for the reverent ceremony which followed.

When they were officially married, the minister sent them on their way with this beautiful benediction from Isaiah 55:

For you shall go out in joy
And be lead forth in peace;
The mountains and the hills before you
Shall break forth into singing.
And all the trees of the field
Shall clap their hands.

• • •

THE END

MORE FROM CHUCK GLEASON

If you enjoyed *Mystery Daughter*
You might enjoy:

Widow

A heartwarming love story.
This is the story of Peggy Waldren whose husband was killed in a car accident the day before the story begins. Peggy is left with an eight-year- old son, not much money and a broken heart. The stirring novel describes how she deals with her grief, gets a job, avoids a lecherous boss and eventually finds a second love.

Fired Angels

Three young women start a charter school in East Lansing Michigan. They incur the wrath of the Detroit based Teachers Union, who are very adept at throwing obstacles in their path. Eventually, the community rallies to support the school. In the midst of the struggle, each of the omen discover their true love.

Collision Course

Two college freshman, Keli and Lincoln, argue in class. They have a minor war for two years. Finally, Lincoln persuades Keli of his love for her. She admits she loves him. Then Keli meets The Dragon Lady, a potential mother-in- law from hell. Can Lincoln surmount this obstacle?

CPSIA information can be obtained
at www.ICGtesting.com
Printed in the USA
LVOW12s0512170317
527554LV00001B/15/P